Also availab
and

To my family for believing in me,
my writing network for supporting me,
my editor (Stephanie Doig) for making me work harder
and my readers for keeping me motivated.

STRICTLY CONFIDENTIAL

Lynda Aicher

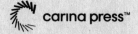

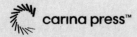

ISBN-13: 978-1-335-65286-7

Strictly Confidential

Copyright © 2018 by Lynda Aicher

Recycling programs
for this product may
not exist in your area.

This edition published by arrangement with Harlequin Books S.A.

® and TM are trademarks of the publisher. Trademarks indicated with
® are registered in the United States Patent and Trademark Office, the
Canadian Intellectual Property Office and in other countries.

www.CarinaPress.com

Printed in U.S.A.

STRICTLY
CONFIDENTIAL

Chapter One

If one more person—man—rubbed against her, intentionally or not, Kennedy was going to scream. Okay, not literally. But the urge boiled within her until she was ready to let loose with a banshee wail of rage. Not that she would.

A Keller wouldn't do such a thing. Not a female one at least. Now her father, he'd probably be admired if he did, but not her. Not when she fought every damn day to be respected in a man's world.

Irritation merged with fatigue to increase the pounding in her head. The exaggerated echo in the oversized convention hall lifted the noise level to a dull roar that resonated on a ready-to-explode scale. She rubbed at her forehead, determined to hold her facade as she wove through the people, smiling when appropriate, noting the location of certain booths, until she reached the end of the aisle where a wave of cooler air beckoned to her from the lobby.

The line for the only coffee shop at their end of the Long Beach convention center was of course long. Men in suits mingled with guys in T-shirts and jeans— unlikely pairings that worked in the manufacturing world.

She eyed up the soda machine, looked back to the coffee line. The choice was easy.

Her sigh was long and encompassing after the fizzing beverage hit her throat. Tucked along the wall away from the congestion, she could finally breathe—and let her guard down. She was used to the battle, but that didn't mean it became easier or less exhausting.

Twenty years of working in the family business, of showing that her intelligence outshined her looks, might've gained her some professional respect, but there was always someone else she had to prove herself to. Especially when one glance at her business card linked her to the company. Assumptions were always made.

Founded by her grandfather, Keller Pallet was a key supplier of custom and standard pallets within the San Francisco Bay Area. Her father made the business a Bay Area success, and now, as the VP of Operations, she was determined to grow it even more.

She set her briefcase on the floor, rolling her shoulders to stretch the tight muscles. There were two hours left before the venue closed for the day, which gave her plenty of time to touch base with three or four more companies.

Their product was far from glamorous. Most overlooked it completely, yet the global market relied on pallets to ship everything from food to electronics to drywall. She liked to compare them to underwear. Everyone needed them, but most hated spending money on them.

One deep preparatory breath, a last glance through her contacts, and she was ready to dive back in. Headache or not, she had a job to do.

A scan of the lobby showed a number of people leaving the venue, some likely headed to private dinners or drinks where deals were negotiated or lost. Her gaze caught and held on a man as he exited the convention hall, his expression switching from cordial to exhausted the second he passed the plane of the doorway. She snickered, identifying with him. He undoubtedly didn't know he was being watched, but she found the silent honesty refreshing and attractive.

Tall, but not overly so, he held himself with the stiff-backed formality she associated with the military. He wasn't in uniform, but she pegged his suit as tailor-made and done expertly. It emphasized the breadth of his shoulders and the trim line of his waist, the material crisp even after a long day.

A flash of lust curled up to tease her. A handsome man in a well-cut suit got her every time. Add in his aura of control backed by authenticity and she was even more enticed. The stony, impersonal act was a tired concept that too many still equated to power. But this guy offered something different. Something…real.

His polite mask shifted back into place when he turned toward the building exit. He cut a path of authority with nothing more than his stride and calm demeanor. His crew cut defined his no-nonsense air, the tablet in his hand indicating his technical savvy. And he was leaving, like she longed to do.

That thought had her mind snapping back to the work she had to finish before she could go. Following him to his hotel room wasn't an option, no matter how much she'd like it to be. Her prospect list was never-ending, even though added sales was just one component of expansion. Competitive pricing, diversified offerings and services, efficiency and customer service were all part of the overall package. One she controlled.

Confidence flowed in on that reminder. She had this.

She tucked her hair behind her ear and headed into the fray. There were men to dazzle and others to commiserate with. She'd listen to every complaint and counter when appropriate. She'd endure the subtle once-overs along with the blatant ones and use her looks as a means of entry.

Resentment got her nowhere, but owning and using her assets gave her power she had no trouble wielding. Her mother thrived among the social elite, and Kennedy had been raised to excel within that set as well. But she needed more than that. She wasn't born to simply exist. She had things to prove and security to achieve—for herself.

Keller Pallet would belong to her one day, a right she would earn, just like her father had.

"We're heading out to dinner in an hour or so," Thad said, glancing her way as he shoved a notepad into his briefcase. His gray hair receded sharply at his temples, complementing the fine lines around his eyes and mouth. Both traits hinted at his age, which edged toward sixty. "Are you going to join us?"

"Are you meeting with anyone?" Kennedy asked, checking the aisle. Most of the booths were shutting down, the flow of people dwindling.

"I don't think so. Craig?" He sent a questioning look to the other salesman.

Craig adjusted his shirt collar before flipping through his tablet. Younger than Thad by a good thirty years, the salesmen balanced each other. Kennedy took pride in that. Where Craig was aggressive and innovative in his thinking and deal shifting, Thad was tenacious in a milder way that displayed his years of experience in the pallet industry.

"I haven't arranged anything," he said.

She kept her relief contained. "I'm going to pass, then." She flashed a smile. "But thanks for the invite."

Thad frowned. "Are you sure?"

"I have some paperwork to catch up on. I'll just grab room service."

"Come on, Kennedy," Craig cajoled as they headed out of the convention center. "You can't work *all* the time." His grin held that open flirtatious edge he leveled at everyone.

Kennedy dismissed his remark without comment. She wouldn't defend herself or refute her work ethic. "How about we meet here at seven tomorrow morning to go through our game plan for the day?"

"Sounds good," Thad said before Craig could respond. The fresh air hit her with a stroke of warmth when they stepped outside. "Can we walk you to your hotel?" He glanced down the block, squinting into the sun.

"I'll be fine," she reassured him. "But thank you."

"Have a good night," Craig said. "Let us know if you change your mind."

"I will."

Responsibility shed itself with each step she took away from the salesmen. She lifted her face to the sun, its warmth sinking through her on tingling waves of freedom. Duty had been engraved in her since birth. The Keller family standards were directly tied to their image, both corporate and social. Forgetting that for even a moment wasn't allowed. Not within the reach of her parents.

But away from them and everyone connected to them...

Her hotel beckoned a block down, its shiny windows reflecting the surrounding landscape. Night was settling in with the slow descent of the sun, bringing with it a slight breeze. The October weather was almost perfect. Not too hot or cold. Yet another reason why she loved California.

She stuffed her convention badge into her briefcase and took a moment to breathe. Her headache had diminished to a dull throb that lessened when she forced her shoulders down. Stretching her neck eased the tension even more. An outside coffee stand tempted her with the alluring scent of freshly ground beans. Her four o'clock alarm that morning was zapping her energy now, but she usually caught another wind if she just persisted through the drain.

The hotel lobby was littered with people in suits, some still sporting their convention badges as they continued to network. The knowledge that she should be doing the same battled her desire to ditch it all. And do what?

She scanned the area for the guy she'd noticed earlier. The one who'd caught her eye and her interest. More than one man openly stared at her, but she ignored them. The speculation she glimpsed on their expressions countered any thought that they were eyeing her up as a potential business contact. Feigning ignorance granted her an element of safety. Plus, bruised egos were hard to overcome in the sales game.

Her steps slowed as she passed the entrance to the

bar. Sectioned away from the check-in area, the wide opening welcomed people in without putting the entire room on display. Softer lighting offered an illusion of quiet supported by the lounge chairs and scattering of cocktail tables. The room was still fairly empty, which only made it more inviting to her.

Her gaze snagged on the profile of a man sitting alone at the far end of the bar, his focus locked on the TV mounted on the wall. A smile formed as she recognized him. What were the odds?

His polite mask was gone, his fatigue visible in the slight downturn of his mouth and the hunch of his shoulders. Once again, she related to him—whoever he was—and admired his openness, along with his confidence that required no front or false projection.

His beard shadow darkened his jaw, adding to his air of unattainable that only made her want to obtain. Was he married? Attached? His roughened good looks had the mature quality of age, which placed him firmly in the questionable zone of taken family man. But then, he could also be single and open to every fantasy circling her mind and nudging her forward.

She entered the bar without another thought. The draw was unexplainable. The urge to meet him had her heading straight for the empty seat next to him. Add in the bonus of getting a drink along with a break from the forced hospitality, and she almost whimpered.

Her prospects for the evening had just changed for the better. At the very least, she'd make another contact and have a chance to relax. But in truth, she was really hoping for more than that—if he was willing to play.

Chapter Two

"Can I get you another?" the bartender asked.

Matthew Hamilton stared at his beer, blinked. "Sure." He emptied the contents in one long swallow before handing the glass to the bartender. "Thanks."

The woman shot him a smile. "No problem." She leaned in conspiratorially. "It's my job." Her flirtatious wink sailed past him before he registered the action. With her blond hair, sculpted features and large breasts accentuated by her tight shirt, she worked the bar like it was her stage.

His chuckle was dry as she pulled another draft from the tap. He scrubbed a hand over his jaw and shook the fog from his mind. "I appreciate it," he told her when she set the full glass before him.

She sent him another suggestive look, her voice softening to a low rumble. "Let me know if you need anything else."

"I'll take a gin and tonic," a woman said as she dropped onto the barstool beside him. Her shoulders visibly sagged, relief swooping in on a brief reprieve before she released a smile and added, "Please."

The bartender straightened, her expression swinging

back to polite in a shift so quick Matt almost laughed. "Bombay?" she asked.

"Sure," the woman responded with a dose of sarcastic enthusiasm. "Sounds great."

He let his laughter out this time. "Long day?"

The woman glanced at him as she lowered her leather briefcase to the ground. "I thought that'd be obvious."

He nodded, acknowledging the truth of her statement as he took in her sleek black pantsuit and white blouse beneath. "Convention drain?"

Her lips twitched, countering her deep exhale. "Yes."

He could commiserate with her on that. For a man who rarely traveled, let alone attended a national convention that drew in thousands of people, the event was a special form of social hell for him. But as the new owner of McPherson Trucking, he saw networking as a required evil if he wanted to expand the company.

The bartender set her drink on the bar, and Matt lifted his glass in a toast to his bar mate, waiting until she clicked it with hers. She took a long drink, her smile full and beautiful when she sat back. "I so needed that."

He froze, his own glass held suspended in the air. He couldn't look away when she leveled the full impact of her smile on him. Her eyes were a striking hue of blue-green that danced with amused relief, mesmerizing him. How long had it been since he'd noticed a woman's smile, let alone her eyes?

Too long.

He chased away his thoughts and interest with a much-needed drink. The TV mounted over the bar provided an excellent distraction, but awareness prickled over his side and teased at desires he shouldn't acknowledge.

She shifted on the stool, crossing her legs as she flicked through her phone, her dark red nails flashing with each decisive swipe. She tucked her hair behind her ear, but the long locks escaped to fall in a gentle wave over her shoulder. Every detail was caught in his peripheral vision until he gave up his pretense and studied her openly.

Her features were young but mature at once in a way that coincided with her mannerisms. She was alone in a bar getting a drink, and she'd chosen the seat next to his when there were empty ones lining the bar, along with plenty of free tables. That bold statement intrigued him more than it should. Yet she hadn't pushed their conversation or initiated the flirting dance.

Her scowl deepened the longer she stared at her phone, the slight pull leaving a small crease between her brows. He itched to rub it away as all signs of her previous relief vanished.

What was causing her stress?

He cut off the thought as soon as it'd formed. It was none of his business. *She* was none of his business.

Normally, he would pay his tab and leave without a backward glance. But he didn't now, not when his desire dug at him in ways he'd thought long gone. Ways that'd been pushing more and more since he'd exchanged his work shirts for suits. Ways that had him craving things better left untouched.

Her thumbs tapped in quick succession as she typed out a message, her lips pursing and releasing in an unintentional tease. A soft glow tinted her cheeks and drew him to the faint smattering of freckles that trailed over her nose. The little imperfections softened her appearance and added an innocence that didn't match the confidence she projected.

"I thought you were relaxing," he commented, unable to hold back.

She looked to him, going still. Her lips curled in a slow crawl upward as she lowered her phone. "Apparently, I'm not very good at that." She hitched her brow in an insinuation of a shrug.

"Maybe you should try harder." He lifted his own brow, enjoying the banter. She was a nice distraction on an otherwise bland evening, that was all. Just a simple conversation. Yet her short chuckle hummed inside him, mocking his lies as it drew his interest forward.

She set her phone on the bar. "There." She folded her hands on her lap. "No more work." The challenge was leveled back at him in her tone, the "what now?" included in her expression.

"That's a start." He indicated her phone but didn't expand even though she clearly expected him to.

Calculation marched through her eyes before she shook her head, looking to the TV. Her thoughts and emotions were masked behind her blank expression, a skill he recognized. Where had she learned it? Why? Eight years as an Army officer had honed it into him, but her...

A couple of men took the seats next to her, their attention lingering as they sat. He stared at them, annoyance building until the closest one noticed. The man's knowing smirk contained a silent apology before he turned away.

She twisted in her seat, turning her back to the two men. "Kennedy," she stated, hand extended, waiting.

He grasped her hand, welcoming her firm grip that

said assertive but not aggressive. "Matt." The foreign knot in his chest loosened as he shoved back the protective rush that'd had him staking a claim where he had no right.

"Nice to meet you, Matt."

"Likewise."

She released his hand, yet her touch lingered with an impression of warmth. His stomach tightened, desire spreading in a slow build that buzzed over his skin and teased him with possibilities.

"What do you do?" she asked, reaching into her suit pocket.

He stalled her hand at the first sign of her business card. "Nope," he said. "No work." She hesitated. "We're relaxing, remember?" He could've—should've—moved his hand away, but he left it resting on hers, almost daring her to object.

She didn't. And that set off a whole different reaction tied to behavior he'd long abandoned—for good reasons.

That tempting smile of hers returned as she slid her card back into her pocket. "All right. I'll play."

Play. He clenched his hand, letting it fall to his lap. The word launched a slew of images that had nothing to do with the innocent way she'd applied it. It took very little to envision her panting beneath him, hands tied over her head, her soft pleas urging him on.

He cleared his throat, washed the ache down with his beer. Nothing good would come of going down that road. But the yearning still lingered, taunting him with what-ifs and why not? It prickled over his skin and pulled dual strings on the control he maintained and longed to wield.

"Tell me, Matt." The emphasis on his name came with a quirk of her lips. "Do you relax in a bar often?"

He held back the sarcastic scoff that raced up. "No." Bars required free time, which he rarely had. "Not usually. You?"

"Only at events like this. Or," she conceded, "when I need to be seen as one of the guys."

The overabundance of men in the now-crowded room emphasized her point. It also highlighted that the most beautiful woman in the bar was sitting beside him, and she had zero chance of being classified as *one of the guys*.

"But then that'd be work," he countered, the buzz intensifying to a firm want that simmered and built the more he talked to her.

Her smile flashed again. "True."

"So it doesn't count." He caught the eye of the bartender and motioned for another round. She didn't object or comment, instead sending him a slightly secret, slightly coy smile before she lowered her gaze.

He managed to keep his groan silent despite the bevy of images that assaulted him. How much control would she surrender? How far would she let him go? How far did he dare let himself go?

"Then how do you normally relax?" She studied him now with a directness that countered any hints of complacency.

His lips quirked. A quick hand job probably wasn't the answer she was looking for. "I run, for one," he said instead. A habit he'd kept since the service.

She wrinkled her nose, the action cute when combined with her freckles. "I could never get into running."

"No?"

She shook her head. "I never found that magic plateau people talk about where it becomes invigorating instead of awful."

He scanned her, confirming what he already knew. Her breasts strained against her blouse, the faint impression of her bra teasing him with lace and secrets. Her waist was trim, legs long. She was fit and most likely sexy as hell beneath her suit.

He swallowed, his interest escaping when he looked up. "Then what do you do?"

Her quick inhalation ignited the connection between them. "I walk. Play tennis. Golf." Her shrug was as much tease as dismissal. "Among other things." Her eyelids dipped, her throaty undertone launching a whole new stream of dirty thoughts.

His dick took note, urging him to take the bait she unabashedly dangled. But to what end? He had nothing to offer her past this night. And he was making leaps she hadn't asked for.

"Do you come to a lot of these?" he asked, changing the topic while he still could. He motioned to the room in general to indicate the convention.

She glanced over her shoulder. "More than I'd like, but it's part of my job. I—"

"Nope." He cut her off. "No work."

"But—"

He swiveled his head when she started to object, holding firm to his directive. Information led to expectations, which he couldn't have, let alone give to her.

"You're tough," she stated, but her scowl held no heat.

That was all it took to have that old urge racing forward, demanding he show her just how tough he could be. His shoulders drew back as the power filled him. It flooded his chest and triggered a wave of memories unleashed by his latent control kink. The one he'd denied since his wife had walked out, seeking more than he could give and leaving their two kids behind.

She turned away to take her new drink from the bartender, unaware of how close he was to ditching every rule, every restriction, every self-imposed mandate he'd laid down over a decade ago.

"Thank you." She shot him a smile as she squeezed the lime into her gin and tonic. "For the drink."

"It's the least I can do," he said, exchanging his empty glass for the full one. His casual pretense did nothing to calm the lust and longing that was slowly silencing his will. "In the interest of relaxing."

"Of course. Relaxing." Her nod was slow and cunning. "But there are other ways to do that." Mischief gleamed in her stunning eyes.

That confidence, that directness, that lack of pretense or the typical over-flirty games was too damn alluring. Her strength pulled him in, tempting him to take what she offered. That awareness sunk beneath his skin to entwine with his darkest wants.

He let her implication hang between them on the sultry note it was before he finally said, "There are."

Lust flowed into her expression, her lips parting before she closed them to swallow. "Can I ask you something?" That tiny frown line appeared between her brows. He stilled, his defenses going up on habit. "This is purely to further define the boundaries," she clarified.

A lightness was back in her voice, but it didn't

change the weight of her words. He narrowed his eyes, assessed. "What boundaries?"

"Between us." She motioned between them before studying his ring finger. "Are you married or attached?" Her gaze was firm when it landed on him.

His smile grew without his consent. The boldness worked for her. "No." He left it at that.

"No," she restated, smiling slightly. "Can I ask why?"

He inhaled, debated his response. "Time. Desire." He dismissed those with a lift of his shoulder. The real answer went too deep for a simple discussion at the bar with a woman he'd just met. "What about you?" he countered, pointedly looking to her left hand.

She wiggled her fingers before him, all of them bare. "No."

"Can I ask why?"

"Time. Desire," she mimicked, that humorous tone carrying to her expression.

He looked away before his gaze dropped to the inviting curve of her lips. Yet he could still picture the arch and dip, imagine the feel of them beneath his own, on his skin, kissing down—

"Are you here with others?" He tossed out, scanning the room, noting every man who studied her. He was playing with fire and couldn't get himself to pull back.

"A couple of sales guys, yes."

"And they're where?"

"At another hotel." Her tone was as steady as her gaze. She was on the same track as him and had no qualms about letting him know. "I like the distance."

"They're that bad?"

"No. Not at all." She let that rest for a beat before adding, "I just value my freedom."

Like the freedom to engage with a man she'd just met in a bar? The freedom to be direct about her interest? The freedom to go up to his room and let him do the explicit things to her that refused to leave his thoughts?

Kennedy presented an opportunity, one he longed to accept. She was openly seeking what he wanted to give her, at least partially. Would she have looked at him if he'd been in his usual jeans and T-shirt? The suit conformed to his CEO role, yet it wasn't his norm.

Only it had been lately.

It'd become his new uniform when the other was safer. Power came with the suit. Expected authority and unearned respect were granted based on nothing more than his appearance. He'd forgotten how emboldening that could be. How it urged him to live up to every expectation, and then be better. To be the one who could provide. Who cared.

Who was more than just an overbearing Army officer.

Sex was clearly on the table, but what did she truly need from him? Would she give him more than a quick fuck and thank you? Would she let him take control? What if her answer was yes?

Visions of her naked, her power entrusted to him as he hunted out her darkest desires, crushed his lingering hesitation.

He leaned toward her. The intoxicating blend of her perfume wove through him, painting a picture he longed to uncover. Dark, seductive without being obvious. He let every lustful thought and all of his suppressed hunger tumble into his voice. "What do you do with that freedom?"

No one he knew was here and few here knew him.

His lips quirked at the status he'd been cursing when he'd left the convention hall after hours of introductions in his hunt for every possible opportunity. And here one sat, unexpected, but the potential was wide open.

The only thing holding him back was his own damn rules. Ones he could bend or break—or redefine.

Chapter Three

Matt's eyelids lowered just a notch, his head tilting as he waited for her response. The look pulled her in, daring her to object while encouraging her to concede. His authority prickled over her skin like little darts of permission she longed to explore.

How would he wield the strength he exuded? Would it be tempered with the gentleness that'd been in his touch? Would he demand too much or not enough?

Desire mingled with the calculated risk. She knew nothing about him, yet their mutual anonymity enticed her more. That in itself was a freedom she reveled in.

She could be anything—have anything—with him.

"Lots of things," she finally answered, her elusiveness weighted by the huskiness that'd fallen into her tone. She savored the anticipation that flowed openly between them. Possibilities spread out on a chance she rarely took but had no desire to deflect. "Do you have any suggestions?"

There was no mistaking the predatory hunger simmering below his control. "I have a few ideas."

"Such as?" Where would he go with this? Did the game excite him as much as it did her?

He lifted his shoulder, his gaze dropping to her lips.

"Some things are better discovered than told." His eyes had deepened to a molten brown when he met hers. "Wouldn't you agree?"

A soft laugh escaped, want crashing forward. Her pulse kicked up, nerves fluttering. "What are you suggesting?" What was *she* suggesting? At some point, her interest had shifted from simple sex to something riskier and far more tempting.

The corner of his mouth quirked up before he finished off his beer. He set the glass on the bar with a precision that dismissed his casual front. "I wouldn't presume to suggest anything." The heat in his eyes said otherwise.

"Of course not," she conceded. She waited a beat, desire overtaking discretion. "But if I was?"

Some men fled at this point. Others bumbled the pass, while way too many fast-tracked her to slut status. Their demeanor always gave them away. A dose of blatant assumption paired with a leer would end their discussion.

Nothing changed on his expression, but his thoughts were instantly shielded behind the mask that slammed down. Gone was the heat and suggestion. In its place was a cold wall that emanated nothing. No disdain or interest. Just…nothing.

The shift was swift, but she managed to hold in her disappointment. She let her own mask slip in as she recrossed her legs. The move created distance, but that didn't stop the heat from simmering over her skin.

She wouldn't be shamed. That emotion had been purged from her years ago. At least in regards to her sexuality. But screw him for trying.

"I'd be foolish to decline," he said when she reached for her briefcase.

Her snort said everything. "There's nothing to decline." Not anymore.

"Kennedy."

His light touch to her arm shocked her still. Awareness vibrated outward from the touchpoint, both chilling and warming her. She didn't attempt to hide her annoyance when she looked to him.

"I'm sorry," he said, honesty softening his expression and tone. "I didn't mean to offend you."

She studied him, mouth dry. Desire hummed counter chords of want and warning. She should move her arm away from his touch, just like she should end the conversation and leave. Instead, she asked, "What happened?"

His brows dipped, nostrils flaring in the long moment before he responded. "You make me want things I shouldn't."

She could say the same. "Like?" She wet her lips, distinctly aware of the slow stroke of his thumb on her arm.

A sound that edged way too close to a growl rumbled past her. She squeezed her legs to hold back the hunger that blazed to life. That had to have been her imagination. The bar noise distorting sound. Right?

He leaned in, and she turned her head, giving him her ear. A stroke of heated air ghosted over the sensitive skin, sending a wave of goose bumps down her neck. "Like crushing you against the door of my room and finally tasting those tempting lips of yours. To start."

Oh...my... "And then?" she whispered, longing reaching out to caress a desire she barely acknowledged.

What would it be like to give him what she never relinquished to anyone, ever?

"And then…" He blew a gentle stream of air over the shell of her ear. "I'd uncover each secret hidden beneath that expensive suit of yours and tease them out until you gave me everything you're afraid to ask for."

Her swallow hitched on the knot that'd formed in her throat. The image he'd just planted in her head uncurled and spread in a tantalizing shift of power. One she'd only entertained in her most secret fantasies but never dared to explore. Not within her circle of influence. Not with someone who could exploit submission as a weakness.

He eased back, hunger brazenly displayed. Her nipples tightened in a cry of yes. She wanted every drop of the carnal energy radiating off him. Never, not once in her life, had a man affected her like this.

And she was far from innocent.

"Why shouldn't you want that?" she managed to ask when she was certain her voice wouldn't waver.

He studied her for a long moment before releasing a slow breath. "I put that part of my life behind me long ago." He drew his hand away and motioned to the bartender for their tabs.

She missed his touch almost immediately. Would it burn over her skin, sink into her bones to turn her legs to jelly? Would he release that predatory growl if she ran her hand over his chest?

"What part?" she asked after she'd yanked her thoughts back to what he'd said. "The sex part?"

His chuckle held little humor or sound. She saw it more than heard it. He scrubbed a hand over his stubbled jaw, amusement wiping away the darkness that lurked around him. "Yes and no."

That intrigued her even more, but she didn't need his life story to have sex with him.

"Maybe it's time to add it back into your life." She raised a brow. "I hear it's a really good way to relax." She made a bad attempt to hold back her smile, failing almost before she tried.

He shook his head in a slow swivel that countered the smirk growing in stunning increments. It erased the cool reserve and transformed him from dangerous to... gorgeous. The thought of his sexual frustration being unleashed on her turned her interest to instant want.

"It is, is it?" He paused to sign the tab, sliding hers into his folder before she could object. He flipped the folder closed, the pen tucked inside, and grabbed his tablet before he stood. His hand grazed over her shoulder in a touch that could've been accidental but wasn't.

She stared up at him, caught in his game despite her attempt to play her own. Her pulse skittered even as she maintained her calm. She wouldn't chase, and she was pretty certain he wouldn't either.

"Would you care to join me?" he asked.

"For?" she asked with a smirk of her own, already sliding out of her chair, her briefcase and phone in her hand.

He turned away without answering, but her grin spread as she followed him from the bar. His proud carriage enticed people to clear a path without so much as an "excuse me" from him.

She tracked the breadth of his back down to the impression of his ass beneath his suit coat. It wasn't the suit, but the confidence he projected within it. The command that flowed naturally from his demeanor and movements that had her so close to relinquishing what she protected the most.

He turned to her as they emerged from the bar, sliding his tablet into his inner pocket. The sun had set, and she distantly acknowledged that she should be hungry, but food was the last thing on her mind.

"My room?" he asked. No preamble. No hesitation. Whatever doubts he'd had before were gone now. That heat was back in his eyes, his intent clear.

"Sounds good." It was easier to leave than to kick a man out. And that thought should've had her stopping altogether. She was far from naïve, though, and she trusted her instincts. But… "Are you here with anyone?"

He frowned slightly. "No. I'm looking for a new salesman—or two."

"Are they hard to find in your industry?"

"Not that I'm aware of." The vagueness didn't surprise or worry her. Not when he shot her that "no work" look.

"Fine," she relented as they entered the elevator. "Just promise me something."

He waited for the doors to close before turning his full attention to her. "If I can."

She choked back her scoff. At least he was honest. They were alone for the first time and the significance lit up every cell teetering on the edge of all in or out. She could almost feel him touching her despite the two feet of space between them.

"No means no," she stated, firm on her demand.

"Of course." Annoyance wrinkled his forehead.

"At any point."

His expression softened, understanding easing over it. "I promise."

For some unexplained reason, she trusted that. It was just words, but he came across as a man of honor. "Thank you."

He settled his hand on her lower back as he guided her out of the elevator and down the hall. His touch was almost impersonal, yet it scorched through her clothing to imprint his palm on her skin. A flutter rippled through her stomach in a twist that leaned toward excitement.

Matt was new. He screamed of power and control. He was an indulgence she would never allow herself at home. Not like this. Not where image was everything.

He slid his keycard from his pocket, pausing. "You're sure?"

Yes. No. Her heart thudded in her ears. "Are you?"

He gave away nothing as he skimmed the back of his fingers down her cheek. The caress was gentle, a promise without words. It settled into her, easing the nerves that'd surfaced.

Neither of them answered, not verbally anyway. This was nothing more than sex between adults. Hopefully wild, passionate sex that left her gasping for breath. The thrill came in the unknown. Anything could happen once she entered his room. He could be a total dud, or he could fuck her blind and then do it again.

He grazed the tips of his fingers over her lips in a touch so soft she almost sighed. "I can't promise gentle."

"Did I say I wanted gentle?"

His breath hitched. "How much will you give me?"

She flicked her tongue out to skim it over his fingertips, leveling her hesitation with the daring she'd ridden her entire life. "More than I ever have with another."

His eyes narrowed, head tilting slightly as his fingers stilled. "Do you have any idea what you're doing to me?"

She managed a small head shake. Anticipation trembled down her back and scrambled in her chest. They were dancing around a subject that probably should've been articulated, but defining it would make it too real. "I can only hope."

His eyes fell closed. He swallowed, his Adam's apple bobbing beneath the force. A fierce need darkened his eyes and called to her when he opened them. A whisper of fear skittered near the desire drawing her forward. She couldn't identify it or why it was there, but it held. Not in warning, though.

She was stepping into the unknown in ways she couldn't clarify. Yet she wasn't turning around. Not now.

Not when she was so close to potentially fulfilling the craving she'd ruthlessly denied for years. She'd been taking her power from men since she'd first discovered how to wield it, but she'd never willingly given her power to anyone.

Not until now.

Chapter Four

Matt swiped his keycard over the lock, heart pounding with measured excitement. Could he control his hunger? Did he have to? Need to?

And after? What then?

He inhaled long and slow when she passed him to enter his room. Her scent drew him in, the fragrant spice begging him to touch her and savor every hidden curve and secret.

Damn how he wanted to—was going to.

He closed the door behind him as he snagged her hand and pulled her around. He had her back to the door, his body pressed against hers in the next instant. Her soft gasp pinged at the restless urgency that'd been building since she'd taken a seat next to him. Warm breaths chased his own, kissing his lips in teasing acts of foreplay.

She stared at him through the shadowed darkness. Her bottom lip slipped between her teeth only to fall out in a slow roll. He choked back a groan. Could he prolong this moment, this entire encounter with her? He shouldn't—and that argument had fled when he'd led her from the bar.

He slid his fingers along her jaw in a slow caress up

and through her silky hair. Patience tempered the urgency with a reminder of the sweet payoff to come. He gripped the back of her head and jerked her forward.

Her lips parted, a breathy grunt teasing him further. Her hand came to his chest, her breasts pushing against him with each breath. She didn't object to his rough handling, though. Not even a little.

It only took a bit of pressure to tilt her head, raising her mouth to his. Power pulsed on the enticing call of control.

He could own this. Her. His...dominant need.

The one that'd slid into his marriage on the drive to help his overwhelmed wife only to morph into a lifestyle he didn't want and his wife needed more of. He wasn't a Dom, but his sexual desires had unwittingly landed him in that role. His blindness had hurt so many, but most of all his children.

But he wasn't blind now. This was just a night—completely separate from his life back home. He wouldn't allow his desires to endanger his kids ever again.

"Say no," he whispered, his willpower teetering on the thin line of jump or fall back. Did she understand what he wanted? Would she yield to him now, when it was real instead of implied?

A long moment passed before her soft "yes" came out.

He crushed his mouth to hers, desperation crashing with the frantic need throbbing in his chest. Her moan vibrated on a long rumble of pleasure when their tongues clashed. He drove deeper, finding hints of gin and the same hunger ravishing him. It clawed at his restraint in a persistent chant that overwhelmed everything else.

"Damn," he mumbled when he came up for air, breaths heavy. He didn't wait for a response before he dipped back in for another taste. His head swam with lust, his craving rejoicing in its freedom.

Kennedy gripped his nape and gave back everything he took. She didn't fight but merged with him, her hips shifting into his, head tilting further as he drove her into the door. Her gasps peppered with his in their frenzied surge of instant want.

He had to get her naked. Had to see her writhing beneath him. Had to feel her clenching him as she came.

His erection throbbed beneath the layers of clothing separating them. The ache was so damn good. Heavenly after years of denying this very base need. Yes, he'd fucked in the twelve years since he'd taken full custody of his kids, but not like this. Not…

He reared back, chest heaving. "I'm going to fuck you so damn hard." His admission tumbled out, but he wouldn't hide from the truth.

"Good," she purred, her own breaths quick and shallow. She trailed her fingers down his jaw, his beard stubble rasping beneath the tips. The tenderness reached in to unleash yet another longing he'd crushed in the name of duty.

A longing he still couldn't have. Not yet. Maybe someday, but not…now.

He grabbed her wrist and trapped it against the door before he eased her briefcase from her other shoulder. He set it gently on the floor, cursing the hard rectangle of his tablet digging into his ribs.

She let him raise her free wrist, sliding them both over her head until her arms were stretched high. Her breath caught, but she didn't look away.

"Does this bother you?" He tightened his hold a fraction, intent on every twitch or hitch that came from her. This was as close to stating his true wants as he could get. Anything more explicit would define his downfall too clearly.

She tested his grip, just a bit, before relaxing. Her head rested against the door, tension easing from her muscles so beautifully he almost groaned. Her final sigh held that amazing note of submission he'd missed so damn much. "No."

Her response unleashed every dream and false hope he'd harbored for the last hour. His kiss bordered on harsh when he dove back in. The carnal want blazing through his system urged him to take full control. To relinquish every doubt and embrace the side of him he'd starved.

Adrenaline pumped its addictive blend of power and invincibility through him as he claimed her. He'd own this moment—her—and walk away.

A night. He could have a night.

He forced himself to step back, drawing her with him into the room. The curtains were open to display the king-sized bed dominating the space. His clothes were neatly hung in the closet, his suitcase on the stand tucked within it. He released her hands and flicked on the small desk lamp. The yellow glow softened her features, or was her mellow expression because of him?

Her lips were puffy, her lipstick dulled. A blush colored her cheeks, which highlighted the freckles dotting her nose. Anticipation hummed a low tune the longer he stared at her. It resonated deep in his chest, dancing with his favorite song.

"Undress." His voice came out on a low rumble of

authority that echoed like an old friend. His subordinates had jumped to attention the second his officer tone emerged.

She didn't move for a long moment, her expression unchanging. He didn't give either. This was another subtle definition of boundaries. He should lay them out, have a "discussion."

But they were just fucking now. Having fun.

Rules and definition would change it into... something else.

Her eyelids lowered, a sultry heat overtaking her expression as she slid her suit coat off. Power blazed in her movements. She could've objected or changed the game by simply reaching for him. But she hadn't.

Desire simmered in a hot knot in his groin. She laid the coat over the back of the desk chair before undoing the buttons on her blouse in slow movements. Each inch of revealed skin was another tease—and she knew it. Awareness lit her eyes, passion feeding every action.

She owned this, every single decision and deed, and that was so damn hot. Her strength fed his own.

He should hold back. He should make her finish. He should...

Three strides and his hands were around her waist, her skin sliding beneath his palms. Soft and warm, he reveled in the simple touch. Skin to skin contact was a luxury he rarely offered himself.

"I thought—"

He cut off her question with another kiss. It burned hot the second their lips met. He tried to restrain himself, but his willpower had fled. She was soft and strong, giving, yet able to hold her own. And she was in his arms.

He shoved her blouse away and sought out the soft

mound of her breast. He caught her cry and the rumbled purr that followed. The lacy fabric of her bra abraded his fingertips before he cupped the fullness beneath.

She tugged him closer, thrusting her chest up. Her silent request urged him. He could've made her beg, but he didn't want that. At least not yet.

He flicked a finger over her nipple. She flinched, stilled. He eased back enough to catch every response. Need mixed with hunger and desire in a flush that spread down her chest, which was speckled with the same smattering of freckles that graced her nose. The urge to count them all, to find every last one, had him stripping her bra away.

She took a step back to undo her pants, pushing them over her hips until they pooled at her feet. Her shoulders were back when she straightened.

He sucked in a breath, his erection hard and insistent. She was gorgeous. Her dark hair fell like silk over her shoulders to tease the curve of her full breasts. Rosy nipples were puckered and waiting for him to bite. The lacy white wedge of her panties accentuated her trim waist and the length of her legs.

Confidence radiated, from her posture to the steady way she held his gaze. Absent was any hint of shyness or discomfort.

"You like this," he stated.

Her brow flicked in a coy dismissal. "Like what?"

He gave her a slow once over, control settling over him in an unwavering calm. "Showing yourself to me."

The truth of that was displayed in the slow roll of her shoulders and the hooded look that seared him with its heat. She slid a palm over her abdomen, her pinky finger edging the line of her panties.

"So do you." She dropped her eyes to his erection. The damn thing twitched beneath the weight of her gaze.

"What else do you like?" He put the focus back on her.

Her hand shifted in little movements just over her pussy, her pinky finger inching lower. She bit her lip, hips rocking lightly.

"Do it," he ordered. Lust boiled in his balls and threatened to unhinge his control. "Touch yourself."

Her chin lifted, a flash of defiance adding a dark edge to her features. She never looked away as she eased her fingers south. Her lips parted. A soft moan tumbled out, and still she held his gaze. Heat burned over the distance that separated them. Sweat collected along his spine. That fucking hunger ate at his chest and reminded him of how starved he'd been—was.

Her little show of obedience buzzed with the power she had and gave him. And that right there was more than he'd ever had before. More than his wife in their six years of D/s games had ever given him.

He yanked her in, tipping her back until he could feast on one of those plump nipples. The tip rolled under his tongue before he drew it deeper, sucked harder. Her cry held a slice of pain, but she curved into him, her nails digging into the back of his head as she held him to her chest.

She was wild and…

He clamped his teeth around the tender bud and pulled away. Her back arched deeper, her whimper a heavenly note. Her pussy was slick and warm when he slid his fingers through it.

His dick strained against his slacks, and his tie draped down her side. A part of him loved the contrast of being fully clothed when she was almost naked. Yet another part ached to feel her skin against his.

"Matt."

The panted breath of his name rang as an exclamation and plea at once. His dominant beast hummed its own demanding response. The need crawled over his skin and sunk into cracks he'd thought sealed shut.

He spun them around to guide her backward, that lustful heat scorching him. Her gasp cut sharp when her back hit the window. She jerked away before slowly settling against it.

The half window had a small ledge that hit her hips, jutting them forward at a perfect angle. One he couldn't refuse.

He slid his erection in a long line over her mound. The action tortured him as much as her. Want pulsed in his groin and scrambled through his chest. His stifled groan tore at his control while hardening his determination to hold back.

For just a bit longer.

He dipped to torture her nipple with more bites tempered by teasing licks. Her rumbled moans scrambled down his spine to grip his balls. Hunger ate at his restraint, yet he ignored every crazed instinct urging him to fuck her now, letting it build as he drove her higher.

"Please," she begged as she attempted to shift him to her other breast. He'd deliberately focused on just the one to get this exact response. He wanted her off balance.

He sucked long and hard, flicking the oversensitive tip when he pulled back with it firmly trapped between his teeth. She bucked, arching with him until he held her in place.

Her soft curse curled in his groin and hardened his dick even more—if that was possible. He let the bud slip from his mouth with a sudden pop. She gasped, sagging back with heavy breaths. The soft glow of the lamp enhanced the deep red tint of her abused nipple, which was plump and swollen compared to the other one.

One little graze with his finger had her shrinking back, wincing. But her pants increased along with the heat burning in her eyes. The blue in them seemed to shine instead of darken, every want telegraphed.

She wet her lips. "You're a very naughty man."

He didn't deny it, not when every thought in his head confirmed her assessment. Her breath held when he slid his hand beneath her panties to run his finger through her folds. The wetness tore a silent curse from his lips. She was so ready for him.

He leaned in, pausing when his lips grazed hers. He rolled her clit beneath his fingertip, caught her gasp. Her eyelids lowered, her swallow noticeable.

"And you love it," he stated, almost daring her to contradict him.

A long moment passed in held expectation before she whispered, "I do."

Chapter Five

Trapped against the window, the world gone except for Matt, Kennedy gave him everything. Her control and deepest desire. Her worries and fears. The stress, pressure and expectations she'd lived with since birth.

And in return, he gave her a freedom she'd never known before.

Her cry vibrated in her throat, trapped by the hard crush of his mouth. He timed the carnal assault with the deep thrust of his finger into her. Her walls clenched around the invasion, *yes* echoing in her head.

She clung to him, wanting closer and so much more. Matt was everything she wouldn't let herself have. Strong, controlling, sexy and just kind enough to make her chest ache. Longing buzzed around the emptiness she ruthlessly ignored most days.

Hell, for most of her life.

But this wasn't about past wants or hurts. No, this was about sex. Wild, unadulterated pleasure. This, she could own.

The sharp edge of the wall dug into her lower back and she rode that pain like she did his finger. Every nerve ending sparked in heightened awareness that somehow numbed her mind. He worked her body like he'd fucked her for years, plucking each chord with a mastery she responded to.

He added a second finger, the thickness sensitizing her vagina with the temptation of more, every thrust slow yet hard. The precise movements were maddeningly intense but not. The urge to scream in frustration was countered by the luxury of letting go. Her blood pulsed with the abandon he'd somehow tapped into with just a look, a touch, a command.

She wrapped a leg around his thigh to get closer and give him more access at once. His thumb worked her clit with every plunge of his fingers. The insistent drum of her heart throbbed each beat in her sore nipple, which ached for more abuse while the other wept for even a small touch.

"Matt," she whispered when he finally freed her mouth. She tried to chase his retreating lips, already missing the intoxicating flavor of passion and demand, but his firm hold kept his mouth just out of reach.

His fingers stilled inside her, the unmoving fullness a tempting torture all its own. She longed to yank his tie free and shirt off, to dig her fingers into his chest and run them over his skin. Yet she loved the strength he exuded in his suit.

A symbol of authority when worn with confidence. The uniform of success and, on some men, power.

It was a weakness she barely acknowledged, one she'd never give away either. But she could secretly revel in her little fetish and let the rush fill her.

He slipped his hand down her neck, a wake of goose bumps shimmering behind the deliberate movement. The light grip on her throat forced her chin up, her breaths short. His expression didn't change despite the clear statement he was making.

The power belonged to him.

Old fears rushed forward before she let her resistance go, a strange peace settling in when her hands hung loose at her sides. It eased through her on a whisper of surprise and relief.

He could have it—the power—for now.

His curse was mouthed, but she read it clearly. Desire raged in a flash of heat in his eyes, his hold tightening with a quick flinch. He slid his fingers from her, leaving her empty and wanting.

She sucked in a breath when he trailed those fingers up her abdomen, her juices tracing a wet path to her neglected nipple. He held his finger poised over the bud until it throbbed in a stinging cry for attention. But he swiveled his head, lifting his fingers to suck them between his lips.

His eyelids lowered in time with her moan. Her mouth watered, and though she'd never had an overt desire to taste herself, she did now. It tore at her throat and dug at a longing she didn't try to understand.

His nostrils flared, that wonderful rumble emanating from his chest as he eased his fingers from his mouth. He said nothing as he slid his fingers deep within her once again.

Her leg trembled, and she gripped the window ledge for support. Her muscles tightened around the intrusion, relief quickly shifting to need.

His intent was clear when he slipped his fingers from her. That dark desire flared when he held them over her lips. The pungent scent of her juices hit her nose with the blatant declaration of her desire. It pumped into her awareness and set off a chain reaction back to her pussy. Juices dampened her panties as she parted her lips in anticipation.

"You are so damn…"

She lost track of his words when he slid his fingers into her mouth. She sucked on them immediately, eyes falling closed. A wild hunger overtook all logic as she lapped up every harsh drop. The bitterness coated her mouth yet she savored the taste without questioning why.

Her head buzzed in a static state of nothing that left her free to simply do. Be. In this moment, she could give herself to him without recriminations—especially her own.

Her eyes flew open when she was spun around, her hands coming up to catch herself against the glass. Her heart raced in a mix of fear and excitement when he ripped her panties down her legs, but she automatically helped him as she kicked them free.

He pressed her into the window, that damn ledge cutting a sharp path across her hips as it forced her bottom out. Her nipples contracted against the cool touch of the glass, yet that same coolness was refreshing on her forehead.

He slid the hard line of his erection up her butt crack, sending off another rush of hunger. The material of his suit brushed her skin in a tempting reminder of the power he held, that she'd given him. It hummed through her need and mellowed her thoughts in ways she couldn't explain.

"Can you see them?" he growled near her ear. "Down there. Walking on the path. Going about their lives?" He dug one hand between them, the other coming around to pinch her nipple. The sore one. The one that already throbbed from his abuse. Pain laced its way to her pussy on a path of pure joy that countered every natural instinct.

"Answer me, Kennedy."

His demand snapped in to pluck at her base need to please. To be praised. To be...seen.

"Yes," she answered, her roiling emotions camouflaged behind the firm timbre she forced into her voice. "I see them."

He teased his fingers through her pussy, spreading her juices over every fold and crease. She bit her lip to hold in her moan, but her knees still dipped, hips rolling back.

"What if they look up?" The naughty rumble behind his words enticed her to imagine that very thing. "Would they see you plastered against the window?" He circled a finger over her anus, pressing slightly.

A shocked cry slipped free. Her muscles clenched around the unexpected touch. He twisted her nipple, her thoughts successfully pulled to the spark of agony that had somehow morphed to pleasure. She wanted more of the erotic torture when logic said she shouldn't.

"Would they see me taking you?" The digit slid deeper. "Fucking you?" His voice deepened on the last question, his own need scrambling through.

What if? She stared at the people far below and tried to picture what they'd see. The passion or the force? The wild depravity or the control? Her being taken or willingly giving?

"I'd love it." The truth slid free without thought. The rush of being claimed so thoroughly, of owning every moment of it, sang through her on another wave of breathless release.

"I could fuck you here," he taunted, pumping his finger in short strokes that hit every nerve ending designed to protect that opening.

"You could," she choked out, her mind scrambling to process her response even as he growled his approval. She wasn't a stranger to anal play. She'd done it to herself plenty of times. But offering it up to a man whose last name she still didn't know? That was new.

But so was this entire night.

She hunted for even a hint of regret—about any of it—and found none. Would it come later? She didn't care, not now.

She was thirty-six years old. She could get screwed against a hotel window if she wanted to. And she so wanted to.

Her nipple throbbed in relief when he suddenly released it. Her mind fuzzed out on the pulsing beat until he stroked a finger over her clit. She jerked, breath catching as he upped his movements. Want crested to a frantic obsession under his knowing touch. The continued tease of her anus timed with the equal attention to her clit had her pussy clenching to be filled.

Once again, the obvious neglect only intensified the ache. Would he fuck her?

"What if someone is watching from one of those darkened windows?"

Panic spiked a snarled knot in her chest that had her frantically searching every window in her sight. Logic didn't penetrate for a long moment, her hunt pinging back nothing but a sea of dark reflections, the lower ones peppered with white and yellow lights from the harbor.

The windows were mirrored. No one could see them.

But the risk still danced in her awareness. What if they could be seen? What if the reflective quality was only an illusion?

The exhibitionist in her reveled in the idea. He knew it and was exploiting it. The knowledge only heightened her lust when it would've killed it in any other situation.

"Do you think they'd wonder what I'm doing to put that look on your face?" He lightened his touch to a soft brush on her clit and slow circle over her anus that succeeded in driving her need deeper.

She wanted to come. Wanted to cry out with her release, but he wasn't giving it to her—yet. She shook her head, but it didn't clear the fog within it.

"Wonder if I'm teasing you with my fingers or my dick or a toy." Heat covered every word and singed her neck as he spoke them into her ear.

Her breaths were short and heavy, each telling hitch giving away what she wasn't saying. She turned her face toward his, swallowed. "Your dick would be nice."

He cut off his chuckle by taking her mouth in another consuming kiss that twisted her neck and contorted her spine. She reveled in that too. In the mindless take and wild strokes of his tongue. It screamed of his own desire, of the control he struggled to maintain.

He wasn't detached from the moment, not even slightly.

Air raced into her lungs when he jerked back. That same air swooped in to chill her back. She missed his heat almost immediately.

"Stay there," he ordered before stalking away.

She let her eyes fall closed and focused on his movements behind her. The flick of the bathroom light, a rustle of items. Her thoughts ping-ponged around possibilities only to settle at the distinctive crinkle and tear of a condom wrapper. She had one in her wallet—and she'd totally forgotten about protection.

She never overlooked safety, especially her own. That was yet another first of many for this evening.

Material swished, a belt slicked through loops before being set on the desk, the buckle clicking its dismissal. The purr of his zipper became a cry of forewarning. It prickled over her nape and raced to her pussy.

She could turn around or open her eyes and possibly catch his reflection in the window, but she didn't. Instead, she savored the anticipation, let it build along with the easy languidness that'd settled into her.

The first long stroke of his palm down her spine calmed her even more. The press of his chest against her back spread a rush of answered longing through her chest. The heat was like silk, his skin a balm she hadn't been aware of needing. Her head fell back, hips hunting for the heavy thickness of his erection. It scorched a path through the slick crease of her pussy when he pulled her tight to him.

"I'm going to fuck you, Kennedy." She choked on her gasp, caught in the spell he'd so expertly woven. "Against this window. Your passion displayed to the world but owned by me." He rolled his hips, his dick sliding over her aching folds until the head caught on her entrance.

Her whimper escaped this time, desire trembling in every muscle. "Yes," she managed to whisper. "Please."

Take me any way you want.

Chapter Six

Heat wrapped around his dick in a heady clench of slickness as Matt finally gave in to the frantic need to have Kennedy. Desire blacked out his good intentions to consume him with thoughts of ravishing her against the window and on the bed and in the shower and...

A scratchy groan scrambled free when he bottomed out before he was ready. The position wasn't optimal for deep penetration, but it was so damn hot. She clung to his sides, her back arched, breast thrust out to emphasize each clipped breath.

He forced the uncomfortable position if only to reclaim his control. Their hazy reflection provided a close-up of the man he'd tried so hard to shut down. The one he'd iced and flat-out ignored for the last twelve years.

Look at him now.

Damn if it didn't feel good, though. Right. Like he'd finally found that missing part of himself. But he'd known where it'd been all along. The fierce intent in the bastard staring back at him mocked his naivety.

This...kink had never died.

And he wasn't the only one here. This was about more than him. Way more.

"You're beautiful," he told her, meaning every word.

A shiver trembled through her to vibrate against his chest. He focused on her reflection, on her soft whimper and hitched breath as he caressed her abdomen, easing lower. The trimmed fuzz of hair provided zero protection from his gaze or his touch. It tickled his fingertips in a seductive warning that only tempted him lower.

Fuck he loved the tease. Nature had provided an enticer, which so many now chose to eliminate. He'd never understand why. He found the slick, smooth heat hidden below, and he chuckled at his hypocrisy. He also loved the unhampered access to her pussy.

And she'd unknowingly given him both.

"Matt," she said with more air than sound.

His chest clenched around the longing it sent off, like it'd done every time she'd said his name in that same breathless want-mixed plea.

"Kennedy," he answered right back, his own blend of need and hunger included. He rolled her clit beneath his finger, his stomach contracting against the rampant urgency building in his groin.

She tried to rock her hips, but he wouldn't let her. One movement would end this moment, this…quiet. Peace settled in his heart without guilt or recriminations for wanting this. For still needing it when it'd hurt the two people who were more important to him than his screwed-up desires.

"Fuck me," Kennedy said, eyeing him in the window. Lust encompassed her features, her strength still visible despite her vulnerable position. Not once had she cowered or scrambled to please him, yet she'd held nothing back. "Please."

That one little word was an enormous gift from her, one made in trust. It slithered over his skin and scrambled to the heart of his craving. That damn drive to control, but to also help. To give someone what they needed to feel better, be better.

And that last soft plea was his undoing.

He shoved her forward, ensuring she caught herself before her face hit the glass. Her gasp, cut short by a low moan, was his signal to let loose. The fervor he'd been holding back burst free on a feral cry. He grabbed her hips and drove into her on long plunges that rocked her forward on every thrust.

Her fingers squeaked on the glass, her breaths leaving a growing fog. Want crested too fast in his balls when he loathed to end this. Not yet. Not...

He slowed, chest heaving. Urgency pulsed in his dick and knotted his stomach, but he wouldn't let it win. This he could own. Control.

Kennedy sagged against the glass, a pleading moan slipping between her parted lips. Any fears that he'd gotten too rough were nullified by the impassioned flush and dazed bliss displayed in her profile.

He shifted his focus to where they were joined as he slowly withdrew from her. Her juices coated his dick, the slickness gleaming against the condom. He slid back in on the same torturous pace. Want drew his balls up and he trembled with the passion he refused to set free. Not...

"Fuck."

The harshness of her uninhibited curse took another chunk out of his restraint. When she lifted her knee to rest it on the window ledge, he gave up all pretense of control.

He had none. Not...now.

He rammed into her with all the pent-up frustration

she'd ignited with one little suggestion. One sly look had unlocked years of denial he didn't want back. Not when he could have this. Own this.

Each thrust released another wave of throttled hunger until there was nothing left but amazement. Of freedom to be himself.

And he reveled in all of it. Her sweet sounds as she pawed the window that meshed so perfectly with the harsh slap of skin to skin. Sex and lust scented the air and flooded his senses until it clung to every thought.

Her leg quivered with the strain to hold herself lifted on her toes, yet she stretched more, each shift letting him go a little deeper. His frustration clashed with his need to get deeper until it chased away the orgasm brewing in his groin.

He hauled her to his chest and swung her around in one quick motion. Surprise gave him the advantage, but he didn't abuse it. Power thrummed through his veins beside the adrenaline that lit him with its incredible high. Was that his true addiction?

Two steps and they were at the bed. She scrambled onto it without a word from him, her ass lifted, pussy displayed between her spread legs. Her plump red lips glistened, her vagina clenching in an open request to be filled.

The urge to taste her for real, to lick up her juices and cause more, warred with the ache to come. Another place, more time, and he would've gladly ate her out until she screamed. But now...

He slid back into her on a low moan that screamed of rightness that couldn't last. Not for good. He couldn't forget that—wouldn't forget that.

He leaned over her, hips locked against her round ass.

Heat seared his chest when he pressed into her back. It stole his breath for one quick second. Longing gripped his heart before he shoved it back, yet he still savored the feel of her. The warmth and connection. The shared moment. The intimacy when he hadn't expected it, had thought he didn't want it.

"Should I fuck that pretty ass of yours?" He left the taunt close to her ear.

She turned her head to watch him from the corner of her eye. She slicked her lips, took a long breath. "Isn't that your decision?"

Her sass mixed with her open submission stroked that dominant flame he'd valiantly tried to snub out.

"Excellent answer," he growled before he claimed her mouth with a sloppy kiss hindered by their position. He didn't care if it was awkward or messy, not when he craved her taste. Not when he drew back to see her dazed expression beneath the lust.

He reared up, landed a brazen slap to her ass. Her cry held more shock than objection. She squirmed into him, grinding her bottom to his groin like the naughty wanton she was. The fact that she owned it was even hotter.

His own shameless want roared its demand as he rubbed his thumb over her anus. It fluttered beneath his touch, her pussy clenching around his dick. His groan tore through his chest to leak between his clenched teeth. He tried to keep his pace slow, tried to draw it out even more, but her pussy was too warm, too slick, too tight. His orgasm too close.

Intent faded beneath base hunger as he drove into her, taking everything she so freely gave. She gripped the bedspread and pushed back to meet each plunge, their rhythm fast, desperate and dirty.

"Touch yourself," he ground out. "Play with your swollen clit."

Her hand snaked down so quickly he almost barked out a laugh, not in humor but appreciation. Her quick little circles vibrated into his dick in a tease so unique he almost came right then. The slight graze of her nail shot a flare of pain up his shaft that merged with pleasure.

He was so fucking close. It boiled now, nudging coherent thought away until nothing mattered except feeling her contract around him, seeing her tremble, hearing her cries—so he could finally come.

"Come, Kennedy." His growled command snapped from him without thought. "Fucking come all over my cock. Show me how hard I made you come. How much you love it."

She shot him one lust-filled look before she curled in on a cry. Each ripple of her orgasm shuddered through her pussy to clasp his dick in its exotic hold. Her gasp displayed every passionate sensation flooding her.

And he was lost. To her. The moment. The impossible he'd thought he'd never have again—could never have again.

His release powered from his groin and blasted him with a punishing rush of intensity. He gripped her hips and rode out the orgasm on a hitch of breath and hard grind. "Fuck. Fuck… Fuck."

His limbs tingled, ecstasy humming through him on a glorious rush that also left him numb. He sagged forward, caging Kennedy between his arms as he propped his forehead on her shoulder. "Fuck." That one barely escaped on a breath.

"Hmmm." Her low purr mimicked his own contentment. His heart pounded in his head and hammered his ribs with demands he couldn't respond to, but he also couldn't reject her. Not after all she'd given him.

"Let me clean up," he murmured before pressing a kiss to her spine. A shot of tenderness laced around the possessive want he couldn't acknowledge. Separating from her required pure will. He slid free on a clench of regret, but not for what they'd done.

He ducked into the bathroom, deliberately avoiding the mirror. He didn't want to see his expression. His default stony flatness was most likely gone given the riot of emotions banging away inside him.

She was sitting on the side of the bed, her back to him when he stepped into the room. The window served as a mirror to display her uncertainty before she noticed him. Her smile came quick, a falseness attached to the brittle edges.

"Hey," she said, not turning around. "That was—"

"Don't do that." His words came out harsh, close to a reprimand when he hadn't intended them to be. Her back straightened, and he slid onto the bed, wrapping an arm around her waist before she could stand. "Don't," he said near her ear. "Please. Don't cheapen this."

She stilled, her breath held for a beat before her shoulders dropped. "Okay."

He smothered his relief beneath the kisses he trailed across her shoulder. "Thank you." He released a long breath when she relaxed into him, the stiffness leaving her muscles. The entire evening had been an unexpected gift he wanted to treasure, not diminish or dismiss.

She didn't resist when he shifted around to tug the blankets free and urged her to lay down with him. The knot in his chest released when she curled into him, her head resting on his shoulder, one leg threaded between his.

This was...almost better than the sex. The simple power of human contact should never be underestimated.

"Why are you doing this?" she asked after a bit. Her breaths had evened out, but a stiffness remained. A wariness.

"Doing what?" He skimmed his fingers over her hip, savoring the softness that went with her curves. Her hair fell in a soft wave down her back that tempted him to touch it too.

"This." She gestured over them.

His chuckle remained mostly in his chest. She started to rise, but he held her tight, holding a kiss to her head until she relaxed. Her disgruntled sigh put a smile on his lips.

"Because it feels good," he finally told her, underscoring his statement with a gentle rub on her back and ribs. "I have no expectations beyond this."

She twisted around to study him, her chin propped on her fist. That telling line was present between her brows, her eyes narrowed.

"What?" he asked, amused. He used his thumb to rub at the frown line, smiling when it deepened.

"You're...unexpected."

"As are you."

She shook her head, lips twitching. "So...do you do this often?"

"Do you?"

"No." Her lips pursed. "Never like this."

It was his turn to frown. "Like how?"

She studied him for a long moment, hesitation clear

before she blinked it away. "I don't usually pick up guys in a bar and let them fuck me against a hotel window."

He didn't respond at first, sensing there was something more she wasn't saying. But was it really his business? Did it matter if she did pick up men and fuck them on a regular basis? No. It didn't.

Or it shouldn't.

His flash of jealousy had no place in this arrangement. One where he refused to know her last name.

He ran the back of a finger over her cheek, his knuckle grazing the edge of her freckles. "And I don't usually pick up women and fuck them against hotel windows." Actually, he hadn't hit on a woman since college, let alone pick one up for sex.

The few hookups he'd had since his divorce were instances of mutual opportunity instigated by the women more than him and strictly vanilla. No commands. No roughness. Just safe, basic sex.

His dick and its demands had taken a backseat to his kids, both of whom were now teens edging closer to adults. They were fine. They wouldn't be hurt by him dating. But his priorities had been set for so long he didn't know how to shift them without changing himself.

"Could we call this a mutual anomaly?" The corner of her mouth quirked up.

He smiled. "Yeah. We could."

Amusement danced in the blue of her eyes before her smile slowly died. Regret laced her voice when she spoke. "I should go."

Logic smothered the denial that raced up. He couldn't argue when he had nothing more to give.

She rolled away, but he followed, stopping her before

she stood. Question lifted her brows when she turned to him. He answered it by drawing her in for a long, slow kiss. He brushed his lips over hers, circled her tongue with his own, careful to keep each touch, each stroke, gentle. What he couldn't say, he could try to show her.

This had been more than a simple fuck to him, despite that being all it could be.

She moaned into his mouth, cupping his cheek as she drew him closer, deepening the exchange. He locked in every sensation along with her passionate flavor, every purred appreciation and soft breath.

Her eyes were guarded when she eased away. She stroked her fingers along the edge of his hair, her eyes tracking the movement. "Thank you."

He curled his fingers in to keep from drawing her back. She gathered her clothes and stepped into the bathroom, the latch connecting with a soft click that managed to kick at his chest.

He squeezed his eyes closed, rubbed them to get rid of his wild thoughts. He'd been prepared for her to ask for more details about him, had half expected her to toss out her own. But she hadn't done either, and he didn't know how to feel about that. Relieved? Disappointed? Annoyed?

And he was being stupid now. This was nothing more than a really good fuck. The kind he hadn't let himself have for exactly this reason. Intense sex had a way of spilling over into life, at least for him. Even the slight chance of that happening again had made the risk too high.

The ache near his heart only proved that his fears had been valid.

He was standing by the window, his slacks on, when

she exited the bathroom. Her professional demeanor was back in place, from her pressed suit to her tamed hair and impersonal smile.

She slid her briefcase over her shoulder before she lifted to kiss him softly. Her hand lingered on his chest until she drew it away on a slow glide down. "Maybe I'll see you tomorrow."

"Maybe." And then what? They couldn't repeat this.

Her nod said she understood. "Thank you for sharing your relaxation technique. It was very effective." The hint of mischief in her smile urged a reluctant one from him.

"You're welcome." It was on the tip of his tongue to offer his assistance in the future, but what good would it do when they both acknowledged the state of this arrangement.

She left his room with only a quick glance back. He stood at the window, watching the door for a long while after she was gone. His mind dashed from one thought to another before it stopped on nothing.

He turned around to stare into the darkness beyond. There was little to be done about where his life was. He had two kids who still needed him, even if they were mostly grown. He had a business to run and expand, along with a mountain of issues and problems that came with taking over an established, if stagnant, trucking company.

Fucking women against windows had no place in his life outside of a one-off fluke of luck and opportunity.

Kennedy...

Would remain in Long Beach when he returned to Daly City. And that was the end of it.

Chapter Seven

The jerk and hitch of the plane touching down yanked Kennedy from her thoughts. She glanced around, blinked. The short jaunt from LAX had passed without an ounce of work accomplished.

"Welcome to San Francisco. The weather is…"

Kennedy tuned out the rest of the flight attendant's welcoming monologue. She'd heard it often enough to have it memorized. The older gentleman next her was busy searching through his briefcase, the same studied frown on his face that'd been there when she sat down.

She switched her phone from airplane mode and forced every thought of Matt from her mind. He'd already consumed too much of her attention. Way too much, if she included her lust-soaked dreams.

She closed her eyes, impressions from the previous night shivering over her with their persistent reminders. His commanding touches and filthy mouth, his heated kisses and wild fucking. His tender strokes and soft caresses.

The last ghosted over her jaw in a phantom pass that tightened the knot in her chest. She snapped her eyes open, breaths short. Heat soaked her nape and dampened her spine despite her refusal to acknowledge why.

Just like she wouldn't admit why she'd caught the first flight out of LAX she could get that morning.

Her phone buzzed in her hand, and she relished the distraction—until she saw her dad's name on her screen. The ache in her temple pulsed with everything she was trying to ignore.

She silenced the vibration and slid her phone into her bag. Only then did she notice that most of the first-class section had emptied. She was spacing like a school girl high on her first crush—something she'd never done, not even when she'd been a school girl.

She hiked through the busy airport on autopilot. No thoughts. No reliving a night she shouldn't have instigated but couldn't regret. Not even now. Nope. Just get to her car, check her email, call her dad back.

Work.

There were a dozen tasks waiting for her, every one marked important. She couldn't afford to be distracted. Her focus and drive were two of her biggest assets. One night of sex wasn't going to derail that.

The fresh air hit her with a smack of exhaust fumes and reality. Her smile was locked in when she handed her ticket to the valet.

He checked her number into his computer, nodded. "I'll be right back, Ms. Keller."

She made a concerted effort to go through her email while she waited. She flagged a few work items and deleted a solid fifty or more from her personal account before her sleek, black luxury car rolled to a stop in front of her, the valet jumping out with a smile.

"Here you go," he said, holding the door open for her.

She left her travel bag by the trunk, which she popped open when she sat behind the wheel. The valet took care of it, his efficiency and manners rewarded with her tip. Her mother had educated her on the return value of a generous tip.

Traffic out of the airport was its usual late-morning clog of annoyance that thickened once she hit the highway. Given her lack of productivity on the plane, she clicked her phone to the dash mount and checked her messages via voice commands and the wonder of Bluetooth speakers.

"Call Dad at work," she said after discovering that he hadn't left a voicemail.

"Ken?" His gruff baritone matched his image to a tee. "Where are you?"

"On the one oh one almost to the San Mateo bridge."

"What are you doing here?"

She let his snarled reprimand roll off her shoulders with practiced ease as she checked her mirrors and followed the exit to the bridge she crossed almost daily. Locating the company in the outskirts of Oakland had been a financial decision made over fifty years ago, but living there had been out of the question, even for her grandfather.

"Thad and Craig have the convention under control," she breezed. "I hit my priority contacts yesterday and decided to head back to focus on the new workflow layouts we're considering." Optimizing production was always important, and with every new piece of equipment or specification requirement, they took a hard look at efficiencies.

"Did you speak with Owen?"

"Yes." She kept her expression contained to her eye roll. "He says you need to get to Santa Barbara soon so he can kick your ass on the green again." Her dad's deep chuckle put a smirk on her face. He might ride her like she was a newbie in the business, but she'd mastered the art of managing him before she'd stepped through the company doors. "You and Mom are welcome anytime, just give him a call."

Owen Nickle was an old college buddy who'd traveled the same trek as her father through his own family business, only his was in medical supplies. That industry had proven to be far more profitable than the pallet business, a tidbit her father resented, but only behind closed doors after one too many drinks. Connections provided eighty percent of their business, and Owen had passed them some of their most valuable customers, including their newest prospect, Calloway Industries.

"What about that lead he referenced?" her dad asked.

"I'll update you when I get to the office." When she wasn't distracted by traffic. "Are you free for lunch?"

"No." He didn't bother to expand, and she hadn't expected him to. As the CEO, he ran the company on a need-to-know basis, even with her. "Come to my office at two." He disconnected after that.

She tried to hold back her sigh, but it still escaped, her mumbled "yes, sir" falling out with the heavy sarcasm carried over from her youth. She'd marched to his demands since she'd learned to walk, while steadfastly blazing her own path. Or she tried to anyway.

Her curse snapped out when traffic came to a stop three exits from the office. And of course she'd just passed an off-ramp. She dropped her head back, hands clenching on the wheel. She flicked the radio on. Flicked it back off two seconds later.

She didn't have time for this. Not when her thoughts drifted straight back to Matt. Nope. Not happening.

"Call Dani." Her voice slashed through the car, but it didn't vent an ounce of her frustration.

"Ken." The obvious warmth in her best friend's voice released a large dose of the tension strung tight through her neck. "How are you?"

Kennedy was well aware that her laugh held a defeated edge she rarely exposed. "Good," she said. "You?"

"Hmm." Knowledge vibrated on that long note. "What's going on?"

God, she loved Danielle Stables. Their friendship had been almost guaranteed from the moment they'd met at boarding school even though Dani had been three years older.

Their male nicknames had linked them in a place where everyone struggled to be unique yet loathed being different. Dani and Ken—a match made from a cool factor defined by bored teens. Their weak connection had strengthened when they discovered how similar they truly were in ways that stretched beyond the poor little rich girl routine.

Their mutual lack of inhibitions and sexual curiosity had cemented their bond through different colleges until they landed in the same MBA program at Stanford. Thankfully, Dani had remained on the West Coast instead of returning to her East Coast roots after graduation.

Kennedy set her doubts loose on the only person she trusted to keep them. "I might've made a mistake last night."

"What kind of mistake?"

"A fucking amazing one." Literally. And that was her problem. The night had knocked her back while setting her free. And she couldn't repeat it. Not with Matt or any man.

But she wanted to—with Matt.

"Details."

The snapped command pulled a defeated chuckle from Kennedy. "I picked up a man in the bar at a convention..." And they'd had sex, which was no biggie in itself.

"Did he hurt you? Are you okay?"

"He didn't harm me." Kennedy's guilt charged forward for scaring her friend. "I'm fine. He was fine. Better than, actually." Heat raced a path up her neck and over her cheeks at a speed too quick to stall. *What is wrong with me?* She placed a hand on her cheek, relishing the coolness that did little against the burn stinging it.

"Oooh?" Speculation popped in Dani's voice, and Kennedy could picture her eyes going wide. "Do I get details?"

Gossiping about their sexual adventures had become a mundane task back in boarding school that'd continued as they'd explored their sexuality. Any shyness she might've first had fled beside the undaunting confidence Dani exuded. She'd educated Kennedy on the power that came with owning her desires.

A lesson that'd proven to be one of the most important ones she'd ever learned.

Traffic started a slow crawl forward. "It kind of wrecked me," she finally said after a short internal debate. The how of it wasn't important to the big picture. It didn't matter that she'd submitted to a man for the first time. Nope.

"And that's bad?" Dani teased, or at least Kennedy thought she was teasing.

"Not in itself."

"So…?"

"I can't stop thinking about it."

"Oh."

Yeah, oh. Sex was something to be enjoyed, not analyzed. Repeatedly. Until her panties were wet and nipples hard.

"So…maybe you should have it again?"

"Sex? Definitely," she snarked, switching the air conditioning up a notch.

"With that guy."

Dani's flat delivery blocked her attempted dodge. She heaved a sigh but kept it silent. It didn't help that her friend doubled down on her grilling by staying quiet. And there was a lesson in the art of drawing out the truth.

"I can't," Kennedy finally huffed. "I didn't get his information." On his insistence. Which was good, knowing what she did now. "And I don't think a repeat would help my situation."

"And what situation is that?"

"I'm horny as hell." Maybe she should've swung by her condo and gotten herself off before heading to the office. She'd turn the car back now if she thought a round of masturbation would help.

Dani's laugh rolled through the car. "Poor you." Her false sympathy got the smile her friend was probably going for.

Kennedy checked the time, winced. "Am I keeping you from something?"

"I have a meeting in ten." Their mutual VP titles

meant they each worked too much, both to get where they were and to stay there. Phone calls and texts had become their main touch point despite living just miles from each other.

"I'll let you go."

"I've got a few minutes," Dani said. "What was different about last night?"

The straight shot should've been expected, yet it still caught her by surprise. Her mind flashed to being pressed against the window, breaths short, a finger rammed up her ass. *I could fuck you here.*

She would've let him fuck her any way he wanted. She had.

She cleared her throat, squeezing her legs together. The ache in her pussy intensified, but worse than that was the want that sang within her. She wanted that freedom again when she couldn't have it.

Once had been too much—too dangerous.

Losing control was one thing. Giving it up was completely different.

"Hey," she said instead of answering. "I actually have to go. But thank you for listening."

"Kennedy."

The reprimand in Dani's voice stalled her from disconnecting. She fisted her hand in her lap, annoyed at herself for even calling. "What?" She laced the word with innocence.

"Do what you need to do to get over whatever's hanging you up," Dani advised. "Take your power back. Do your thing in the Boardroom."

Do your thing in the Boardroom. Of course. She sagged into the seat, the obvious smacking her in the face. Why hadn't she thought of that? "Thanks, Dani."

"Anytime."

She ended the call after a round of goodbyes, her thoughts flying through her options and schedule in tandem. Relief filled her now that she had a plan, or was it a mission? She'd given her power to one man, and he'd managed to strip her of something else.

Thankfully, she had the ability to change that.

Dani had introduced her to the Boardroom not long after she'd become a member herself. The exclusive sex group was every man's desire and woman's fantasy. Anything was possible, within reason, if someone else was interested. It provided freedom for the sexually open—or deviant—under the insurance of privacy.

She'd once joked that the group had been made for her. It fit her so perfectly. She thanked her friend every time she utilized it without backlash or recriminations of any kind from anyone.

Sex without ties or accusations. Public sex.

That revved her up like few other things did, and she had Dani to thank for that too. The brazen confidence required to not only flaunt her sexuality, but revel in it in front of others, had bled into every facet of her life.

Dani had shared that power with Kennedy when she'd been a sweet little sixteen-year-old. Maybe the sweet part had been nothing more than a front she'd worn in deference to her parents, because it hadn't taken much to shatter it. A few nights. That was it.

Nights among Dani's crowd of influential teen socialites spent executing dares to stave off the boredom, and she'd never turned back. Never questioned how one of those dares had ended with her spread on an obnoxiously long dining table, masturbating, while getting high on the lust-filled looks around her.

Strictly Confidential

She cleared her throat, reached for her water bottle only to curse its absence. She'd managed to progress halfway to the next exit during her conversation with Dani. At this rate, she'd be lucky to make it to the office in time for her meeting with her father. Okay, that was an exaggeration, but time was ticking, and she'd already wasted too much of it.

A couple of forced maneuvers across lanes crawling at a snail's pace took longer than the length of her patience. Her hallelujah shook the interior when she reached the exit ramp. If luck stayed with her, she'd hit the office in time to snag the production manager before he took his lunch break.

A smile broke over her face as her sense of purpose returned. No way was she letting one man break her stride. Mystery Man Matt had turned out to be a fantastic lesson on what she should never do again.

And if nothing else, she was a very quick learner.

Chapter Eight

"Yes!" Matt jumped to his feet, his cheer blending with the crowd around him. "Go, Beach!"

His grin was huge as he watched his daughter charge the court to celebrate with her volleyball teammates. As a freshman at CSU Long Beach, she still rode the bench like she'd expected when she'd accepted the scholarship. But that hadn't diminished her joy for both the sport and the team she was a part of.

As for Matt, he was just relieved that Dawn had locked into an activity that'd given her structure and a support system that'd propelled her from junior high to college. Now if only his son could find the same...

He filed out of the stadium with the rest of the spectators to wait for her. A part of him couldn't believe she'd grown up. In his mind, she was still that scared little girl he'd scooped up from social services. The sucker punch still hit him whenever he thought back to that day.

Of traveling for twenty hours with no sleep, weighed down with a shit-ton of guilt and anxiety strapped to his back. Only to find his kids—his two small children—huddled together in the corner of a stranger's home, tears streaking their cheeks, betrayal radiating from their eyes.

He scrubbed a hand over his face and tried to shake off the memory even though it was securely lodged in his long-term storage bank. For years, he hadn't wanted it to fade. He'd seen it as his due penance for being so blind to what had been going on in his own home. Now, it only cropped up when his guilt pulled it forward.

The reminder of exactly how dangerous the dominant path could be had been enough to end any wayward desires he'd had—until the other night. Now that old guilt-inducing memory appeared to be making friends with his newest, the one of Kennedy's lust-filled gaze staring back at him as he slammed into her.

His dick twitched, that empty ache charging forward to taunt him with wants he couldn't acknowledge.

Only he had. With her.

"Dad!"

He spun around, arms spread to catch his daughter up in a hug. "Hey, Sunshine. You guys did great."

She pulled free, her eye roll so familiar it was actually endearing in that moment. "The team did, yes. Me…" She wiggled her hand in a so-so motion.

"Nah," he contradicted. "Don't cut yourself down."

"I'm not." She shrugged. "I'm just being honest. You taught me that." Her side-eye contained just enough snark to have him chuckling.

"I believe I also taught you that being a smartass would get you into trouble." He hauled her into a side hug before she could object, her laughter making his grueling week worth it.

She rolled out of his hold, dancing back. Her hair bounced in her customary pony tail, her wide grin infectious. "Only if I get caught," she taunted, laughing at his fake scowl.

"It's a good thing you're too old to ground," he grumbled.

"Ha!" She tucked her hands into her hoodie pocket, head tilting as she studied him. "How are you doing?"

"I'm fine." He bolstered his automatic response with a smile. Her narrowed eyes said she didn't believe him. "And you? How are classes? Did you get that test sorted out in biology?"

"Ugh!" Her head dropped back in an exaggerated display of youthful annoyance that'd once driven him nuts, but he now treasured. She was growing up so fast in so many ways.

He listened to her ramble for the next hour, shifting from one topic to the next as they sat on a bench outside the stadium. The campus was quiet at night, but the lighted paths chased away the darkness. He'd liked the vibe when they'd toured it last year, and he was relieved to know Dawn was enjoying the school.

He gave his watch a quick glance, regretting it and his wince when she cut off her sentence.

"You have to go." Her statement didn't need a response. They'd only managed to have dinner together once that week despite being a few short miles from each other. Her being in Long Beach had been an added motivation for him to attend the convention.

"You're still coming home for Thanksgiving, right?" he asked instead of answering.

Her scowl communicated her thoughts on his question. "Of course."

That guarantee was only good for a limited time, though. Soon she'd have other places to be and her own

life to live. "Good. Your grandmother would be disappointed if you didn't."

"Just grandma?"

He nudged her. "Ben too."

Her bark of laughter came out bright and doubtful.
"Sure." She sobered. "How's he doing?"

A cloud of worry swooped in to dampen the moment. "Good, as far as I know." The conversation level
of a sixteen-year-old boy tended to consist of grunts
and forced one-word responses.

Dawn frowned, concern showing. He sat up. "What?"
he asked, insistence leveled in his tone.

She stared at the ground, shoulders rolling forward.
"Nothing."

"Dawn." His mother had used the exact same warning tone in his name, the one that said don't push me or
you'll not like my response. He'd hated it as a kid but
valued the effectiveness as a parent.

She jerked around, her scowl hard. "Nothing," she
insisted. "He's just…" She squirmed. "I don't know."
Defeat sagged through her. "Quiet." She gave him a
side-glance. "He barely responds to my texts anymore.
I know we're both busy, and I don't reach out as much
as I should, but…" She shrugged. "It makes me worry."

"Ah, Sunshine." He pulled her in, willing his embrace to be enough to cure her concern. "I love you." He
kissed the top of her head, damn amazed that he'd managed to raise a kid who still worried about her younger
brother when her own life was filled with exciting dis-
tractions. "I haven't noticed anything outside of the normal teen angst."

But that didn't mean anything. He wasn't so old that
he didn't remember his own teenage years. Tempta-

tions were everywhere. Combine that with horny, still-developing bored brains and it didn't take much to go down the wrong path. He'd had sports and his mother's discipline to keep him steady when many of his childhood friends had toyed with drugs and gangs.

That constant nugget of worry twisted in his stomach as he sped down the path of possible trouble. There were no guarantees, though, no matter how invested he was or how much of himself he'd devoted to his kids.

Dawn leaned into him. "Okay."

Her easy acceptance of his lame reassurance didn't help his own concerns now that they'd been pinged. "We're all looking forward to having you home for a week." He reluctantly stood, checking the time again. "Do you have enough money?"

She stalled his hand as he reached for his wallet. "I'm fine, Dad." She squeezed it. "But thanks." Her grin returned. "I had this amazing teacher who hounded in the value of having a budget and sticking to it." She flashed another quick wink that succeeded in getting a chuckle from him.

"Good." His nod was supposed to be stern. Her laugh said he'd failed. "Let me know if you need anything."

"I will."

He gave her a last hug before walking her to her dorm despite her insistence that she was fine on her own. His heart ached as he watched the door latch behind her. She sent a last wave to him through the window before heading back to her life.

Where had the time gone?

He cycled through answers during his late flight back to San Francisco and walked to his car. Time had a way of dragging through a day only to speed by during the month as routine blended everything together. And now he was a forty-one-year-old man rushing toward fifty on the same cycle of daily existence that'd gotten him through those first hard days and months after he'd reclaimed his kids. Twelve years had flown by in a blink.

He slammed his car door, savoring the echoing silence that followed. He took a moment to simply breathe in his own space. No one hounding him. No one waiting for him, expecting something, wanting more of his time, his thoughts, him. Just quiet.

And into the nothing wove the enticing image of Kennedy. That saucy smirk and directness countered by her beautiful submission that'd never become dependent. With it rose the addictive rush of power that'd laid its familiar tracks, reminding him of old needs he'd thought dead.

No, they were very much alive, especially now.

He tugged at the collar of his T-shirt, rolled his head to ease the tightness in his shoulders. A stale coffee scent permeated the air from the travel mug he'd left half full when he'd arrived at the airport days ago. Another late-night traveler trudged through the parking garage, taillights flashing on a car further down the row.

The normalcy grounded him. He had responsibilities to his kids, his mom, his company. He couldn't get lured into the dark side of his needs. The ones that teased at the authority he'd learned to wield as an officer and the fulfillment that came from giving another what they craved.

He whipped his car into Reverse, focused on getting home. His responsibilities called and they started with touching base with his son. Ben was a little too much like him. A little too headstrong. A little too cocky.

A little too blind to the things he didn't want to acknowledge.

The clench in his groin mocked him.

Screw that. He could fuck without the edge, get off without controlling every aspect. He'd managed fine for over a decade. He owed it to Ben to remember that. His personal needs were secondary to those of his kids.

The kitchen light was still on when he pulled into his driveway twenty minutes later. He was proud of the little semidetached house he'd slowly remodeled into a cozy home. It didn't offer much in square footage, but the location in a good school district and kid-friendly area made it golden. Plus it was just down the street from his mother, who, even now, played a vital role in raising his kids.

He might have no idea who his father was, but he'd gotten damn lucky with his mother.

He found her curled up on the couch reading when he came in through the garage door. "Hey, Mom."

Her smile still had the magical ability to hug him from a distance. "Matt." She tucked a bookmark between the pages of her novel, stretching as she stood. "How was your trip? And Dawn? How's she doing?"

With her hair studiously cut close to her scalp and her preference for efficiency over style in her clothes, she presented the same practical image he remembered from his childhood. Her hair might be grayer now and her middle a little rounder, but she still marched through life determined to kick it instead of being kicked down.

"It was good." He set his bags down, exhaustion swooping in. "And Dawn's good. She sends her love." He rubbed his eyes, covering a yawn. "I didn't expect you to be here." A frown crept in. "Is Ben okay? He's here, right?"

She waved his concerns away with a flick of her wrist. "Everything's fine. I just got lost in my book and then decided to wait." Ben had outgrown the babysitter age years ago. It was Matt who hadn't wanted him home alone the entire time he'd been gone. Ben had argued differently.

"Let me walk you home." He held the front door open, snatching up her overnight bag from its spot on the floor. The brisk night air woke him up with the bite of cool fog that loved to creep off the Pacific and hang over their coastal city.

She tugged her sweater tighter around her and took off at her customary crisp pace that hadn't slowed as she'd aged.

"Did Ben give you any trouble?" he asked.

"Nothing worse than you did at that age."

Matt snorted, draping his arm over her shoulder to give her a squeeze. "That doesn't reassure me."

"Bah." She wiggled out of his hold. "You turned out just fine."

Thanks to her. As a young single mother, she could've fallen into any of the social traps and stereotypes of the time. Instead, she'd worked hard, skimped and bullied her way into a better life for both of them. She was a hard act to live up to, but she'd also been his inspiration when he'd landed back in town with two little kids and no idea what to do next.

The short walk down their quiet street brought back a slew of memories. He'd lived most of his life within this two-block radius. His only departure had been during his time in the service, and that had ended in dismal failure. He'd loved his job, had loved the military with its structure and chain of command.

He also blamed it for honing and tuning his desire for control.

"I could be better," he mumbled.

His mother stopped, and he instantly regretted his moment of weakness. Her scowl was part annoyance, part concern. "Why would you say that?"

He debated a number of answers before admitting, "Because it's true."

Her single nod was executed with precision. "You're not that bad." Her tone was dismissive as she started to walk again, her strides slower. "But it's good to recognize that there's always room to grow."

She didn't bother to turn around when he remained planted in his spot. Her retreating back held the same straight posture she'd employed to take on life. *Be proud of who you are. Walk tall and people will think you are.*

Her words of wisdom had threaded their way through his life, inspiration that might've lacked warmth but had been given with love. Tenderness was not her strength, not when she'd had to fight for everything she'd earned.

He caught up to her in a few quick strides, his heart a little lighter. "I give all the credit to my teacher." He winked at her scowl tempered with a half-smile.

"You're too hard on yourself," she said. "You always have been."

"Again…" He shot her a knowing look.

"Humph." Her chin hitched up, but she didn't counter his implication. A defensive edge tightened her voice when she spoke. "I only wanted the best for you."

In poured another dose of guilt. He closed his eyes,

wincing at the twist in his chest. "I know," he said softly, contrite. "Thank you."

She waved him off again. "It's what parents do. That's why you stew so much about your own."

He couldn't deny it, but what was the personal cost for such focused dedication? His mother had never married, and she'd rarely dated, even after he'd left home. At least not that he knew of.

"But what about now?" he asked, digging his hands into his jean pockets. "Do you ever regret giving up so much for me?"

She turned to him, her earnest intent highlighted by the soft glow of the streetlights. "Do you? Regret what you've given your kids?"

"No. Not even a little."

Her nod confirmed her agreement. "Then why would you think *I* do?"

Another round of doubts screamed through his head, all triggered by one powerful encounter that'd unlocked longings he couldn't shut down. Or did he really want to?

He had no idea why they'd reemerged now and a part of him didn't want to snuff them back out. That was the issue.

"What about *you*, though?" he pushed when he could've let it go. "What about what *you* want?" He glanced down the street, seeing the years of sacrifice that'd trapped her there.

"I have exactly what I want." She started walking again. "I have a family. A family *I* built." The last snapped out to remind him of her history. Her own mother had basically abandoned her, leaving her to be raised by her grandmother after her father had died. A grandmother who'd tried but hadn't had the energy to create a nurturing home life.

He scrubbed a hand over his scratchy jaw, kicking himself. He had no right to question her choices, not when each one had been made for his benefit.

"I'm good," she reassured him when they reached her door. "I have no regrets. I'm happy with my life and where I am." She squeezed his arm, pressing home her point in the same manner she'd used for as long as he could remember. "If you're not, then you need to look at why and change what you can."

"I'm fine," he rushed to say.

"Are you?" She raised a brow, shaking her head when he nodded. "Then why all the questions?" She found her keys in her purse and turned to unlock her door. "You only dig when you're trying to uncover something."

He chuckled at her play on words, choosing to ignore her observation that hit too close to the truth. "Thank you again for staying with Ben." He brushed a kiss to her temple before he ducked his head inside the door to give her home a quick visual sweep. He handed her bag over, gratitude clogging his throat. "You're the best."

"As are you." Her smile held the love she rarely uttered with words. Actions had always been her method of expression, and she'd passed that trait onto him. "And don't worry so much about Ben. He's got a good head on his shoulders. Trust that he knows how to use it."

He waited until her locks clicked into place before heading back to his house. His thoughts continued to race in a disconnected path until he shut them down. Tomorrow would bring another day of routine and with it the normal he relied on. That had been enough for so long he had no idea how to change it even if he wanted to.

And why should he when there was nothing inherently wrong with where he was? He had a good life. His kids were fine. He had a company to improve and employees counting on him to keep them working.

He'd forget about Kennedy and the feelings she'd stirred up. There were more important things to stress over than how he got off.

A lot more.

He'd focus on each and every one of them until the longing disappeared—or he took Trevor James up on the offer he'd laid out a few months back.

Had that been the trigger? The casual invitation to an exclusive sex group had rolled off the tongue of the Faulkner Investment Group president after a few drinks over a business dinner. He'd declined, yet…why? It wasn't like Matt had a moral or ethical objection. Maybe there was something there, something he should explore before outright rejecting the invite.

Maybe he would if his dick didn't stop twitching every time Kennedy's sweet submission and engaging banter invaded his thoughts. She'd given him so much while maintaining her strength, and that's what got him the most. She was different. No matter how hard he tried to dismiss her and the night, he couldn't. He couldn't shake the what-ifs and if-onlys that refused to be silenced.

He'd resisted the urge to look her up or dig into who she was. Knowing her personal details wouldn't change his situation. They'd had one evening of fantastic sex. Nothing more, even if part of him craved a different ending.

Chapter Nine

Kennedy slid her bra down her arms and set the garment on the chair. Her blouse hung over the back, along with her suit pants. She probably should've worn something more…alluring, but no one was there to see her undress.

The cool air danced over her bared skin. Goose bumps spread down her arms and puckered her nipples. She ignored them as she draped her suit coat over the chair and nudged it into the corner. The room offered little in warmth and everything in industrial luxury. She'd worked hard to ensure their boardroom walked the fine balance between modern and classic, the latter a nod to their manufacturing roots.

She set the vibrator on the table, a snicker teasing her throat. The dick-shaped toy went out of its way to impersonate the real thing, right down to the flesh colored bulbous crown, complete with a slit and impression of veins lining the shaft. It was far from her favorite, but the tease factor made it perfect for the Boardroom. Every man who watched her ride it would imagine his dick pumping into her.

A condom and lube landed next to the vibrator. She highly doubted she'd need them, but again, the tease factor made them a valuable tool. They laid down possibilities without promises. Public masturbation was her kink, and it usually ended at that—unless she changed her mind, and she rarely did.

A devious smirk curled over her lips and fed its mischief into her. God, she needed this. It'd taken three weeks to get this scene arranged. Three long, frustrating weeks of circular thoughts chased by conflicting wants and desires.

Matt continued to haunt her thoughts no matter how hard she tried to move on. She'd given up all attempts to distinguish between the man and the longing he'd set free. And there was no one she trusted enough to test out if the two were truly connected or simply linked by the circumstances.

Submitting to anyone, even sexually, went against everything she projected. Changing that perception wasn't an option. She couldn't change it. Not if she wanted to retain her hard-earned reputation.

She sent a text to Trevor before turning off her phone and tucking it beneath her clothes. He'd bring the other guys into the room in five minutes. Anticipation trembled down her spine before it settled in her core. The distant slam of a door had her jerking around, a hand raising to cover her nakedness before she caught herself.

The boardroom door was closed. The building was locked. Everyone had left—including her father—hours ago. Trevor was with the other guys. He'd take care of any issues. He'd shoot first if it meant protecting the group and everyone associated with it.

Her pulse raced despite the logic that'd kicked in. Doing this at Keller Pallet was a risk she willingly accepted. Getting off on her daddy's custom-ordered mahogany table was a bonus she couldn't pass up. Not when she was this agitated.

Which was also why she'd waited until Trevor could participate. As the Boardroom's brainchild, the buck started and stopped with him, and Kennedy trusted that. He'd never let anything happen to her that she didn't want to happen. Not under his watch.

She had little worry for her safety within the Boardroom, but after Long Beach, she didn't trust her sexual judgement. And that was new, not to mention unsettling.

Doubting herself or her actions wasn't a habit she wanted to get used to.

She fluffed her hair, checked her reflection in the window. The image was fuzzy in the limited light from the small lamp, but it boosted her morale. She would rock this scene and remind herself of the power she held.

The table was cool on her bottom when she sat on the edge. Scenarios skated through her mind before she scooted back, lying down when there was room to brace her heels on the table, her knees bent. She closed her eyes, inhaled long and slow. The chill on her back was quickly diluted beneath the heat building within her.

This was hers. She owned her desires. She decided how the scene went. She controlled her orgasm and incited the men's.

She let that sink in as she grazed her fingers over her abdomen. Her muscles clenched, anticipation firing. Unwanted, visions of Matt raced in. Of teasing him just like this. She hooked her pinky under the line of her panties in an exact replica of her show that'd enticed him to dive in and take what he'd wanted.

And she'd let him—no, she'd given him that right and so much more.

Now she was taking it back before she forgot why she could never do that again.

The non-descript building sat just east of the Oakland airport in an area cemented firmly in the industrial category. There was nothing that screamed exclusive in the basic whitewashed three-story structure. The long line of rolling garage doors reminded him of his own building, as did the basic economy of its appearance.

Matt studied the front door as a clean-cut man in a suit waited to enter. The lighted parking lot cast its glow on the guy, but his features remained indistinct given the distance. Matt had parked in the back of the empty lot, still undecided on if he was going inside. He should turn around and never look back. Yet...

Here he sat, stomach knotted, anticipation sparking over every nerve ending. He drummed his fingers on the steering wheel, the low patter doing nothing to settle his thoughts. He should go home—and Ben was most likely in bed by now.

He rubbed his eyes, pressing back the guilt that came from working too late. But he'd needed to finish a contract and that'd led to reviewing the budget before he'd read through another chunk of resumes that'd been culled by his HR manager. And then there'd been this appointment.

His phone rang, blasting its demand for attention through the silence. Trevor. He answered with a gruff, "Hello."

"Are you coming in?" No introduction, no preamble. That's how Trevor worked, and Matt liked it.

His response sat poised on his tongue. He could still decline.

"No pressure," Trevor said after a moment. "But I'm not standing at this door for much longer."

The front door of the building swung open for the guy who'd been waiting. Trevor stuck his head out, phone pressed to his ear as he stared across the lot directly at Matt's car. Of course Trevor had seen him. The man missed very little.

Matt shoved his door open, disconnecting the call. His dress shoes clicked out his path over the asphalt, confidence fueling his stride. He buttoned his suit coat, rolled his shoulders back, chin lifting as his decision settled over him.

One scene, that was all he was committing to.

He wasn't participating, according to Trevor. He had a voyeur-only role for a woman who loved to get off in front of men. He'd signed the damn paperwork, submitted all the medical tests. He might as well see what the Boardroom was about.

Trevor had given him the rundown on the exclusive group two weeks back, after his dick continued to pop to attention with even the slightest thought of Kennedy. Solo hand jobs were no longer enough to knock back his sex drive that'd returned with a vengeance. Maybe this was nature's payback for years of denial.

Trevor nodded as Matt passed him in the doorway. The lobby of Keller Pallet was clean if sparse. The few chairs were standard waiting room construction, the small reception desk basic. It pretty much matched every manufacturing business that focused more on output than putting on airs. He related to that, but it wasn't exactly the high-class atmosphere he'd tagged for a group of Bay Area executives.

"This way."

Trevor led him through another set of doors and up two flights of stairs to the top floor. An open set of cubicles took up most of the interior area, with offices lining the back wall. The silence echoed through the space and beat into his calm.

His pulse notched up as they entered a small conference room. Four men were already there, all of them in suits and ties like himself. Every one of them eyed him with a glance before turning their attention to Trevor.

"Gentlemen," Trevor greeted. "I trust that you've all read the scene rules." He waited for the other men to nod before continuing. "She controls the scene. No touching without permission. No demands. You can jack off, but don't come on her."

Trevor had shared the scene details with Matt when he'd invited him to participate. The hands-off scene combined with the convenient proximity to his own office had cemented his agreement. However, he couldn't shake the strangeness that prickled over his nape. He pinned it back to his years of military training and the simple fact that he was here to watch a woman masturbate.

Good thing he hadn't added that detail to his calendar.

Trevor glanced at his phone before he turned it off and set it on the table. The other men did the same, and Matt followed along without being told. He'd read the rules before signing the extensive NDA, but this was also basic security.

He never would've come, let alone joined, if his identity and participation hadn't been protected. Based on the general air emanating from everyone in that room, they all had a lot to lose if their connection to the Boardroom was ever leaked.

And he was here, why?

His dick gave an interested twitch when his thoughts raced back to Kennedy plastered against a window, her moans hungry as he claimed her. He cursed his damn inability to let that night go. Need added its persistent crawl over his chest and hunkered down in his balls.

The line of windows behind a few of the men reflected the interior back at him. The darkness beyond added to the unknown and pinged his old instincts. Were there other sightlines into the building? Were they being watched?

He had to trust that those risks had been mitigated. *Trust.* He was handing every one of these men his, and they were doing the same. The unique bond tied them together even though he recognized none of them. Possible business contacts rolled through the back of his mind before he dismissed them.

He wasn't there to deal or think about work. No, he was there purely for pleasure. Naughty, blatant, sexual pleasure.

The men filed out of the room in silence, a few wallets and a belt left on the table along with the phones. His shirt collar seemed to constrict with each step he took. He ignored it, though. He couldn't show discomfort, not if he wanted to maintain his tentative place on the bottom rung of the hierarchy pole.

Control demonstrated authority, which led to power. The path to success had been laid down for him in strict military precision from the time he'd entered the ROTC program, his sights set on becoming an Army officer.

Trevor led them into another room, the long table and leather executive chairs defining it as the company boardroom. The only light was provided by a small lamp located on a cabinet along the far wall. A smattering of distant lights peppered the darkness through the windows, reminding him of the airport beyond.

Those details were immediately cataloged and dismissed for the woman lying on one end of the table. Her dark hair spread in a fan of silk over the gleaming tabletop, her pale skin stark against the wood. Her naked breasts were topped with deep rose nipples already pebbled into hard tips. But his gaze caught on the freckles that peppered her chest, some so faint, others darker declarations that triggered the very memories he'd been trying to forget.

His swallow choked back the burst of want that zinged to his dick and launched a dozen images, both old and new. Her hair, the freckles, the long legs and brazen ownership of her desires were all too similar. It was like Trevor had seen into Matt's fantasies and dropped the reality in his lap.

He resisted the urge to move closer, to shift down the table to get a glimpse of her face. The odds were so long, so impossible that it was better to sink into the fantasy than be disappointed by the truth.

But what…if…

Her hand worked an obvious rhythm beneath the scrap of white lace that acted as panties. She trapped a nipple between her fingers, squeezed.

Lust simmered in his groin and flooded him with unwanted longing. He curled his fingers to keep from mimicking her actions when he could already feel the hardened softness beneath his fingertips.

Her low moan trembled through the room on the husky rumble of desire. The note kicked down the door he'd steadfastly resisted opening. It triggered another round of memories, of that same distinctive rasp falling from her parted lips before she'd pleaded for more.

His breath stalled, pulse thundering a possessive beat when she turned her head. The telltale line of freckles over her nose gave way to the lush swell of her lips painted a deep red. The smoky seductress played her role with perfection. Her eyelids lowered, her tongue snaking out to wet her lips as she eye-fucked the man standing in her line of sight.

She was stunning. Even here, in this sterile environment with six guys watching her get off, every societal norm stating this was wrong was lost in that moment. Power and seduction bled from every action. She was the show, and she knew it. Owned it.

Fuck, did that turn him on.

Especially when he knew exactly how giving she could be.

Kennedy. *His* Kennedy.

Heat flooded his nape before it raced down his back. How was this possible? His gaze snapped to Trevor, who stood by the only door, his arms crossed over his chest. Appreciation shone in his eyes, but his expression gave away nothing. Did he know about them? How? Was this a joke? A setup?

He took in the rest of the men, all of them focused on her. Various forms of open lust, want and desire painted their faces in honest displays that showed nothing devious. Was this truly a coincidence?

The erection in his pants said it didn't matter. She was hotter than he remembered, and he still ached to sink into her one more time. To see those lips part on a silent gasp, feel her arch beneath him before she clenched him tight.

His throat ached for liquid, his dick suddenly so hard it was impossible to ignore. Yet he remained stuck in his spot, out of her view. Did she know he was here? Had she secretly arranged it?

He ripped his focus from her stunning display to assess Trevor once again. Either he had the best poker face in the world, or he was truly unaware of Matt's connection to Kennedy. Trevor turned his head, gaze holding on him. Inquiry reached across the distance, his eyes narrowing the longer Matt stared back.

He was acting like a suspicious fuck when there was no proof of a conspiracy.

Kennedy's throaty purr filled the room with its lust-filled yearning that so perfectly mirrored his own. He closed his eyes, inhaled. The heated scent of her arousal seemed to fill him when logic said she was too far away. Yet he knew it. The musky edge that declared her excitement.

There was no one but her when he reopened his eyes. She rocked her hips, the motion snaking up his spine in a sensuous undulation that left her head tilted back, passion owning her expression. She used both hands to slide her fingers beneath her panties, easing them down. His mouth watered at the first sight of the dark triangle of hair on her mound.

A sultry smile curled over her lips when she looked to that guy again. The one she'd eye-fucked earlier. "A little help?"

Her request drove a spike through Matt's calm. Jealousy raged unjustified as the man stepped between her legs and slowly eased the lacy panties down her legs. She hummed her appreciation, trapping her lip between her teeth as she lifted each leg so he could remove the material completely.

Matt clenched his fist tighter, desire battling his control. He swallowed his growl, yet he couldn't shake the urgency pressing on his chest. He should just walk out. At the very least, stay put.

The other guy placed the scrap of white lace on the table beside the dick vibrator and returned to his spot after one last lingering gaze at her pussy. That sweet pussy he knew to be clean shaven, her lips plump and red with her arousal.

Matt edged down the table without conscious thought. The only signal he responded to was the one to get closer. To see every gorgeous curve and have that tempting strength aimed at him again.

He just wanted to see. That was it.

His dominant bastard laughed at the false tale he was trying to perpetuate. The hands-off approach had never been his strength, but he was also a rule follower.

Her fingers dipped between her legs, a full swipe drawing a low gasp from her lips. He caught her scent now, clear and distinct, that spicy heat mixed with her sultry musk a combination he could never define yet instantly knew.

But stronger than his desire to have her was the one to help her. He'd never disrespect her or override her control, especially here. This was her scene, and he was just a spectator, like every other man in that room.

His breaths pumped from his lungs, his control snapping back in to stop his blind trek. He wouldn't harm her—ever. And anything he did here could do exactly that.

Which meant he'd do nothing.

Chapter Ten

A long, sensual moan floated from Kennedy on the same languid flow that filled her. She stroked a finger over her clit, her pussy clenching with the hit of pleasure. Desire built in a slow crawl that she drew out for her own enjoyment and that of the men watching her.

A smile teased her lips, her eyes fluttering open to catch a glimpse of the lust she knew would be there. The first heady hit nailed her with the shot of power she relished. The heavy-lidded eyes watched her with open want, every wish inscribed on his pinched brow and parted lips.

The table bit into her shoulder blades when she arched her back, rocking her hips in a suggestive motion. She rode the slow grind with a wicked smile and dirty intent. He wet his lips, a hushed "yes" escaping when she pinched her nipple. She rolled the tip between her fingers, drawing out the spread of tingles that glided over her breast before sinking deeper.

She played them all, seeking her desire while driving their own. She imagined the hunger on the faces she couldn't see as she closed her eyes, another moan floating free. Her fingers slid through the slickness created by her own arousal. Heat had chased away any thought of being cold. It burned from the inside out on an enticing simmer of her own doing.

She rotated her hips, slowly rubbing her clit. Her orgasm collected in tiny spasms beneath the sensitive bud. A hard, persistent stroke would yank her release out in under a minute, but she wasn't here for fast and dirty.

Although that did have its own appeal.

Like when Matt had powered into her, lost in his own need to come. His hands digging into her hips, his order for her to touch herself hitting her need to own her destiny even as she gave away her control.

Matt. Would his eyes darken as he watched her, like they had before? Would he wet his lips, hunger marking the slight frown that would form?

She lifted her hips and made a show of easing two fingers deep within herself. Silky wetness entrapped the digits in its distinctive hold. Her hum rumbled her appreciation even though she longed for more. Something bigger, harder. The fake dick would be used tonight. Maybe it'd wipe out the ache that none of her other toys had been able to appease.

Like this scene was designed to achieve.

A rustle at her side had her turning her head in a slow roll that matched the dreamy flow of sensuality that'd overtaken her. She let her eyelids drift open, her gaze catching on the two men staring back at her. One was new, the other the man she'd seen a moment ago.

Her mind hitched, thoughts shuffling before recognition clicked with reality. *No!* Her pulse jumped, breath holding for one long moment of indecision. React or not? Show her cards or pretend they don't exist?

She closed her eyes and withdrew her fingers to rub

her juices over her clit. The slick movements battered
the rush of nerves that threatened to ruin the scene.

Matt was here. Now.

How? Why? The Boardroom was private, which
meant he belonged or was a guest—and Trevor trusted
him or he wouldn't be here. But…it still didn't compute.
Was this a setup? Had he known who she was at the
hotel? Had he planned all of this? But she'd approached
him in the bar. She'd hit on him.

She pinched her nipple until the sharp bite cleared
her jumbled thoughts. It dug into her reserves to pull up
the fierceness that'd driven her to claim her spot next
to her father when everyone had tried to box her into
the mold of her mother.

She wouldn't let Matt derail her.

Determination rushed in on a wave of savage conviction. She cupped her breast, drawing it up in a firm squeeze
before she let her fingers drift down over her abdomen.
Her naughty streak burst to life, a cunning smile forming.

Her walls hugged her fingers when she pumped them
into her vagina. She savored the build, rolling her clit with
her other hand. Her breaths were short, her seductress in
full form when she lifted her slick-covered fingers.

Her pulse echoed in her ears, the beats increasing
when she locked her eyes on Matt. Lust and want pierced
her. His hunger blazed back filled with everything he
knew, yet he remained silent. Still. His chest lifted with
each quick breath, heat searing her from his intensity.

She was his sole focus, and she reveled in that. This
was her, and she wasn't shying away from it when she
never had before. If he expected differently, he'd be se-
verely disappointed.

She held her fingers over her nipple but didn't touch

it. Her breast tingled with the anticipation she'd created even as she drew her fingers up, her gaze never leaving his. His lips parted. A growl rumbled from his chest when her fingers reached her lips.

Another groan hit the air from the other side of the room, but her focus was trapped on Matt. She inhaled long and slow, her eyelids falling a notch as the musky scent of her sex teased its way through her. It bumped up the eroticism and pushed her more.

How dirty could she go? Would he break?

Her juices hit her tongue in a burst of exotic flavors. She sucked her fingers into her mouth on a low hum, her hips rocking as she absorbed the sensual hit.

"Christ."

The mumbled curse from Matt fueled her even more. She was playing with fire and couldn't get herself to stop—or care.

She drew her fingers from her mouth, flicking her tongue over them to get every last drop. A spark of deviousness had her dipping her fingers back into herself to cover them once again. Heat lit her pussy and curled its way through her as the full extent of her wickedness took hold. It triggered her smirk and egged her on when she knew she should stop.

She slicked her tongue over her lips, heart pounding as she extended her fingers to Matt. She raised a brow, the dare leveled. His sharp intake of breath cut through the tension before ratcheting it right back up. It prickled down her arm and tightened around her chest the longer he made her wait.

Another rumbled curse blew through the room with an envious edge. Want flared in Matt's eyes, stirring the brown depths into pools of lust. His nostrils flared, his chest expanding in a display of power that fed her kink and teased the desires she wanted so desperately to deny.

His suit fit him perfectly. Authority dripped from his bearing, the scruff on his cheeks adding to the dark element that'd intrigued her from the beginning.

He stepped forward. Her heart raced. He dipped, pausing with his lips a hair away from her fingers, his own dare extended in his gaze. Her breath stuck, want hammering her as she traced her fingers over his parted lips.

His eyes closed. His hands fisted where he braced them on the table. Her arm started to shake before she dipped her fingers into his mouth. The rush of wet heat tore a moan from her before she could contain it.

He flicked his tongue, sucking hungrily. Each draw seemed to pull her wants from beneath the pile of rejection she'd shoved them under. Longing trembled in her chest to fortify the need coiling in her groin.

Power laced with open lust blazed when he opened his eyes. The firm drag of his teeth over her fingers as he eased back sent a shiver straight to her unchecked fantasies.

"Yes," she mouthed, desire overtaking logic. She wanted him. Still. Here. Now. But...

Her heart pinched when he stepped back, hunger still rampant on his features. He held his hands behind his back as he lifted his chin, his feet shoulder-width apart. So formal and commanding. Holy...

She ripped her gaze away, reaching for the vibrator as her pussy clamped down on the rush of need he'd ignited. Her hips rocked, muscles clenching, a moan tearing free before she even touched it. Images of Matt taking her, filling her, driving her wild on this table took hold until all rational thought disappeared.

She could have that. It was hers to define. She could have any of the men here, if they agreed. She only had to ask.

She drew her gaze over the men she could see, the vibrator poised between her legs. One guy already had his dick in his fist. Another rubbed his erection through his slacks. A third eyed her boldly, a trace of envy lining his scowl.

And then there was Matt.

He watched her with open passion, his control locking him down. His lips twitched when she ran the head of the fake cock through her folds. Her stomach clenched, her eyelids dropping. She rubbed it over her clit, mouth parting on a gasp. His chest expanded, his swallow forcing his Adam's apple into a hard bob.

She flicked her eye from him to the space between her legs. Her pussy contracted around the empty ache pulsing within it. Her breath caught, legs trembling when she braced the tip at her entrance, yet she didn't press it deeper.

Matt moved then, stepping around to stand at the end of the table. Kennedy tracked him, her pulse going wild. Blood roared in her head, want and fear chasing each other in a vicious loop of indecision.

He loomed between her legs, wielding his power on a silent note of command. Defiance had her thrusting the vibrator deep. She hunched forward as the pleasure burst through her. The fullness stretched her walls and rubbed against nerve endings begging for friction.

She lay back, breaths short as she eased the toy out only to shove it back in. It slid in smoothly, sparking a wave of carnal lust. And Matt watched it all, each withdrawal and plunge, every quick pump that teased her opening before she thrust it deep.

She had him. He wanted her. He didn't try to hide the truth of that. His hard frown burned with desire, his eyes heavy with the need he kept locked down. And she wanted it. Him. All of it.

To be ravished. To be controlled and cherished at once. To be his—again.

The vibrator slid from her on a distinctive squelch before she set it aside. Her pussy pulsed with the emptiness, her lust racing in to fill the hunger.

Trevor moved into her peripheral vision as Matt lifted his hand. He held it over her knee, restraint rolling from him. His eyes narrowed, head tilting ever so slightly as he stared down at her. But he didn't touch her, didn't so much as graze his fingers over her skin as he waited.

A wave of tenderness did its best to smother her. She choked on the emotion, so unaccustomed to feeling it she barely recognized it for what it was. He wasn't taking, even now. In truth, he'd never taken from her.

No, he'd given her exactly what she'd wanted. And he was waiting for her to tell him what she wanted now.

She caught Trevor's frown and ignored it. This was her scene, damn it. And she wanted Matt. God help her, but she did. She could have him and maintain her control if she balanced it right. She wasn't giving anything up.

Not if she owned it.

She tossed her restrictions to the wind, setting her need and desire free on three little words. "Touch me, Matt."

Chapter Eleven

"Touch me, Matt."

Kennedy's words shot through the room to nail Matt with the hunger encased within them. He bit back his groan, his control strapped tightly around the lust scrambling to break free. The rest of the room didn't exist, not anymore.

He lowered his hand to her knee in a deliberate move, his eyes never leaving hers. Her flinch was small, more of a twitch that pulsed in a single beat before she relaxed. Her eyelids drooped in that way that smoldered with sex.

She was driving him crazy, and she knew it. Even here, now, she didn't shy away from what she wanted or the knowledge of what she was doing to him. Who was this woman? Where had she come from?

He skimmed both hands down her inner thighs, stopping when he reached the V of her pussy. She sucked in her abdomen, hands fisting at her sides as she bit her lip.

Want surged with the high of the power she'd given him. Not any of the other men. Him. Trevor hovered at his back, but Matt dismissed him. He'd take care with her—take care *of* her.

She was his now. All his.

He watched, intent, as he swiped a thumb over her clit. Another flinch, a held breath. He rubbed it slowly, her sigh tumbling out on a muffled moan. Her hands uncurled, hips undulating. He held her there, on the impasse of good but not great until she squirmed, her whimper begging for more.

He understood that, understood her.

Heat surrounded his other thumb when he slid it into her. Her wetness eased his entry as she clamped down, holding it tight. His dick ached to take the place of his thumb. To fill her so completely she couldn't think of anything but him.

She had him so entrapped in her spell he didn't care about the promises he'd made to himself. His primal instincts spilled forth without an ounce of hesitation.

He dragged his other hand up her stomach. The softness of her skin was exactly as he remembered. His calluses scrapped over each dip and rise as he skirted between her breasts to reach her neck. Her chest rose and fell in a rapid pace that fueled his own. Her freckles spread in an inviting sea beneath his palm, and he still longed to count each one with his tongue.

Fire blazed in those dazzling eyes of hers, the blue sparking with desire. She lifted her chin, challenge issued before he eased his palm around her throat. *Fuck.*

Her sigh breathed into him, her acceptance shimmered, setting his dreams free. Could she really be this perfect? This stunning? A resounding *yes* clamored in his head and pounded in his chest beside the more pressing question: Could he really let her go again?

Her hand shot up, wrapping around his tie in two quick twists before she hauled him to her. He fell forward, catching himself before he crushed her. His pulse raced with his confusion as he stared down, fascinated by the raw emotions shining so clearly in her eyes. Hunger, want, lust and right there, on the edge but just as clear—fear.

He froze, overwhelmed by the onslaught of anger at himself for putting it there and a crazed need to make it go away. She pulled him closer, eyelids lowering as her lips grazed his. He hunted for air, sweet joy dancing over his heart at her gentle hit. Her breath sensitized his jaw with each little ghost of a touch until she reached his ear.

"Not here," she whispered, insistent. "Not now."

He caught his immediate question before it slipped free. It didn't matter why. Her request was enough. It would always be enough.

He lowered the fraction it took for his lips to hover over hers. Her pupils were enormous, the blue pushed back to bright rings that screamed her aroused state. He wanted to kiss her so badly. His lips pulsed with the need clamoring to taste her again.

The slightest swivel of her head gave him his answer. Disappointment slammed in even as understanding took hold. He rubbed his nose against hers in a gentle pass that he hoped she understood before he dropped down to take a nipple in his mouth.

She dug her fingers into his hair, her desperate sounds growing louder as he sucked and played. He could give her this. He'd gladly give her all the pleasure she could take without overstepping his bounds.

The scene was hers.

The scene was always hers, even when he controlled it. And tonight, now, here, she needed that to show.

He dragged his teeth over her nipple, teased it until

she cried out. Yet her fingers dug into his scalp as she urged him on. He cupped the fullness, kneading her breast before he drew back, her nipple firmly clamped between his teeth.

She gasped, arching her back in an attempt to follow his retreat, her breaths heavy when she stilled. He held her there, suspended in the unknown of what he'd do next. Would he pull more? Let go? Her eyes were closed, that small wrinkle present between her brows. A flush tainted her cheeks and chest, those beautiful freckles darkened beneath the stain.

He freed the tip from his teeth, suckling it gently before switching to her other nipple. He tracked every hitch of breath, rumbled groan and shift of her body as he focused on fulfilling her desires. She was beautiful, bold, and he refused to take any of her strength.

"I've got you," he whispered near her ear when he gave her nipples a break. Her shudder trembled down her body in a small wave he doubted anyone could see. He felt it, though. It vibrated into him on a swell of satisfaction. His own needs were nothing when balanced against hers.

He'd missed this so damn much. This give when it seemed like take. The caring that went with the sex. The connection that came with the trust. The growing bond that had him reassessing the limitations he'd placed on himself.

He laid a trail of kisses down her neck and over her chest, every peck and lick communicating his message. The salty taste of her skin coated his tongue and tempted him with memories of her juices. Anticipation tightened in his groin with each inch closer to his final destination. Her musky scent drew him down while enticing him with a promise of more.

The first hit nailed him with a longing so strong his approval came out as a savage snarl. His head buzzed with the ecstasy flooding him. He dragged his tongue through her pussy again and again, pausing to play with her clit before dipping down to lap at her entrance. She squirmed beneath him, but he held her legs wide, keeping her at the edge of the table.

His balls tightened into agonizing knots of suppressed release that shot up his dick. He savored that too. He wasn't ruled by his dick, even if it had propelled him here.

Kennedy curled forward, her nails digging into his scalp. The tiny bites of pain drove him harder.

"Yes," she mumbled, the word indistinct but clear. She rocked her hips, directing his mouth to her clit.

He followed with ease, focusing on the swollen nub that'd hardened so beautifully. He sucked and flicked, drawing her closer to her crest without rushing. The end would come soon enough and then... He refused to think about that.

He slid his fingers into her on a slow glide that allowed him to savor the clench, coating his fingers in wet softness. He groaned his approval against her clit, his eyes squeezing tight as he remembered how sweet she'd felt around his dick.

He reached for the vibrator, easing back to blow a stream of air over her heated pussy. Her lips pulsed and fluttered, the muscles contracting when he removed his fingers. Her scent surrounded him even after he wiped his mouth with his hand. It took a dose of pure determination to lock down the almost overwhelming urge to free his dick and sink into her. A sticky pool of pre-come dampened his lower abdomen in a declaration of the urgency that crawled through his groin.

A deep breath, another, and his control slid back in on the reminder that this was about her. He stood, moving his hand so his thumb could work her clit. He ran his gaze from her strappy black heels to her exposed pussy and up her torso to her full breasts, her nipples still puckered, and on to her dazed expression, her hair spread in a dark halo behind her.

She was stunning.

And she met his gaze without hesitation, her tongue slipping out to tease him with a pass between her lips. Damn, how he wanted to kiss her, spread her flavor back into her until another groan fell from her lips.

He moved with deliberate slowness as he slid the head of the vibrator over her pussy. Her swallow was pronounced before she lowered her chin, that fierce strength flashing in her eyes. She slid her hand down her stomach until she nudged him away from her clit, taking over. Her moaned purr was cut short when he slid the fake dick into her.

He gritted his teeth to hold back the urge to touch his own dick, just a hard rub or adjustment to ease the ache as he stroked the lifelike phallus in her. Sweat beaded down his back, his heart racing to keep pace with the building tension.

Her mouth parted, eyes going heavy the faster her finger moved. He studied every cue, keeping pace with her before slowing to tease her entrance with small, quick pumps. Her hips lifted, fell before he pushed the vibrator deep, flicking it on as he did.

She lurched up, mouth gaping. A cry broke free when

she fell back, her orgasm breaking in a rush of shudders. She arched, her finger moving wildly until she reached her peak on a choked groan. Only then did he turn off the vibrator and slide it free, her muscles going lax.

Fucking... Matt search for air, finally giving into the need to touch himself. He palmed his rock-hard dick through his slacks, counting backwards until he regained control. The world slammed back in on a harsh grunt and the smacking of flesh.

His head snapped up, gaze tracking the room in a blink. One of the men eyed him, envy clear on his dark scowl as he stroked himself. Another guy was cleaning himself up, while the other two were apparently done or content just watching.

He straightened his shoulders and held the gaze of each man. Possessive pride roared to life in his chest despite him having no claim to it. But he saw the curiosity along with the impressed awe in their eyes. He had zero idea what it was for, yet it still managed to pluck at the strings of authority he'd tried to suppress.

The high buzzed through him when he wanted to reject it. But Kennedy still lay on the table, vulnerable now. His heart clenched at the sight of her closed eyes, her expression soft, her breaths slowing as she came down.

He set the toy aside and reached for her.

"That's it, gentlemen." Trevor's voiced cracked through the room. "Scene's over." He laid a hand on Matt's arm, stopping him before he could touch her.

Matt whipped his head around, annoyance flaring before he caught Trevor's hard glare. Questions assailed him from Trevor's steely gray eyes, his anger clear when he tightened his hold.

What the ever-loving fuck?

Should he give in? Demand answers? Defy Trevor? To what end?

Matt looked back to Kennedy, who still hadn't moved. She hadn't even opened her eyes. Understanding hit him hard. This was it. No explanation. No conversation. Not even a goodbye. His stomach twisted around the sour note as he stepped back.

This wasn't right.

Was she okay? Did she want to be left alone? Could they really expect him to just walk away without ensuring she was fine?

No. He couldn't. He didn't work that way.

He yanked his arm out of Trevor's hold and leaned over Kennedy before Trevor could stop him. "Thank you," he murmured near her ear. He brushed a kiss over her cheek, holding it as he got his sudden rush of emotions under control. He longed to scoop her up and hold her tight, but she gave no indication that she wanted that, and he wouldn't force it. He'd never force her.

He skimmed his fingers down her hairline before he dragged them through the silky ends of her hair. Her eyes fluttered, a breath escaping on a soft sigh.

"Are you okay?" he asked.

"She's fine," Trevor bit out from his spot by the door. The rest of the men had left, and Matt had clearly overstayed his welcome.

He put all his animosity into the glare he shot across the room. He didn't care what he was supposed to do. Trevor could kick his ass from this little Boardroom group if he wanted. Kennedy was more important.

A touch to his cheek drew his attention back to her. A soft smile lifted her lips before it fell away on a tiny tremble. Warmth sunk deep when she cupped his cheek in the softest of connections. "Thank you."

He saw more than heard her words, but each one kicked at the walls he'd held strong for so long. How, when he barely knew her?

"I'm fine," she reassured him. "Really." He frowned, doubt holding. "You should go," she added when he didn't move. The last knocked him back. *He should go.*

She was done with him—again. Of course.

What had he expected? No, what had he been thinking?

He nodded, then dropped one last kiss to her temple before he straightened. "Take care, Kennedy." He was already kicking himself when he turned away. Sex was just sex. He obviously needed to have it more often or go back to his dry spell.

And if it'd actually been just sex, he wouldn't be this conflicted.

He'd barely taken a step before she shot up, grabbing his arm to haul him around. She cupped his face and had her mouth locked to his in the next instant. She licked his lips, sunk deep when he opened to her. How could he not?

He drew her in, doubts and questions gone beneath the sweet heaven of her kiss. Heat and passion chased the carnal assault as she claimed every inch of his mouth. A desperate edge tinted her taste, her soft cry laced with something he didn't understand.

She retreated as quickly as she'd attacked. She blinked a few times, her fingers drifting over his lips. "I owe you an explanation. But..." She pressed her lips together.

"You owe me nothing," he told her, meaning it. Both

of their encounters had happened without expectations. They'd simply been. He had to remember that. "Good-bye, Kennedy."

He walked away while he still could. An ache built in his chest, but he held his resolve. He slipped past Trevor and strode to the smaller room to claim his phone. The more he knew about her the harder it'd be to stay away. And he should, right? Stay away. What could there really be between them?

Yet…

He came up short after he almost plowed into one of the men leaving. "Sorry," he mumbled before he ducked into the room. He grabbed his phone from the table and was turning to leave when Trevor stepped in.

"Got a minute?" His question really wasn't one.

Matt checked his phone, using the excuse to school his features into the emotionless mask that hid his turmoil. He had one message from Ben stating he was heading to bed. Ten minutes ago. If Matt had gone straight home, he could've seen him, talked to him about his day.

Instead, he'd chosen to have sex in a room full of strangers—and Kennedy. Had the temporary high been worth it? His slowly deflating dick said no.

But he couldn't shake the longing that lingered, the awareness that there was another he'd started to care for. Someone he wanted to know better despite the danger she could bring.

When the last guy exited the room on a gruff "see ya," he tucked his phone into his pocket and finally looked to Trevor.

His hands went to their default hold at his back, a position the military had hounded into him. Even now, years later, he found comfort in the stance. His world condensed to just that moment the second he gripped his hand. He became centered, his strength pulling from the core foundations that'd honed and molded him into an officer.

His suit was his uniform now, and he let the security of that sink into him. Rank was only implied here, not openly marked on a sleeve. Authority came in part from confidence, which he'd never lacked.

Trevor slid his palm over the back of a chair with an air of nonchalance that didn't reach his expression. "Do you care to explain?"

Matt bristled at the order stated as a question. "No." He didn't report to Trevor.

Trevor's chin hitched up, mouth compressing slightly. His grip tightened on the chair. "What was that?"

"A scene."

Trevor was in his face in three quick steps. "Do not fuck with me."

Matt held his glare without a thought of flinching. Icy anger shot from Trevor's steely eyes in a display of emotion that hit Matt with its authenticity. He softened then, undone by the raw concern Trevor wasn't trying to hide.

"I'm not fucking with you," he said after a moment. "That was a scene. I followed the scene rules."

"You called her Kennedy."

He balked at that. Regret barged in on his next breath. "I'm going to assume that was against the rules. I apologize."

Trevor's expression hardened. "How do you know her?"

"I could ask you the same thing." Trevor's directness

didn't startle him, but he had no obligation to confide anything.

Trevor stepped back. A smirk that was anything but humorous curled his lip. "Are you sure you want to play this that way?"

Again with the question command. Matt let his hands hang loose at his sides as he tried to dissect Trevor's reaction. This wasn't a pissing contest, but Trevor had clearly marked Kennedy as his territory.

"Are you two involved?" Matt asked. His stomach knotted at the thought. He had no beef against open sexual play, obviously. But he wasn't cool with being used as a tool to incite jealousy.

"Trevor."

Matt whipped his head around at Kennedy's curt reprimand. She stood in the doorway, collected and poised. Her black pantsuit screamed class along with the subtle power she expertly wielded. The only hint that remained of what had just happened in the other room was a slight flush to her cheeks.

"It's okay," she said, her steady gaze locked on Trevor. She stepped up to him, laying a hand on his arm. "But thank you."

Doubt showed for a moment before Trevor looked back to Matt. "You hurt her, and I'll ruin you."

"Trevor!"

He took Trevor's threat as real, but he refused to react. His stony silence was all he offered before he inclined his head. "I believe that's my cue to leave."

"Matt, wait." Kennedy snagged his arm before he reached the door. He stilled, doubt and anger clashing with curiosity. She sent him a pinched looked before turning back to Trevor. "There's no reason for this macho big brother act. I can take care of myself."

Matt made a quick assessment of the two and saw zero resemblance between them. The predominance of gray in Trevor's hair hid what used to be darker, but their facial features were dramatically different.

"Ken," Trevor said before releasing a sigh. He straightened his suit coat and passed Matt on his way out the door. He glanced back to her. "Call me if you need me." He sent one last warning look to Matt before he headed down the hall.

Matt's focus swung back to Kennedy as she faced him. The night had turned into another round of want and confusion centered on her. How? Yet even now, after being dismissed and threatened, he couldn't deny his attraction. Because stuffed behind the formal exterior she presented to him now was a gorgeous, bold woman he suddenly had a second chance with.

Was he truly willing, let alone able, to walk away from her again?

Chapter Twelve

Silence dropped in on an ominous note. The entire night had gotten out of hand and it was up to her to right it, only Kennedy wasn't sure how or what she wanted.

She gave Matt a small shrug. "Sorry about that. Trevor gets a little overprotective with me."

"How come?"

She studied him, ignoring the distant front he was putting off. "We're old friends. I've known him since my teens." Those slightly wild, definitely formative teenage years.

She moved toward him, her heart doing a strange twist and thump she had no idea what to do about. Yet another thing she was lost on when she worked so damn hard to avoid that state. He gave away nothing as she approached. A part of her loved the challenge it presented along with the dark mystery that still clung to him.

His beard scruff was fuller tonight. It complemented his suit with an odd bad boy vibe she bet he hadn't planned. She met his steady gaze, her host of questions falling away to just one. "What are you doing here?"

His brow popped up. "I could ask you the same thing."

She gave him that one. A smile quirked before she pulled it flat. "You're not in the app."

"What app?"

That explained a lot. He was either super new or a guest if he didn't have access to the app where the Boardroom scenes were scheduled. "Did someone invite you tonight?"

"Trevor." He glanced out the door. "But I think he's regretting it now."

Her short laugh came out as more air than sound. "I'm thinking you might be right." She waited for him to look back to her. "But I'm not." A shiver of fear blew down her spine in the beat it took her to comprehend what she'd admitted.

His head cocked just a tad, eyes narrowing. "No?"

The innocuous action took her straight back to their night. To the way he'd assessed her and then taken control. Just like tonight. She smothered the shiver that quaked through her chest and contemplated her options.

She could play it coy, keep it light and let it go. "No." And there went that opportunity. But then, she wasn't known for lying. She laid her cards on the table and went from there.

His slow smile was just as devastating as she remembered. Her stomach took a ride on the Oh Shit roller-coaster as she tried to hide her reaction.

"Did you arrange this?" he asked. The low timbre of his voice skated over her memories to draw up every command he'd given her. Every touch and order she'd so willingly followed.

She cleared her throat, almost laughing at the absurdity of his question. "No. Did you?"

"No."

It really had been a coincidence. What were the odds? "Do you know who I am?"

"Not beyond your name… Kennedy." His low rolling purr enunciated every syllable to add a hint of accusation to the seductive tone.

"If I remember correctly, it was you who insisted on keeping our full identities secret." She wasn't taking the blame for what appeared to be a stunning act of fate.

"I did." He studied her for a long moment before he shook his head, looking away. "Who would've thought we'd meet again, let alone under these circumstances."

"Definitely not me." A smile picked at the corner of her mouth when he looked back to her. She shrugged yet again. What else was there to do or say? "Was there a reason why you were so insistent on remaining anonymous?"

He huffed out a short laugh before he rubbed a hand up his jaw. It was his first real display of emotion since she walked into this room and it touched her in an odd way. What was he struggling with?

"No," he finally said, his hand falling to his side. "Not really. It just seemed easier. No expectations. No worries about raising your hopes on something I couldn't offer."

"And what's that?" she asked. He needed to spell it out even though she was pretty sure she could guess what he was referring to.

"Anything more." His bomb landed with a dull thud.

"Well, you're in luck." She gave his chest a quick pat. "Because I have no desire for anything more."

She strode from the room to add an exclamation point to her statement. Why did men assume women spent their lives looking for a man to sweep them off their feet in a whirlwind of Cinderella fairy dust? She was happy with her life. She didn't want or need a man in it.

But that didn't explain why she'd been unable to forget him. Why he still invaded her thoughts almost a month later.

Her snort was lost beneath the creak of the stairwell door. She didn't look back to see if he was following her, but he caught the door before it slammed shut. She swung around the landing and attacked the stairs as if she was wearing running shoes instead of heels.

She could run in heels, no problem. Just add that to the list of helpful skills her mother had taught her. Grace under any situation, and most of them required matching shoes.

She halted at the front door, her ire flattening into a practiced line of disinterest as she ignored the nugget of disappointment that tried to pry its way into her emotions.

Matt entered the lobby on that same controlled calm that defined him. But she'd seen the passionate side of him too. Along with the one that'd listened to her quiet demand this evening. He could've ignored her or tempted her with the very things she couldn't fully admit to wanting, let alone expose. But he hadn't.

Not even a little.

He'd given her nothing but pleasure, all without taking anything for himself.

He extended his hand, a kindness to his expression she couldn't quite pinpoint but felt. "I'm Matt Hamilton, owner and CEO of McPherson Trucking. It's nice to meet you."

Nope. Her heart did not do that fluttery flip thing just now. She took his hand in hers, momentarily stunned by the warmth that crept up her arm to soften her a little more.

"It's nice to meet you. Matt *Hamilton*." She emphasized his last name. "I'm Kennedy Keller. VP of Operations at Keller Pallet."

He kept her hand enclosed in his, but not by force. She could've pulled it away if she'd wanted to. Yeah, if she'd really wanted to. She couldn't explain why she didn't want to, or how that little hold made her feel safe when she hadn't felt unsafe before.

"Kennedy Keller," he repeated in a thoughtful tone she couldn't decipher. "For the record, you should consider that maybe it wasn't you who I was concerned about wanting more." He paused, his words sinking in with the resounding boom that'd been absent earlier. "Maybe it was me I was worried about. And maybe..." He cupped her cheek with his free hand, his thumb tracing an arc over her cheekbone. "I was right to listen to those concerns."

The rollercoaster crashed in a bloodcurdling descent that shook her old resolves. This was the last thing she'd expected when the evening began. Instead of reclaiming her power, she'd somehow managed to give more of it to him.

Her insides trembled with the uncertainty chasing her longing. "Thank you," she said, pulling away from his touch. She fisted her hands and held them firmly at her sides. "For tonight. For listening to me."

He frowned. "Why wouldn't I?" He didn't move, yet she couldn't shake the perception that he'd inched closer. Or was it her moving closer to him? "I'd never disrespect you like that."

She'd known that, deep down. Despite having just

one previous encounter with him, she'd trusted him to play by her rules when she'd taunted him with her fingers.

"I…had hoped," she finally said.

"I thought those scenes were safe."

"They are. Or I wouldn't do them." Her brows drew down as she circled back to how this situation had happened. "Why did Trevor invite you tonight?"

"I've been questioning that since I realized it was you spread over that table, owning your sexuality and the room." Lust laced his voice and matched the fire in his eyes. "I'd been trying to shake the image of you plastered against the window, taking my dick with such hungry sweetness. And there you were, taking your own pleasure with the same confidence that drew me in from the start."

Her mouth went dry. How was she supposed to respond to that? He'd been thinking about her? Remembering their night like she had?

"How do you know Trevor?" she persisted. He wouldn't derail her with sexy words and a husky tone.

His half-smile showed a spark of admiration. "I hired Trevor to manage my company's investments a while back. We've formed a bit of a friendship since then." He dismissed the details with a shrug. "The Boardroom came up a few months ago. I passed, but my dick couldn't seem to shake your memory, so I took him up on the invite."

She processed that. "You were led here by your dick?"

"I doubt if I'd be the first."

"Touché." She shared a smile with him and tried to not be drawn in by the devastating effects of his. It

softened every hard edge without detracting from the
authority that was an inherent part of him.

"And you?" he asked. "What brought you to the
Boardroom?"

Her laugh was quick. "I'm no different than any man
on that aspect—minus the dick." She paused to see if
he'd react. He didn't. "I like sex. Open, unencumbered
sex. Men don't own that."

"No. They don't."

She hunted for a hint of derogatory or negative sub-
text and found none. She rested a hand on the door, but
her rush to see him go had faded.

"You also like control," he stated. "Both having it
and giving it up."

His blatant declaration was totally true, only most
didn't know about the last bit. Actually, no one did—
except him. "I'd appreciate it if you kept that knowledge to yourself."

"It's not mine to share." His simple response defined
him. Clear cut. Precise. Accurate.

"And you," she said, "like wielding control. What I
don't understand is why you gave it up to me so easily tonight."

"Did I?" He frowned. "I guess it depends on how
you look at it."

"I guess it does." She'd let him stew on that even
though she understood what he meant. He might've
given into her wish of not openly dominating her, but
he'd controlled her in every gentle touch and demanding caress. And she'd asked him to do it.

He took a step toward the door, which also brought
him closer to her. He appeared a little distracted when
he stared down at her. Her breath did that irritating hitch

before she held it. How? Why? He was just a guy. She'd been around powerful men her entire life. He was no different—yet he was.

Which made him very dangerous.

He raised his hand in a deliberate motion that clearly telegraphed his intent. She could've stopped him. Moved away. Deflected. Instead, she stood there and let him run the back of his fingers down her cheek. Her breath gusted out on a telling sigh.

She turned her face into his touch, eyes closing as the longing rushed in. It'd only taken that one little stroke to bring back every ache she worked so hard to deny. Possibilities danced invitingly before her, dangled within her reach by a man she barely knew.

The barest of kisses grazed her temple, soft as a breath. She leaned into it, drawn in before she could think.

"You are a temptation I didn't plan on," he murmured.

She swallowed down her response. Was there really any point in agreeing with him?

"Logic tells me I should walk away. But logic also said I shouldn't have come here tonight."

"Maybe you shouldn't have," she countered. If he hadn't, then neither of them would be wading through the internal debate they were obviously both having.

"But I did."

"Yes," she whispered. "You did." She inhaled a long, slow breath that fed his scent into her. The tangy hint of his cologne blended with the pungent undercurrent of her sex. She didn't need the reminder of how he'd pleasured her with the same focused dedication she'd bet he used for every task. The reminder was there, though. Trapped in the short hairs of his beard. Could he still smell it? Would he wash it out or let it remain?

Her fingers drifted down his lapel, seeming to move on their own. When had she gotten so close to him?

"I have two kids."

The sharp splash of reality doused her errant emotions. He had kids. What? Why did he tell her that? Now?

She jerked back, trying to read him. "Okay..."

"They're both teens. One's in college. The other in high school. I owe them my focus."

Her thoughts flew in the same scattered maze of her emotions. Confused. Shocked. Alarmed. Kids was a topic she generally avoided on all levels. Usually because it led back to when was she going to have them. Just the thought of being pigeonholed into the standard female expectation of motherhood made her nauseous.

"Agreed," she finally offered. She had no problem with kids being a parental priority, especially when she'd never been. "And..."

He studied her, indecision flashing before he shut it down. "You make me want things I haven't let myself want in years."

"And that bothers you." She wasn't about to ask what he wanted. Not knowing was better than digging for a response she didn't want to hear.

He moved closer without answering her. His intent was clear, though. From the smoldering hunger in his eyes to the longing that hummed through the air and incited her own. He swept his hand along the side of her neck, cupping the back of her head and drawing her in for a kiss that left no question to what he desired.

His tongue swept over hers, teased and demanded at

the same time. He took what he wanted and she gave it to him so easily. He was a threat to everything she held dear. Her independence and respect. Her position and autonomy. The place she'd carved out for herself in a field owned by men.

And this was just a kiss. A kiss.

That had her head swimming and her pulse racing. From a simple kiss.

He tilted her head and dove in deeper before retreating to tease her with lighter strokes that managed to curl her toes and leave her clinging to him. Her scent blended with the lingering taste of her on his tongue, or was that her imagination. A reminder of how he'd drawn out her orgasm until it'd burst from her on a blinding rush of stunned ecstasy.

She lifted, determined to give back. To chase his demand with her own.

He drew his other hand down her back and over the swell of her ass. The slightest of pressure had her hips connecting with his. His erection carved a defined line down her lower abdomen. Her moan vibrated in her chest and lit up the lust that should've been sated. Her pussy clenched with the sudden urge to feel him in her.

How? How did he set her off so easily? Sex. It was just sex. A base attraction triggered by hormones. But this was so much bigger. More intense.

He ripped his mouth away, breaths crashing with hers before he rested his lips on her temple. "This," he mumbled. "This right here is why I wanted distance."

She hummed her response, too lost in the dizzying effects of his kiss. But she totally agreed. This— whatever it was—was dangerous.

"But I know who you are now," he continued. "I

know how to find you." He eased back to look in her eyes. His intentions were telegraphed along with his turmoil. "And I don't know if I can stay away."

Warning bells sounded every alarm she'd rigged to prevent herself from falling into this exact situation. Yet he could give her the one thing she didn't trust with anyone else.

Was the risk worth it?

"Then you probably should," she told him, backing away. Regret twisted a sharp knife in her chest before she'd finished her words. She held strong through the whispers of possibilities and what-ifs until she let her hands fall from his shoulders. "Sex shouldn't be complicated," she added, more as a reminder to herself. "And this screams complication."

He blew out a long breath. Nodded. "It does." He shoved the door open. A wave of cooler air swooped in to bathe her heated skin. "Because sex wouldn't be enough with you."

Her stomach dropped. Her lips parted, but no response came out. She refused to acknowledge the yearning created by his hidden threat...or was it a promise? What would more entail?

He pierced her with a long look that spoke to how much he wanted to act. "Goodbye, Kennedy." He left without a backward glance. His strides were crisp, his spine straight as he strode across the lot to the black car parked on the far end.

She stood there, numb, watching him until he pulled from the lot, his taillights providing one last confirmation of his existence before he turned the corner.

Something cracked within her, but she ignored it. She could've stopped him at any point. She could've accepted what he was dangling. And that would've put her in the one position she'd promised herself she'd never be in.

Being beholden to a man would only hold her back. But for the first time ever, she was having a hard time remembering exactly where she needed so desperately to be.

Chapter Thirteen

Matt looked up from his conversation to find Trevor James studying him from across the bay. His curse died in his throat. He'd been expecting a call, but an unscheduled personal visit was even worse.

"It looks good," he said to his supervisor, handing the clipboard over to him. "Keep me updated."

"Got it."

Matt tucked his pencil behind his ear and headed to his guest. He mentally shuffled his tasks for the day, while hunkering down on his loyalties. He'd tried to limit them after his ex, but he'd taken on a ton more when he'd bought the company.

Howard McPherson had started the business with three trucks and the hopes of providing for his family. Forty years and a fleet of vehicles later, he'd more than succeeded in reaching his goal. The brand had a strong local following and association, but Howard's drive to succeed had lessoned with his age. His daughters all had families of their own with no interest in taking over the company, and his wife's dreams of a tropical retirement had spurred his decision to sell.

Matt's military background as a transportation officer had landed him a job here when he'd been desperate to support his own family. And now, he had a few dozen employees all doing the same thing. They were still small-time in the grand scheme of things, but he had visions on how that could change.

As long as someone like Trevor James didn't sabotage him.

All for a fuck. Damn it.

But it wasn't just a fuck. He couldn't demean his interactions with Kennedy like that.

"Trevor." He held out his hand to the man whose expression hadn't changed even a flicker in the long walk Matt had taken to reach him. "This is a surprise." Yet not.

"Matt." Trevor took his extended hand, his shake one of perfunctory courtesy. He glanced around, his tailored suit and tie standing out among the grime of the bay and the standard jeans and T-shirts worn by his employees. He gave away nothing when his gaze landed back on Matt. "Can we talk?"

Matt bit his tongue against the irritating question statement that seemed to be Trevor's default way of demanding what he wanted. Saying no wasn't really an option given he was already there. His San Francisco office was far enough away to make this trip an effort.

Matt led the way into the office portion of the building. Cami glanced up from her desk, brows lifted in a question he didn't respond to. She was the ideal assistant with her love of spreadsheets and organizational skills that kept shipments straight and drivers scheduled.

He wiped his palm on his jeans, already too aware of his attire, but hell if he was letting his lack of a suit alter his approach. His office door was open, and he stepped aside to let Trevor enter, closing the door behind him. He'd never questioned Trevor's dedication to his job, but he doubted this was going to be a friendly chat about investments.

He dragged the pencil from behind his ear and tossed it on his desk before turning to Trevor. "I expected your call three days ago." Each day that'd dragged by since that night in the Boardroom had only drawn out the showdown he'd known was coming.

"Sorry to disappoint." The snark in his tone said he wasn't. "But I had some details to iron out."

"Such as?"

Trevor wandered the small space, gaze tracking over every surface before he stopped by the window. The view of the asphalt parking lot and large warehouse behind them offered nothing like the gorgeous city sightlines Trevor's office provided.

He turned, nailing Matt with a hard stare. "Like how you know Kennedy and what that means."

Matt resisted the urge to cross his arms. The defensive gesture would gain him nothing. "And you have those details now?"

His lips pinched just a tad before they flattened out. "No."

Surprise caught him before he could school his expression. He sat on the edge of his desk and gave up on caring what Trevor thought as he crossed his arms over his chest. "What do you want to know?"

Trevor's eyes narrowed. The authoritative air that never left him tracked a path across the room to prickle over Matt's ingrained habit to stand at attention before a superior, especially given his own dressed-down state. But Trevor was nothing more than a business associate. One Matt had hired.

"First, I hope you remember every line of the contract you signed before walking into that room."

He resisted the eye roll that would've outdone any his daughter dished out. "Yes."

Trevor absorbed his short response with a slight flick of his chin. "Second, you fuck with Kennedy, you fuck with me."

That had the hairs on Matt's nape dancing in predatory warning. "And why would I want to fuck with Kennedy?" He wasn't playing into Trevor's hands, no matter who he was or what influence he held.

"I have no idea. Just don't."

"I wasn't planning on it." Now fucking her again, quick and hard or long and slow, he'd gladly be on board for. And another fuck wasn't all he wanted.

Trevor studied him. Matt stared right back. He had nothing to hide. "Good. She deserves to be treated with respect."

"Doesn't everyone deserve that?"

"It doesn't mean everyone gets it."

"True." Unfortunately. Matt gave him that point, adding, "I have nothing but respect for Kennedy. I would never 'fuck with her,' as you put it."

The tension lengthened between them until Trevor huffed out a sarcastic laugh. "I sound like an ass."

Matt raised a brow but kept silent. A response wasn't required for the obvious.

Trevor shoved his hands in his pockets. The last of the stiffness that'd held his shoulders back drained out on a visible exhale. He hung his head, inhaled, his combative demeanor gone when he looked up. "She doesn't let men do that, you know."

Matt frowned. "Do what?"

"Touch her like you did. Especially in a scene."

She doesn't let men touch her. But she'd let Matt, in more than the physical sense too. His pulse increased, a whisper of relief easing through him when he had no right to feel it.

Trevor turned back to the window. "She opened up to you in a way I've never seen before. I don't know why or what it means, but you should understand exactly how rare it was." He paused, the importance of his words sinking into Matt. "As in every man in that room couldn't believe what they were watching."

The significance settled over Matt, humbling him. What it meant exactly, he didn't know, but the possibilities teased his imagination. He braced his hands on the edge of his desk, a swath of nerves skittering down his spine.

Kennedy. His world had been turned upside down by her, and they'd only met twice. What would happen if he gave into his urge to call her up, ask her out. Seeing her again would only strengthen the strange bond pulling them together.

And she clearly wanted nothing to do with it. But he'd said the same thing.

Trevor leaned his shoulder on the window, his focus never leaving Matt. The corner of his mouth ticked up when Matt remained silent. "She's hard to figure out. At once strong and independent yet somehow vulnerable. But don't ever say that to her. She'll chew you up and spit you back out before you realize she attacked."

"Did she learn that from you?"

He snorted. "She didn't have to."

No, she probably didn't. "Why are you telling me this?"

His frown held a hint of confusion. "Honestly, she'd smack me down if she knew I was here. But…" He raised his shoulder. "She gave you liberties in an open setting that went against everything I know about her. I couldn't let that go until I was certain of you."

"Certain of me?" Matt didn't know how to feel about that. "I would've thought you'd made that determination before you invited me into your group."

"I did. But I have to reassess with every new piece of information. It's how I stay ahead of the game."

There wasn't an ounce of contriteness in the man standing before him. He acted and owned what he did without hesitation. And apparently, he guarded the Boardroom with the same ruthlessness he applied to his business and friends.

Matt respected that loyalty even though it dug at his own. Sharing anything about Kennedy went against his personal honor code.

"And now?" he asked, straightening away from his desk. He eyed Trevor as intently as he was being eyed. He could take his little group and walk for all Matt cared, but he'd be pissed if Trevor also walked away from his business.

"Now…" Trevor shifted away from the window. "I hope my trust isn't misplaced."

He wasn't about to reassure him like a lackey seeking his approval. What he had with Kennedy was between them, not Trevor, no matter how close he was to her.

Trevor turned to leave without another word, but he halted his abrupt departure at the door. "Look for an email that'll have a link to the Boardroom app. It's password protected and only given to members. You'll need to set up a profile and a picture before you can sign into a scene." He waited for Matt to nod his understanding. "I'm also sending you an invite to a benefit I'm hosting to start the holiday season. I'll reserve you a seat. Kennedy will be there."

Matt stared at the open doorway after Trevor left. He should've walked him out, but all thoughts of courtesy had been swept away at that last tidbit.

Kennedy will be there.

He should decline, yet he already knew he wouldn't. The networking at an event like that would be a huge business opportunity. He couldn't pass it over because one woman might be there. Right. He could position it all he wanted, but he'd be going mostly because Kennedy *would* be there.

He dropped into his chair behind his desk, an exhausted sigh gusting out. He plowed his fingers through his hair before scrubbing his face. Kennedy continued to hound his thoughts no matter how hard he tried to dismiss her. She was a puzzle full of traps that could bury him if he didn't watch his step. But he was very aware of where he was going and what he wanted.

He'd given over a decade of his life to his children. Everything he'd done had been for their benefit. And now...

He needed something more.

He couldn't pinpoint when his focus had shifted. Or was it expanded? Kennedy hadn't been the trigger, but she'd become the focal point to what was missing in his life. Could he scratch the itch without it overtaking everything?

In the eyes of his ex-wife, he hadn't taken his dominance far enough. She'd wanted his total control in all aspects of their life, and he'd unwittingly provided it, unware of what he was doing—until it was too late.

Kennedy wasn't anything like his ex.

An image of her spread across the table, her sultry gaze leveled on him as she'd raised her fingers to his mouth, had his dick hardening. Just what he needed at work. He'd shaved his beard off when he couldn't get her scent out, yet one long inhale had the aroma floating through his mind.

Bold and strong, like her.

She wouldn't be overwhelmed by him or anything he dished out. She'd held her own since that first meeting. Why would that change?

He'd made the drastic step of cutting off all dominant sexual play for the safety of his children, but at what cost to himself? Was abstinence still the best path? Especially now, when he'd found a woman who was just as strong, just as confident in her life and desires as he was?

One who haunted his thoughts and had him thinking of more than sex? She intrigued him as no other woman had, and he wanted to explore the potential, and not just sexually. There was something about her he couldn't articulate or define that made her different.

He'd been aware of that since she'd taken a seat beside him in the bar. Only then, she'd been a brief escape. A flirtation he'd engaged in because of the anonymity. But now...

There was nothing to hide behind.

He wanted Kennedy.

Even now, when there was so much at risk. When his past could repeat, and his secret wants could destroy all he'd worked to secure.

But he was smarter now. Older. Not so naïve and unaware.

He could give her something she didn't seek from others. He *had* given it to her. Twice. That alone was a draw he found hard to resist. Especially when just the thought of her satisfied smile or throaty purr or the soft plea in her voice when she whispered his name had his desire crashing forward.

And that was only one part of the entire package.

Kennedy Keller had broken through his restraint on a laugh and broad smile, but she'd charged through his denials on feisty retorts and breathy pleas. And now her gentle vulnerability ate at the long-held rules he'd established to protect his family and himself.

Was she worth it? He'd never know if he didn't try, and to not try was quickly becoming impossible.

Chapter Fourteen

Kennedy lifted her glass of champagne to toast her friend. "Here's to a pleasant evening."

Dani shot her a quick scowl before she clicked her glass to Kennedy's. "What kind of a toast is that?"

The bubbles tickled over her tongue as it slid down her throat. "A safe one."

"Since when has safe ever been a concern of yours?"

She hid the pinch in her chest at her friend's casual dig. The mark hit too close to home when she'd spent the last week assessing the risks she'd taken. At what point did they hurt her instead of bolster her?

She stared out the tinted window of the limo at the passing scenery. None of it registered as she tracked through the exploits of her past. From the outrageous parties of her youth, to the clubs of her twenties, up to the Boardroom. Sex had always been a tool for her, one she wielded with precision to get that untouchable high she reveled in during her public masturbation scenes. The high that'd always been enough—until Matt.

"Ken."

She turned to Dani, her curious smile in place. "Yes?"

Dani frowned, her brows drawing into a pinch of concerned worry. "What's going on?"

What wasn't? Yet nothing outright startling had happened. She'd had sex again with Matt. In the Boardroom. The group was supposed to be her sanctuary. A private domain for the privileged and sexually deviant. And Matt had been there. But more than his presence, was what she'd given him, even there.

Her control.

The one thing she protected with every breath she took.

She fiddled with her glass, taking another sip but not tasting it this time. Her stomach had been snarled in a knot of unaccustomed doubt since she'd watched him walk away. It'd been the right thing to do—if she wanted to maintain her autonomy.

But what if she could have it, Matt and what he offered?

"You're officially starting to worry me," Dani said, cutting into her thoughts. She laid a hand on Kennedy's arm.

She glanced to her. Indecision wrestled with the openness that usually existed between them. Dani exuded the very strength Kennedy strode to emulate, and she'd succeeded for the most part. So why was she faltering now? Over a man?

"I'm fine," she reassured her, breezing into the superficial charm mastered by her mother. She squeezed Dani's hand before dislodging it. The connection was too distinct for the distance she was trying to achieve. "Are you ready for Trevor?"

Dani scowled at the deflection that shoved her own issues in her face. Her eyes hardened, her ice mask of distance slamming down. "When am I not?"

"You're right." Regret consumed her. It sat on her

chest along with the pile that'd been building with the hazardous scavenging of her sexuality. "I'm sorry." This time she reached for her friend's hand and gave it a squeeze. "That was rude of me."

Trevor was one topic Dani rarely talked about. Open landmines littered the terrain surrounding the subject, and Kennedy respected them.

"It was." Dani didn't give her an inch. "But I'll ignore it if you tell me what's going on with you."

The blatant blackmail was justified given Kennedy's lousy attempt at avoidance. Maybe sharing a ride to Trevor's benefit hadn't been such a good idea. And maybe she should stop stewing and just own up to her damn feelings.

"I had another encounter with the guy from Long Beach, Matt," she finally said, watching her friend for every reaction. Her stomach did a small flip, but a bit of the unease slid away. Talking about the issue was one step closer to resolving it.

A smile ghosted over Dani's lips. "And?"

The openness of her response was so her. She could lead without offering judgment better than anyone Kennedy knew, and it was exactly what she needed.

"And...it was in the Boardroom."

"Oh." Surprise echoed over her expression. "That's unexpected."

"Tell me about it." She slugged down the last of her champagne before refilling her glass. Dani shook her head when she offered the bottle to her.

Nerves started an excited rush that tingled over her skin and trembled through her hands. She gripped her glass tighter, trudging on. "He's a new member. I didn't know he'd be there."

Dani settled into the seat as the car entered the city. "I've never seen you this unsettled over sex."

Because she never had been. "He's…different." There was the bomb of truth that'd been troubling her since their first interaction. He was very different from any sexual encounter she'd had. And if the draw had been limited to sex, she wouldn't be this conflicted.

"Is that bad or good?"

"I don't know." Or she didn't want to take a stance on it. Defining it would highlight what she was still avoiding.

She was saved from revealing more when the car pulled up to the theater. Trevor had outdone himself this time. A red carpet was laid out leading to the entrance in an extravagant declaration of opulence. The ticket prices guaranteed only the wealthiest and most influential would attend, and he delivered to expectations.

White lights twinkled in subdued elegance around the entrance that was also decked out in holiday splendor. Thanksgiving hadn't arrived yet, but that seemed to be the norm now. The rush to the next sales cycle eclipsed the current one until they were all pushed ahead to an annoying point.

Dani joined her side once they'd exited the car. She paused, took a deep breath. "Ready?"

"Are you?" Kennedy asked back.

"Always." Dani strode down the carpet with the same confident swagger she'd had since they'd first became friends. Any nerves or insecurities were so deeply buried no one would guess she had any.

Kennedy chuckled to herself as she caught up to her friend. She admired the hell out of Dani and would do anything for her. She looped an arm around her shoulders and gave her a quick side hug. "We can bail after dinner."

"Hmm." Dani stepped away to greet a man Kennedy recognized from the Boardroom. There'd be a lot of members there, and that'd never bothered her before. One of the luxuries of the group was how no one publicly acknowledged its existence. She didn't have to greet or mingle with any of them, and they'd never think negatively of her for not doing so.

She slid by with a brush on Dani's arm to let her know she was heading in. The grand lobby was packed with loitering guests dressed in their finest. She took in the period décor, complete with looming ceilings sculpted with details from an era long gone, before she spotted the bar.

Getting drunk wasn't her intention, but one more glass would relax her enough to actually enjoy the event. The open bar was provided with the hopes that it'd loosen more pockets before the silent auction. It usually worked.

The benefit was for Trevor's personal cause, and she was a hundred percent behind it. He'd been a supporter of the nation's largest anti-sexual violence organization long before it'd become hip. She'd asked him about it once, only to get a vague response as to why. Of course there didn't have to be a motivation other than recognizing that nonconsensual sex of any kind wasn't okay.

She bypassed a group of her parents' friends and waved at a business associate but didn't pause to talk. The energy required to be social, even superficially, was missing tonight. There was no reason for it other than the drag of overanalysis she'd been cycling through for the last week.

She could've called Matt. She had his information now. She'd even looked him up on the internet. His company profile had confirmed her assumption about his military background, but it'd given little in personal details.

"Kennedy."

His voice trembled down her neck before it scampered straight to her core. She sucked in a breath, eyes closing for a moment before she turned. Had she conjured him up from her imagination? A nervous laugh slipped out on that thought.

"Matt," she managed with a clear voice. "What a surprise."

His brows rose, a smile appearing. "It's nice to see you." He extended his hand as if they were nothing more than polite acquaintances.

She studied the offering a bit too long before laying her palm on his. The rush of warmth coincided with that stupid flutter in her chest. "You too." Her words came out breathier than she'd intended, but there was no changing it.

His thumb caressed the back of her hand as he made a pointed scan of her. Appreciation smoldered in his eyes when he finished. "You look stunning."

The open honesty in both his voice and gaze brought a rush of uncommon shyness. "Thank you," she murmured. "As do you."

His tuxedo fit him perfectly. The classic cut in basic black with a traditional black tie was the perfect statement of refined formality. His beard was barely there tonight, more of a shadow than actual scruff, but he still had that dark and dangerous aura that'd drawn her from the start.

He brought her hand to his lips and brushed a soft kiss over the backs of her fingers. The gallant action would've made her chuckle if any other man had executed it. On him, though, it came across exactly as he'd most likely intended. Dirty and lust-filled when combined with the smolder in his gaze.

Her knees melted beneath her floor-length gown, but she managed to hold her composure. A part of her brain knew she should look away from him, but she couldn't get herself to do so. "What are you doing here?"

He gave a quick glance around as a smirk grew. "I believe I was summoned to support a very noble cause."

"Summoned?"

"I was informed by Trevor that he'd reserved me a seat."

A laugh slipped out at his explanation. "That sounds like Trevor."

"Did I hear my name?" Trevor said as he stepped up beside them. His smile was locked in that perfected charm mode she found easy to identify but most didn't.

"I was just informing Kennedy of the warm invite you extended to me for this event." He held Trevor's gaze for a beat, something unspoken exchanged between the two. "I'm glad I accepted."

Trevor glanced to the hold Matt still had on her hand. How had she not noticed that? Yet she didn't pull hers away.

"You look lovely, Ken," Trevor said, bending to brush a kiss on her cheek. He squeezed her shoulder as he pulled back. "Thank you for coming."

"I wouldn't miss it."

He nodded, a true smile settling on his face. "I

know." He turned and greeted another guest on his next breath.

Matt drew her away with a light touch to her back. "How about a drink?"

"Perfect," she agreed, her nerves settling beneath the simple enjoyment of being near him. Yes, she was succumbing to the things she swore she'd never feel around a man, but right then, she didn't care. Tingles spread up her back from where his hand rested, and she welcomed the sense of security he projected. She didn't need it, yet she relished it anyway.

Or was it belonging? Here, among the very crowd she'd been raised in, she enjoyed the sense of being connected to him.

"Gin and tonic, right?"

She smiled. "Good memory."

A spark flared in his eyes before he turned to order from the bartender. She took the opportunity to step away and tried to find her bearings. She was bound to run into him again, she just hadn't expected it to be so soon. Especially in a setting she usually mastered but had been distracted from before she'd even entered.

Because of Matt.

She tossed up her chin, rolled her shoulders back. This was her domain. Matt's presence didn't change that. A scan of the room showed the Bay Area elite at their finest. Diamonds glittered, dresses sparkled and money dripped from every pretentious gesture. And then there was Matt.

He meshed, yet his sober calm set him apart. She caught multiple people eyeing him up. He was a new face in the sea of standards. New money? Someone passing through? A guest? She could see the questions forming, although no one approached. He was a mystery…except to her.

She smiled at that, loving the knowledge she held.

"Thank you," she said, accepting the drink from Matt. "Are you here alone?" The question just occurred to her. Her stomach took a dive at the thought of him having a date. Why, though? She normally didn't care.

"Yes." He put his arm around her again as they drifted away from the bar. "You?"

Warmth spread when she recognized his disgruntled tone. "Yes." She shot him a side-glance, lips teasing upward. "At least for now." There was her game.

He leaned into her. "Not anymore."

And there it went. She stared at him, eyes wide in playful shock. She should contradict him, yet… He raised that brow in a dare she recognized. Goose bumps chased each other over her chest, her nipples pebbling. Hopefully, the lace on her bodice hid the inappropriate display.

"Don't get cocky," she warned as she turned to study the room. There were people she should talk to. Networking was a continuous obligation. "Come on." She looped her hand around his arm. "Let me introduce you to some people."

He didn't object as she led him to a group of Area businessmen. He joined the conversation like a pro, saying the appropriate things without pushing himself or his company. She admired his tact while wondering about his background. McPherson had been sold some time back, but she'd only heard a trickle of information about the man who'd bought Howard out. Not that Howard McPherson had been big in these circles.

But here was Matt. Friends with Trevor. Invited to

the Boardroom. Crashing one of the wealthiest bene-
fits of the year and all without a whisper spread about
him. That in itself was something to admire or be suspicious of.

They'd circulated through a few more groups before
she ran into her parents. She sucked in a quick breath,
then stepped up to sweep a kiss on her mother's cheek.
"Hi, Mom." She turned to her father. "Dad." She sent
him a smile, skipping the hug he wouldn't want.

Raymond Keller was a stout man built on determination and a solid work ethic. His receding hairline only
added to the air of stubborn bluntness that defined him.
Even dressed up in his best tux, he couldn't quite shake
the rugged edge.

"Kennedy," he barked. "I thought we'd see you here."
He turned to Matt, frowning. "And you are?"

She laughed to cover her father's directness. "Dad,
this is Matt Hamilton. He's the new owner of McPherson Trucking. We met down in Long Beach and have
been talking over possible collaboration efforts that
would benefit us both."

"You have?" Her dad hit her with his customary
scowl. He didn't like being left out of the loop on anything. "This is the first I'm hearing of it."

"We're still in the opening phases," Matt said, extending his hand to her father. "It's nice to meet you.
Kennedy's spoken highly of you both." He included her
mother in his glance.

Her father couldn't not accept his handshake without looking like a total ass. He mumbled a greeting in
return before Matt focused on her mother.

"I see where Kennedy gets her beauty." He managed

to pull off the tired line with a charm that worked perfectly on her mother.

"Thank you," her mother said with all the grace of a royal. Andrea Keller never passed over a compliment, especially from a handsome man. Her mother's rigid routine of facials, exercise and spa treatments kept her appearance youthful. Petite and always stylish, her gown was a declaration of sophisticated elegance. "You're very kind." She shot Kennedy an approving smile that shouldn't have pleased her, but it did.

"I only speak the truth."

"What are these dealings you two have been talking about?" her father charged back in. He shot a suspicious eye between them.

"I'll brief you next week," Kennedy hedged, unconcerned but irritated at the unnecessary lie she'd created. All to avoid questions about why she was with Matt.

"Why not now?"

"I believe we're being summoned," Matt interjected, motioning to the flow of people entering the theater. "It was a pleasure to meet you." He nodded to her mother before he focused on her father. "I look forward to seeing where our companies can help each other."

He guided her away with an authority that managed to shut her father down. Her chuckle rolled free when they were out of earshot. "That was fabulous," she told Matt, laying a hand on his arm. "I'm impressed."

Amused question showed on his expression, but he didn't respond as they wove through the people and tables. The large hall had been decked out in more holiday finery that managed to be beautiful instead of tacky. A large stage dominated the front of the room, the tables arranged to provide optimal views.

"What table are you at?" he asked, leaning in to be heard over the din of the crowd.

She had no idea what the number was. She only knew that it'd be near the front, like it always was when she sat with Dani, who'd purchased the entire table. Kennedy supported the benefit through a donation and auction bidding.

She scanned the tables as they closed in on the front. Dani stood next to Trevor, looking poised and stunning despite the concern on her face. He ran a hand down her bare arm. Her eyes closed briefly, lips parting in a way that had Kennedy increasing her pace.

Whatever was between them never leaked into public even though their connection was common knowledge. No one messed with Dani unless they wanted to incur Trevor's wrath. In many ways, Kennedy fell within that same circle, as did every female in the Boardroom, but Dani was in her own protected class.

"Hey," Kennedy said, blatantly barging into their conversation, taking a lesson from her father. "I've been looking for you." She flashed a smile at Trevor before eyeing Dani. "Have you looked through the silent auction offerings? You've done an amazing job, like always, Trevor."

His lips compressed before he nodded, stepping back. "I need to check on a few things. If you'll excuse me."

Dani tracked him as he left, her gaze slowly shifting to Kennedy's. Sadness coated her eyes in a brief hit of honesty before she inhaled. Whatever she'd been feeling was gone when she turned to Matt.

"Hello. I don't believe we've met," she said, extending her hand. "I'm Danielle Stables."

"Matt Hamilton," he said, pure grace and formal honor once again. "It's a pleasure to meet you."

Her smile took on true warmth. "You're my mystery guest. Well, welcome. I hope you're enjoying the evening."

His gaze landed on Kennedy. "I am. Very much so."

Heat swept from Kennedy's cheeks clear to her toes. Matt was sitting at their table. How? Why? Had her friend known who he was?

Dani glanced at her, curiosity clear. "We have time to check the auction items," she said, grabbing Kennedy's hand. "If you'll excuse us a moment, Matt." She didn't wait for a response before she stepped away, Kennedy at her side. "Matt?" she inquired when they were two tables away.

"You didn't know?" The tension that'd locked down her airway eased.

"Know what?" Dani stepped around a group of people and started perusing the auction items.

Kennedy maintained the same distant air, barely seeing the items before her. "About Matt. Who he was—is."

Her lips quirked. "I'm going to assume that's your Matt, then."

"He's not *my* Matt." Yet a soft glow bloomed at being linked to him.

"But he is *the* Matt, right?"

She didn't need to say yes when Dani already knew the answer. She tried to scowl, but there was no heat behind it. "Why is he seated at your table?"

"Trevor asked me to add him."

That was it. No further explanation was given or needed, really. Trevor had orchestrated their meeting here, but he hadn't forced them together.

She'd stayed near him by choice. She couldn't ignore that fact any longer.

Matt had her rethinking her entire life after two encounters. What would happen if she continued to see him? If she let herself try?

There was only one way she'd find out—if she dared.

And when had she ever backed away from a dare?

Chapter Fifteen

The evening was winding down. Dinner had been cleared a while ago and the stage productions, which had consisted of various scenes performed from the upcoming season, were finished. The entire evening had been a demonstration of opulence that reminded Matt of the military balls, only more extravagant and less formal.

Kennedy laughed at his side, holding his attention like she had all night. The throaty tone had deepened through dinner until every rumble sounded like sex. Want buzzed its demand through every cell, but he curbed it. This was Kennedy's domain, and he had no desire to undermine the image she presented.

He ran his hand along the back of her chair. She smiled at him, that coy play leaping out to grab him by the nuts. He wrapped one of her curls around his finger, not saying a word. The upswept hairstyle gave him all kinds of ideas about running his teeth over her nape until her eyes rolled back and she softened beneath him.

"I'll drive you home," he said after a moment.

The dark navy color of her dress drew out the blue in her eyes, which widened slightly. Her lips twisted in a resistant smile. "I don't need a ride."

He leaned in, and she shifted to meet him. "I didn't ask if you needed one," he said by her ear.

Her side-eye held amusement along with challenge. There was the fire he loved too damn much. "Assumptions will get you nowhere."

He chuckled, sitting back. "I can say the same to you."

The slow scan she gave him contained the familiar taunting intent she'd used at the bar. She was drawing out a game they both knew the ending to. And he couldn't get mad, not when he was enjoying it.

"What am I assuming?" she asked.

He shifted closer once again, savoring her quick inhalation along with the tempting draw of her perfume. "That I'm going to fuck you any way I want." Her shiver was slight but it shot down every pretense she was playing at. "I'll be in the lobby."

She tracked him as he stood. Her expression remained studiously blank despite the spark that lit her eyes. He said goodbye to Danielle, thanked her for hosting him and made his departure. He'd quickly picked up that his seat at that coveted front table had been Trevor's doing. But why?

The heat level dropped a good ten degrees when he entered the lobby. Smaller groups mingled in clusters, some in wraps and coats preparing to leave.

Trevor caught him as he was exiting the building to give his ticket to the valet. "I'm surprised you're going home alone."

Matt studied him, taking his clouded challenge and leveling his own. "I'm surprised you're so interested in my life."

"It's not yours I care about."

His eyes narrowed, his protective instincts kicking into high gear. "Why *do* you care so much?"

Trevor looked away, lips compressing. "She's like a sister to me." The truth of that showed in his eyes when he turned back. "And I think you'd be good for her. Don't prove me wrong." He strode away before Matt could respond, executing another irritating move in his arsenal. Matt was familiar with the tactic and unimpressed.

Again, he wasn't a subordinate or someone currying favor. But alienating the man would hurt him—along with everyone who was counting on him to keep the company going.

He shoved his annoyance aside when he caught sight of Kennedy leaving the theater. Her quick scan of the lobby held on him when she found him. Her focus drifted outside before she turned away to engage with the woman at her side.

He was struck again by the simple elegance she presented. Her gown glittered in understated glam when the light hit it just right. It hugged her curves from the lace bodice down to her heels, leaving her arms bare. His fingers itched to run them over her skin until she shivered with want.

The night air cooled his lust a notch. The slow burn of control clipped up his spine with its own powerful allure. The entire evening had been an act of foreplay he relished. She could've walked away from him at any time, but she'd stayed by his side, introducing him to influential contacts, leaning into his touch.

She still wanted him, and she knew exactly what he wanted.

He was waiting by his car when she swept from the

building. She executed her stride down the red carpet with a confident assurance that only came from someone certain of their place.

Longing spread through his chest before it sunk into his groin. She headed straight to him, nodding when he opened the door for her. She slipped into his car without a word, tucking her skirt in before he closed the door. Relief faded into anticipation with each step he took around the car. His economical sedan didn't compete with the line of limos, town cars and luxury vehicles lining the street. He didn't care.

She watched him as he settled into the driver seat, her expression wiped clean. Goose bumps dotted her arm, and he turned the heat up before he pulled into traffic.

"Where am I heading?" he asked.

She didn't respond right way. He glanced over, caught the mischief in the tiny curl of her lips. "No breakfast with the kids for me?"

His laugh choked out, strained. "Are you saying that's what you'd like?" Her snort caught him by surprise, but the honesty in her response had him grinning. "I thought so." They were a long way from that, yet the idea didn't spark an instant rejection.

"The two-eighty to Menlo Park is the quickest."

Her clutch rested on her lap, her legs tucked back in the perfect display of propriety. The dichotomy of that, of the image she'd presented all night, against the hungry seductress he also knew her to be, only increased his desire. He didn't want to think of her opening up to another man. Not in the Boardroom or elsewhere.

He recognized the dominant possessiveness for what it was, yet he couldn't shake it. He found her hand and brought it to his lap, threading his fingers with hers. He felt her stare, but kept his eyes forward as he stroked his thumb over her palm.

They didn't speak on the drive down the peninsula, and the silence drew out the anticipation with each mile that clipped by.

He passed his exit with only a glance and a thought given. Dawn had arrived home that afternoon for Thanksgiving break. His kids would be fine. He'd be home before they realized he wasn't there. A small dose of guilt wormed into his thoughts, but it didn't override his growing need for Kennedy and all that she offered.

The clock on the dashboard said it was after midnight when he followed her directions off the highway to her place. The end-unit townhome was basic from the outside, but the two-car garage hinted at the luxury within. The quiet neighborhood gave off an air of sophistication his street would never conquer. Groomed landscape, swept drives, every unit painted in the same shade of unassuming beige. Uniformity at its best.

"Are you coming in?" she asked when he didn't move to exit.

He studied her in the dim glow provided by the outside lights. "Am I invited?"

An element of uncertainty crossed her features before she shut it down. "Yes."

"Then, yes." He drew her in only to ghost his lips over hers. Her quick hitch of breath spoke of the promises yet to come.

Hunger gnawed at his need as he exited the car. The full force of his dominant side locked in before he helped her from the car. It shifted his headspace to one of complete control. He was responsible for her and everything she wanted right now.

He brushed a lock of hair from her cheek, tracked his hand around the side of her neck. Her freckles spoke of innocence she didn't possess. Did they fool others?

"Are you mine now?" he asked. No assumptions.

She grabbed his wrist, squeezed, but her eyes never left his. Anticipation hung suspended in the long moment before she answered. "Yes."

He swept in to finally take the kiss he'd wanted to claim the entire night. He took with a barely controlled demand, teasing out her moan and finding the last hint of the gin that lingered on her tongue. His chest ached with restraint, but damn how he wanted her. Needed her.

Her breaths were short like his when he backed away. His head buzzed with the carnal craving she'd freed as he guided her to her door. He'd given up trying to figure out what it was about her that incited the urge he'd smothered for so long. It didn't matter anymore.

She paused, her key in the lock, turning to him. "I might be yours, here, tonight, but don't abuse it."

He took every word with the seriousness in which they were delivered. "I wouldn't dream of it." She studied him, uncertainty flickering. "I treasure everything you give me. I'd never diminish it," he added. He ran his fingers down her jaw, his honor surging up. "I'll leave, if that's what you want." In a heartbeat. Her needs came first. Always.

"I don't want you to." Her soft response registered as she turned back and opened her door.

He locked it behind him before following her down the hallway past the open living room. Her home was a statement in efficiency. Clean lines, glass tables, white furniture set against beige carpets and walls. The mono-chrome pallet was offset by a pop of yellow pillows that were fluffed and centered on the couch.

The fastidious neatness would pass any military inspection and fail every kid-filled home. A moment of doubt slowed his steps. Was there a point in going forward if she was only interested in now? His dick screamed yes, his heart hesitated.

She laid a hand on the bannister and had one foot on the bottom stair when he spoke. "Wait."

She halted, turning back to him. That little line appeared between her drawn brows. Damn his heart and his dick too.

He turned on the row of light switches on the wall with deliberate flicks. Lamps lit up and the overhead light blazed, knocking back the shadows. Power curled between his shoulder blades along with the drive that constituted his foundation.

He titled his head, eyes narrowing. What did she need? How could he help her?

"Take off your dress." The lowered timbre of his voice rolled through the quiet.

Her eyelids dipped, that frown line disappearing. A small note of victory chimed next to the hunger that continued to grow.

She set her clutch on a step, a lush softness overtaking her features when she straightened. "I'll need help with the zipper." She pivoted to present her back, her smile full of that devilishness he loved when she peered at him over her shoulder.

He stopped his progress toward her when he was centered before the large sliding glass doors. The darkness beyond offered no hint to what was behind her home.

Was there a fence? A section of the golf course they'd driven past? More homes?

"Come here."

She glanced at the window, bit her lip, but pure lust shone in her eyes when she strolled toward him, hips swaying, chin lifted. She owned that strut just like she owned the choice she made to obey him.

And that right there was hotter than any dress or figure or piece of lingerie.

The corner of her mouth lifted in a taunt, her eyes dropping to his lips. Her slow turn was yet another tease that fired the want already roaring in his chest.

"You're asking for trouble." He had no doubt of that.

"I believe I'm only following your orders." A hint of stubborn innocence laced her tone.

He couldn't deny that. Her sass was implied more than blatant. It hit that right note of defiance without defying that worked for him. He'd known men who'd wanted total submission from their partners. His wife had given him that when he'd never asked for it.

He wasn't a Dom. He didn't want to be a Dom, but he did love control.

He drew a finger down the line of her zipper. Her back rolled in a slow curl that matched his descent. A smattering of loose curls danced at her nape, enticing him as they'd done at the benefit. Now he could finally give into the urge that'd taunted him all night.

He eased his finger back up, drew her zipper down a fraction. A hiss of breath escaped her when he dragged his teeth over the tender stretch of space on the back of her neck. It fed his craving, his chest expanding with things he still hesitated to fully embrace.

"Kennedy," he whispered, trailing a line of kisses to

her ear. He nuzzled the sensitive spot just below it before tracing the shell. "The things you do to me."

Her breath released on a long exhale, her head tilting. She ran a hand over his hip, her low hum speaking for her. It rumbled with appreciation and agreement. This thing between them was mutual, he had no doubt of that.

He forced himself to step back, drawing her zipper down in a long path that ended at her tailbone. A series of freckles trailed between her shoulder blades to provide another source of temptation. They thickened near her shoulders. Brought on by the sun? There was so much about her he didn't know. So much he wanted to learn.

He eased her dress from her shoulders until she took over. She let it fall down her arms, glanced back. There was that mischief again, sparkling in her eyes before she turned away. The dress caught on her hips, but a little swivel and push had it falling in a pool of dark silk at her feet.

He tracked the length of her legs up past the skimpy thread of her thong. The single strap of her bra cut a clean line across her back, hindering his view. He unhooked it. She inhaled. The item dangled in his hand until he let it fall beside the discarded dress.

His erection ran thick and hard against his lower stomach. She made him hard when she was clothed. Now…

He took her hand to help her step from the material. She slid free of the heels in the process, leaving her in nothing but the thong when she finally faced him.

The sultry seductress was in full attack mode when she looked up at him through her lashes. Her tongue slid over her bottom lip. "My dress is off."

A dozen different thoughts breezed through his mind, each of them dirtier and more wicked than the next. Some would bend her over the couch and spank her for her insolence. Others would tell her to pick up her dress and then ignore her.

Him, though, he only wanted to sink into her long and slow until they were both lost.

"It is," he finally agreed.

He drew his gaze over the stunning sight before him. Her nipples were peaked, her breaths slow, her hands held relaxed at her sides. She was comfortable, confident even. How lovely was that?

He let his focus shift to the window, slowly brought it back to her. He caught her quick glance following his point. Her breaths picked up.

"What's behind you?" he asked.

"A golf course."

"No watchers, then." He drew a finger down her chest.

"Probably not."

He circled his fingertip around one nipple, careful not to touch it. "And if there were?"

She closed her eyes, shoved her chest out, but he avoided her swivel to get his finger where she wanted it. Her frown had that line digging in between her brows. He bit back his chuckle, loving her frustration.

"Then they'd see you doing nothing," she snapped, her eyes flying open to scorch him with her annoyance.

He let his laugh out as he looped his finger over to her other nipple so he could slowly circle it. "But I'm not doing nothing."

She dropped her head back, hands fisting. "You're not doing enough."

"No?" He trailed his finger down to tease the edge of

her thong. He dipped beneath it, but only drew it back and forth in a mimic of how she'd once taunted him. "What would you like me to do?"

She raised her head. Her eyes had darkened to match the hunger in her expression. "Whatever you want," she said with an edge. "Just as long as it ends with your dick in me."

The harsh crassness picked at the dirty raunchiness rooted within him. He plunged his hand into her panties, grazing her pussy before he shoved two fingers into her. She gasped, hands flying up to grab his arms as he gripped her nape with his other hand and drew her in.

She stared up at him, her panted breaths hitting his face. There was only lust in her eyes, though. Lust and want.

His kiss contained all the longing she'd pulled from him. He swept his tongue into her mouth with the same forceful strokes he used in her pussy. She stiffened at first, her whimper reaching him, but it held surprise more than desire.

He cursed, easing off until she gripped him tighter, halting his retreat. He gentled his kiss, teasing her lips with light strokes and her clit with little flicks. Her next moan was pure desire. It fed his need and eased his worry.

He could give her this. Give her rough and gentle. Lust and passion.

"I'm going to fuck you, Kennedy," he murmured between kisses. She moaned her agreement when he swept his tongue back in to play with hers. She drew him closer, her hips undulating against his hand.

He could take her there, but he wanted something better than a quick fuck against a wall or over the couch.

He had her all to himself, and he wasn't going to squander it.

She chased his lips when he pulled back, slipping his fingers from her tempting heat. She stared at him in dazed confusion when he took her hand.

"I'm going to fuck you in a bed." He drew her toward the stairs. "Hard, long and so damn slow you'll never forget me."

Her gasp floated through the quiet. She stared at him, a flush rising on her cheeks. They were halfway up the stairs before her mumbled whisper floated to him. "That hasn't been a problem so far."

Chapter Sixteen

That flutter in Kennedy's chest did a double kick and sigh as Matt led her into her bedroom. He flipped the light switch, illuminating the room. The bedside lamps gave off a soft glow that left the perimeter in shadow.

He guided her to the edge of the bed as he made a quick scan of the room. She knew it was as impeccable as the rest of her home. Even here, in her most private space, she upheld the standards set down by her mother. Everything had a place and it should be in it.

She'd tried to dispel the old habit multiple times only to find she couldn't. And now, with Matt standing in her room, she didn't have to worry if there was dirty laundry on the floor or if her sheets were clean.

He drew the duvet down, flipped the gray covering back, along with the top sheet. His movements were precise, like so much that he did. Very few men had seen her home, even fewer had seen her bedroom. Bringing a man home usually led to expectations she never wanted to mess with. Yet here Matt was.

Nerves scrambled in her stomach, but they were in anticipation more than concern. Her nipples ached for contact, her breasts heavy, panties damp.

She was basically naked, him fully clothed—again.

The power dynamic fulfilled that silenced desire she only released with him. And he hadn't abused it. Not in the Boardroom and not this evening.

She reached for his tie when he faced her. His brows drew in, but he didn't stop her when she loosened the knot and drew it free. The classic tie instead of the traditional bowtie worked on him. It held that edge of different he embodied without thought.

He took the tie from her, setting it on the nightstand. His eyes were dark when he turned back. Lust smoldered from them along with something softer. Kindness. That'd been there too. He held himself to a strict code of honor that both fascinated and comforted her.

He continued to study her as she slid the buttons free on his shirt. He brushed the back of his finger over her cheek in a touch she was beginning to crave. It was soft and tender, caring.

"You're beautiful."

His words weren't new, but the honest wonder behind them curled her toes and had her heart fluttering again. He was so damn dangerous to her, and yet, here she was, charging in anyway.

She lifted up to press her lips to his. The contact simmered over her before it faded into the growing ache. He cupped the back of her head when she started to drop back down. He held her there, inches away, eyes piercing hers.

Desire thread its insidious demands through her core. She had never let it own her, instead owning it. But now, she gave it all to him.

She let her muscles go lax, her trust handed over.

"Kennedy," he whispered before he crushed his mouth to hers.

Yes. God...yes.

His control swept over her with each thrust of his tongue. He held her tight, her nipples chafing on his shirt. The delicious tease balanced the full assault on her mouth. He played with her tongue, plunging deep before backing off with softer brushes. Every lick sent a rush of pleasure straight to the building urgency.

Her pussy contracted, and she clutched him tighter, digging her fingers into his scalp in her hunt to get closer even though there was nowhere to go. He did that to her. Unleashed the crazed side she usually kept locked down.

He ripped his mouth free on a curse, and she sucked in a needed breath, head spinning. Wet kisses trailed up her neck, his breaths heating her skin. Goose bumps prickled over her chest, setting off a buzz of blind want.

His hands were everywhere. Cupping her ass, running up her sides, dipping beneath her thong. He teased her crack, bit her shoulder in a wild shot of pain that blended with the sweet joy consuming her.

She tumbled back at his urging, the bed catching her as she stared up at him, breaths coming too quickly. That dark predatory edge of him shone through in the wicked curl of his lips. He made a slow scan over her, her skin tingling everywhere his gaze landed.

"Should I fuck you hard?" he asked, hooking a finger at the edge of her thong. He yanked the flimsy material down before she could respond. It dug into her skin, catching on her hips, but another jerk freed it. He discarded the material without a thought to where it landed, and for once, she didn't care.

She rested her feet on the edge of the mattress, scooting back as he discarded his suit coat. He undressed with sharp tugs and quick snaps that hinted at the lust he contained. She caught her breath when he stood over her, naked and so damn sexy. She adored a man in a suit, but this…was even better.

He was raw power beneath a hard chest and tight abs. She followed his treasure trail down to his erection, which stood proud between strong thighs. Her mouth watered, yet her throat was so damn dry.

He propped a knee on the bed, nudged her legs apart before kneeling between them. She spread them willingly. God, anything to get him in her.

He grabbed her knees and shoved her legs up in one quick motion. He held her suspended in the curled position, her pussy open and fully exposed to him. Air teased every crevasse in a declaration of vulnerability.

Heat whipped through her core straight to her cheeks. She wasn't shy by any means, but this was… humbling—until he ran his tongue through her pussy.

She cried out, shocked and undone by the action. One swipe, that's all he made, then a slow-blown breath over the very track he'd just set on fire. She squirmed beneath the tease, her muscles tensing, too wound up to stay still.

"You have a fucking gorgeous cunt." The low rumble was filled with admiration. "It's begging for my dick."

Her walls pulsed, that damn heat bursting into flames. His groan tore away any hint of embarrassment that'd dared to creep in. Wonder lined his face right next to the hunger that flared his nostrils and shortened his breaths. She clenched again.

His eyes darted up to nail hers. "You are so naughty."

She started to shake her head only to stop. Her lids lowered as she owned his accusation. "So are you."

His response was to suck her clit into his mouth on a

long, hard pull. Her hips rolled up, her mouth dropped open in silent acknowledgement of the surge of pleasure. He flicked the sensitive nub, sucked again and again before he returned to a persistent hard rub with the flat of his tongue.

Her orgasm roared to a head on a hitched gasp and hoarse cry. "Matt." She reached for his head, holding him in place as she strained for that last...little...edge. "Yes!"

She crashed into the blinding release with a freedom she rarely took. It trembled through her limbs on little shudders after the initial tide subsided. Her muscles relaxed with her huge exhale, the room floating around her.

"That." He placed a kiss on her hip. "Was." Another kiss landed on her stomach. "Absolutely." He sucked a nipple into his mouth. Her back arched. She gasped. "Gorgeous." He took the other nipple in, needling it with his teeth. Sharp darts of pain laced her chest on heightened receptors that enhanced and softened at once.

"Oh, God." She couldn't keep silent, not when her body was on fire. Endorphins floated through her on a mellow note, yet another release was already building.

He grabbed her hands and pulled them over her head. She whimpered in protest, but only because she wanted to touch him. His legs brushed hers, the hair on them adding another sensation.

He swallowed deep, his throat bobbing in a telling display. His breaths grew short as he lowered his hips to hers. His dick threaded a searing path through her pussy before he eased it back up.

Her walls clenched yet again, that empty ache growing more intense. "Matt." She strained against his hold before going lax. She panted her frustration, but he didn't relent. Not even a little.

Something darkened in his expression before he made another slow pass through her pussy with his dick. The taunt was maddening and wonderful at once. She had no control. There was no need for her worry. He'd take care of her.

Like he always had.

Her heart pounded in time with the blood roaring in her ears. He swallowed again, turning his head as he closed his eyes. Awe etched across his face in a reflection of what was spreading through her.

He shifted, opened his eyes to stare down at her. The head of his dick was tucked into her entrance, right where he'd lodged it.

The emptiness echoed through every part of her. It taunted her with what she could have, with what could be if she only…what? Asked? Dared?

"Please," she whispered.

"Fuck." His curse rang in her ears as he drove into her.

Her cry chased his, that hungry, demanding ache temporarily satisfied. She caught her breath, only to lose it when she refocused on him.

Tendons strained on his neck. His arm trembled, his restraint so clearly displayed. But she was lost on why he was holding back.

"You are so damn…" He dropped down, releasing his hold on her hands to brace himself on his elbows. His lips were a breath away when he said, "Mine."

He waited a beat, one that thundered through her thoughts and resonated in her chest before he powered into her again.

Oh. My. God. Pleasure engulfed her from head to

toe. She wrapped her limbs around him and gave him more than she'd thought possible. This connection, the complete contact sunk deeper than her skin.

"Yes," she mumbled. She was his in more ways than she wanted to admit. He understood parts of her no one else did, and yet he knew so little about her.

His kiss drove everything from her mind. There was only him, his touch, his control, his understanding. Desire built in an unrelenting beat on each plunge. Hard and fast broken by slow and agonizing until her expectations fled.

He claimed every part of her while never consuming, because somewhere in the tumble of lust and want, she understood that it was still about her. That she could pull away right now, and he'd let her.

Her stomach clenched, her walls tightening around the wonderful glide of his dick. He filled her so completely she doubted she'd ever get enough of him.

He grabbed her leg, hitching it higher on his hip as he pulled his legs beneath him. The position gave him leverage to drive harder. His pelvis hit her clit on each descent, adding another blast to the orgasm condensing in her core.

She gasped, arching to meet each thrust. To find that end hovering so close.

"Kennedy," he groaned by her ear. He nipped her shoulder, added another bite to the side of her neck. The hit of pain migrated to wonder when she craved more.

"That," she encouraged, stretching her neck in silent indication. "Please."

A harsh growl proceeded the defined bite on the juncture of her neck. "Oh, my God." Ecstasy exploded behind her eyes as she absorbed the contradictory signals. Pain and pleasure became one huge tumble of sensation that shoved her to a level she'd never imagined.

She shook, every muscle tensing until she couldn't breathe, and still it came, rolling through her on a neverending rush. Agony pierced her chest. It cut through the rise and allowed her to tumble into the next wave on a gasped breath. Her eyes fluttered open. She registered the hard clamp of his teeth on her nipple, but it didn't process into an objection. Not when the burn was so damn good.

"Matt," she moaned through the last of her orgasm, lost to understanding. Lost to caring. Lost to him.

He buried his face in her neck, driving deep one more time before he let go. He tensed above her, holding, grinding until he exploded in a harsh cry and a series of rapid thrusts. He sagged against her, his weight a comfortable cloak she welcomed.

This right here, this moment of floating freedom was the one thing she chased, only she'd never found it with another. She'd tried at one point, searched and came up empty.

But with him, she could still breathe.

He laid a kiss on her neck. It highlighted the stinging throb that broke through her reverie while soothing it too. She'd have a mark, which meant a week of scarves and collared shirts. Yet the thought of wearing his mark soothed instead of irritated.

"Kennedy."

Her name trembled over her chest with the same wonder she floated in. She didn't want to question it even though she should. She dragged her fingers through his hair, drawing him in for a slow kiss. She didn't need words for this. Every soft brush of his lips and graze of his tongue spoke to what they both withheld. It trans-ferred between them on the light nips and hushed brushes until he swooped back in to steal her breath yet again.

Her throat stung and her eyes burned when he finally pulled away. She let him go, regretting the loss when he slid out of her.

He glanced around, and she pointed to the short hall that led to the master bathroom. Sweat glistened on his back when he walked away, the tight globes of his ass flexing with each step. Yeah, she stared and admired every inch of him.

A scar traced a jagged line below his shoulder blade that disappeared around his side. The thin bump had registered beneath her fingers, but now she understood it. Did he have more wounds? Where? From what?

She sat up when the bathroom light flicked on. Un-certainty wedged in for the first time since he'd declared he was driving her home. What came next?

She was sitting on the edge of the bed, staring at her thong on the floor when he returned. His expression gave away nothing when he approached. His steps were absorbed by the plush carpet, the silence ringing with questions. They should part now. The scene was done.

But it hadn't been a scene.

He slid his hand up to cup her cheek when he stood in front of her. That one touch, the simple confirmation melted the fears she hadn't acknowledged. Comfort eased in on the soft acceptance of what she no longer wanted to fight.

She wanted more of this, of him and the possibili-ties he presented.

Chapter Seventeen

Kennedy was everything Matt should avoid, but he couldn't. Not anymore.

Was it possible that he didn't have to? Could they navigate this thing that continued to grow between them? He had to try. There was no other choice.

Walking away would be impossible.

"Turn around," he urged.

Confusion flickered before she heeded his request. Her face was still flushed, her lips full and lush, tempting him to taste them again.

She slid around on the bed, hitching one leg up so her back was mostly to him. The low glow of the lamps lent an air of softness to the room that transferred to her, yet it hid none of her beauty or her pride. With or without clothes, she was comfortable in her own skin. He admired that and the strength it took to achieve it.

He ran a finger over the bite mark he'd left on the tender juncture of her neck. The little dents left by his teeth had turned a dark red that foreshadowed the bruise to come. He didn't try to hold back the possessive surge when it blazed in his chest. She'd let him do it. Begged him to do it.

And had come when he had.

A shiver tracked down her spine on a telling tremble, but she tilted her head to give him better access.
Intentional or not?

"I'll want a picture of this," he told her. The demand
skimmed past his reservations before he'd thought to
hold it back. He was treading down a scary path, but
he knew what was ahead this time. He could manage it.

She gave him a quick scan over her shoulder, that
hesitation still in place. She flicked her brows up before a sultry smile hit her lips. She turned back around
without responding, and he let his grin free. She would,
he didn't doubt it. But even better would be to see it in
person.

He found a pin in her hair and withdrew it before
finding the next. She tensed before a soft laugh flowed
out. "Seriously?"

He ignored her, studiously hunting down the seemingly magic clips holding her hair up. He'd collected
a small pile of bobby pins in his palm before strands
started to tumble down in segments. The softness caressed his skin when he drew his fingers through it.

She rolled her head back when he massaged her
scalp, a throaty moan stating her appreciation. "You're
spoiling me."

Again, he didn't respond, but he agreed with her. He
couldn't stop even if he tried. She was firmly wedged
into his sphere of responsibility, and this act here was
simple. Peace found a soft spot inside him and settled
in beside his slowly growing hope.

He set the pins on the nightstand, hesitating for a
moment, responsibilities torn.

"Are you leaving?" she asked. Nothing in her voice

gave away how she felt about whether he was or wasn't. That in itself had him moving to the doorway.

He caught her gaze, letting his intention show. She swallowed, that tiny smile that spelled relief and hesitation showing before he hit the light switch.

Darkness plunged in. It took a moment for his eyes to adjust, but she had moved over when he reached the bed. His pulse did a little jump at her acceptance even as he questioned himself.

That sense of peace returned on a long inhale and equally slow release when she curled into his side. He drew her closer until her head rested on his shoulder, and her leg was entwined with his. Her low hum rumbled into his ribs and calmed him further. This was right.

He kissed the top of her head, skimming lazy strokes over the soft skin on her arm. She traced an indistinct path over his chest with a touch that soothed.

"You continue to surprise me," she told him softly.

Time wove out on the lethargy that'd crept in. "As do you."

"When do you think that'll stop?"

"I don't know. Maybe never."

She huffed a short laugh. "I doubt it."

"Why?"

Her shoulder hitched beneath his hand. "Because most people are predictable."

"True," he conceded. "But that doesn't mean they can't surprise you."

This time, her hum was an undefined purr between agreement and not. He tried to track her thought process but couldn't find a clear path. He drew her hair between his fingers, finding comfort in the silky softness.

"So you know," he started. "This isn't common for me."

Her laugh was rich as she turned to face him. The darkness hid the details of her features, but he didn't need to see them, not when he knew them all by heart. Her breast pressed against his chest, her leg grazing his dick and nuzzling his balls in a statement of comfortable intimacy he'd missed more than he'd realized.

"I believe you've told me that before."

He smiled at her teasing tone. "True." But this was different than their hotel encounter. Very different. "It applies now too." He ran his fingers along her hairline, brushing strands over her shoulder as he sorted through his words. "I don't go home with a lot of women."

"No?"

He shook his head, wishing he could read her expression, yet also relieved his was hidden.

The silence drew out before she said, "What if I told you I don't bring a lot of men home?"

Happiness broke free at her soft admission. God, if only... Yeah, if only. "No?" he said, ensuring his tone was light.

She swiveled her head, her smile clear even in the dark. "Should we call this another anomaly?"

"No." His firm response was out before he'd thought about it. She stiffened. "I hope it's more than an anomaly." He was pushing, but he couldn't deny that he wanted more from her. He'd been clear on that after the Boardroom scene and nothing had changed.

She dropped down to rest her head on his shoulder. He breathed a small sigh of relief when she didn't pull away. This was progress. He didn't know what it meant or where it would take them, but it was a step forward.

And she was still with him.

* * *

Questions chased each other in an endless loop that left Kennedy with no answers. *I hope it's more than an anomaly.* What did she do with that?

Nothing in her background had prepared her for Matt. Not the years of casual sex or the relationships she'd observed. Her parents might still be married, but intimacy had never ventured into their relationship. They lived mostly separate lives that intersected when it was mutually beneficial.

This right here—no, everything with Matt already exceeded what she knew.

She bit her lip to hold back the tremble. She'd dove into this with the same determination that she'd tackled everything, and now her foundation was crumbling. Part of her understanding was falling apart, while a new option was forming. One she wasn't certain of.

Her stomach rolled. Fear chased a path from her head to her heart. Listening to her heart was dangerous. Rejection was easily deflected if she placed no emotional value in it to begin with. And expectations couldn't be shattered if they never existed.

"I can't promise much," she said into the darkness. The steady beat of his heart thumped beneath her ear to remind her he hadn't rejected or disappointed her. Not yet.

"Okay."

His simple response had her smiling. That was so him. Her sudden rush of nerves skittered to the background, her doubts dwindling. "What am I going to do with you?" she mused, flicking his nipple. His little flinch fed the mischief that'd helped her brazen her way through life.

He ran his hand over her nape with just enough pressure to kick off an internal shudder. It soaked into her bones and calmed her in a way she failed to understand. Her muscles seemed to melt until there was only him holding her up. Logically, she knew it didn't make sense, yet the physical proof existed in the quieting of her mind and the peace that floated over her.

"Just be," he said. "That's it. Just be with me."

He made it sound so simple when she knew it wasn't. "What about your kids?" She lobbed the dirty bomb with only a flicker of guilt. They were a very real, very solid entanglement he couldn't ignore and she didn't know if she wanted.

He inched his palm around until his fingers hit the tender spot on her neck. She bit her lip to hold in her whimper. Pain hovered in a reminder of the mark he'd left, that she'd encouraged him to give her.

"They're a very important part of my life." He skimmed his fingers over the spot in a gentle caress. "They've been the most important part since—" His breath hitched as he stilled. "Since my CO informed me that my kids had been voluntarily placed in state custody by my wife. I was in Afghanistan at the time."

Questions raced in and out of her head, but she asked none of them. Her parents would never win the most attentive award, and she may have spent a large majority of her childhood in boarding schools, but they'd never dumped her and walked away.

His chest lifted beneath her with his long inhalation. "My kids were six and four." She swallowed back the shot of anger that rose for him. She couldn't imagine what he must've felt. Not a man as honorable as him. "I promised them they'd always come first after that, and I've spent every day showing them I meant it."

"They're very lucky." Did they appreciate what they had? Did they know how fortunate they were?

His sarcastic laugh said he disagreed. "I'm the lucky one. They're good kids. They'd done nothing to deserve what she'd done."

A sliver of jealousy bloomed at the pride and love in his voice. She'd never heard something even slightly close to it from her own father. He wasn't bad or mean. Just...hard. And she thanked him for it most of the time. She wouldn't be where she was now if she hadn't learned how to hold strong against the comments of others.

There was a story behind Matt's revelation, something that'd left a deep mark on him. How could there not be? But as much as she wanted to know, she also didn't. Not...yet. Not when he was already closer than she trusted.

"Sex is good," she told him, rubbing her hand over his chest. Sex was easy. And the thought of having only that with him sucked away a bit of the quiet that'd settled inside her.

"But," he said when she thought the conversation was over. "This is already more than just sex." He rubbed his fingers over the bite mark on her neck, his implication both clear and elusive.

That knot of uncertainty returned with the added kick of desire. How could she want something that she wasn't?

"I'm not a sub." She wasn't naïve, especially regarding sex. She fully understood what he was playing at, and she was not on board with becoming anyone's submissive. Yielding her power during sex was completely different than dropping to her knees on a command.

She pushed away from him, fully expecting him to stop her, but he didn't. She sat up, staring down at him as disappointment took hold. That was the more he wanted. It explained so much. She kicked herself for seeing only what she'd wanted to see.

Or hoping for something she knew couldn't be true.

"Kennedy," he said when she started to scoot from the bed. His firm tone caught her attention, but it was the softness in it that stopped her. She waited, her back to him, the darkness closing in. "I don't want a sub."

Her derisive snort was her response. She'd given him sexual control—multiple times. It was only a matter of time before he'd expect that to carry over into more.

"I don't," he stated without emotion. "I've had a sub, once. My ex-wife. And that didn't turn out so well."

"You think?" she snarked, encased in self-preservation mode. But regret hit almost immediately. He'd opened up to her, and she'd just shoved it in his face with the same callous disregard she detested in her father. His lack of a response spoke louder than words. "Sorry. That was crass of me."

He rolled closer, the bed shifting to warn of his intent. She stiffened, expecting his touch but not receiving it. He came to her side instead. His presence bounced off every nerve ending that tried to absorb and reject him at once.

"We were young," he started, leaning forward to rest his arms on his thighs. His shadow presented a regretful image she tried to hold strong against. "It started out as bedroom games for me. It'd morphed into more before I'd fully comprehended that it'd happened. I was a new officer with a new marriage and an infant on a new base. I'd switched into survival mode, taking over when I saw her struggling, setting down a structure and tasks for the day without thought to what that meant. For her, that ended with me having a sub whose true desire was to be a slave." He turned his head toward her. "All *I'd* wanted was a partner."

Again, her thoughts were a scramble of questions with no clear response. A mix of pain laced through his words. He clearly took responsibility for what'd happened when there'd been two of them in their relationship.

"You can believe me when I say I don't want a sub." He straightened, his bearing returning to one of confidence. "Sexual control is something I gave up—until you. That night in the hotel room was…too damn perfect."

Her urge to snark out a defense was muzzled by her agreement. That night had been…perfect. It was why they were here. Why she continued to think about him and want more.

"And now?" she finally whispered.

"Do you have to ask?" He ran the back of a finger down her arm. Goose bumps popped up in a prickle of awareness that never truly left around him.

She squeezed her eyes closed, struggling to sort through her thoughts and emotions. He upset the defined line of her life. He presented problems and complications that held no promise of good. And yet, she was still sitting there when she could've walked away at any point.

He started to rise. Her heart leapt, her hand snaking

out to halt him. He stilled. Her pulse pounded out each hard beat in the sore spot on her neck. His bite mark.

He slowly lowered until he was sitting again. Why had she stopped him? What did she want? Did she need to define it? Did he?

They should, yet…

Her swallow did little to clear the lump in her throat. Was that fear? Doubt? Self-preservation?

"Sexual control is something I've never given up— before you," she finally said. The admission pounded at the defenses she'd erected so long ago. The pressure to conform to an expected role had been immense and giving even a little had been seen as a weakness to exploit.

His quick intake of breath cut a sharp hiss through the silence. "Why me?"

"I don't know," she told him honestly. "You were safe at first. Someone who knew nothing about me and had nothing to gain from me. You?"

"The same." He waited a beat. "And now?"

She stared at him through the darkness, exposed yet somehow grounded by his words. He had that ability when so few did.

"I think we're good." Her statement came out far more certain than the mess of indecision roiling within her. *Project what you want, not what you are.* Words to live by from her mother.

"Are we?"

I hope so. And when had hope gotten involved? Her lips quirked at her inane thoughts. She had this, right? Fear fled when confronted, and she didn't even know what had her so damn scared.

"Yes. I think so." She ran her hand down his arm to clasp his hand. If she owned it, it became hers to wield.

"There are times when I may choose to give some of my sexual control to you, but it ends there."

"Of course." He shifted to face her better, his voice low. "I never assumed otherwise. In fact, I have no desire for more than that."

The darkness provided safety, but it also hid so much. She had nothing to go on except for his words and her own instincts.

She inched back on the bed, drawing him with her. He came easily, lying over her in a way that was at once too intimate and absolutely right. Her internal sigh left her mystified, yet he was here, and she didn't want him to leave.

She framed his face with her hands and drew him into a kiss. The gentleness in his touch had her heart fluttering despite the hesitation that still lingered. She'd be fine. They'd figure it out. It was only a kiss.

But the tender way he took her that time was so much more than a kiss. The lazy roll of his hips, the soft murmurs, the slow build that hummed over her skin and caressed her heart cried the lie she was trying to tell herself.

Her release came on a gentle swell and prolonged shudder that shattered her fears while building new ones. She gasped, holding him close. Her neck throbbed with the reminder of the power she'd given him. But it was only as strong as she allowed.

And that's what made them equal.

Chapter Eighteen

Matt leaned down to brush a kiss on Kennedy's forehead. She stirred, stretching an arm over her head as her eyes fluttered open. Her frown dug in as her fog appeared to clear.

"Don't get up," he told her before he placed another kiss on her temple. "I have to go. But I didn't want to just leave." Walking out after the night they'd shared was way below his standards.

"What time is it?" She stretched to look at the clock on the nightstand, dropping back with a groan. "It's Sunday."

His internal clock had set itself to the ass-crack-of-dawn long ago. It didn't matter the day or how late he'd been up. "Go back to sleep." He brushed the hair from her face. She was already settling back into the mattress. "I'll let myself out."

Her little smile said "okay" and "that's it?" at once. Expectations hadn't been set, yet they'd covered a lot of ground last night. He took a step back, hesitated. He could leave it like this, as just another sexual encounter. It'd be safer. "Lunch this week?"

A full smile bloomed at that. She closed her eyes, tucked a hand beneath her cheek. "That sounds good."

He shook his head in mixed wonder and happiness. He was too far past safe to stop now. He gave her thigh a playful smack that had her flinching away. But her eyes remained closed and her smile increased.

"Goodbye, Matt." Playful amusement lifted her tone.

"Goodbye, Kennedy." He headed to the door before he succumbed to the temptation to crawl into her bed and turn that smile into a cry of pleasure.

He laid her dress over the back of the couch and turned off the lights downstairs before he left, ensuring the door was locked behind him. The sun was still nestled below the horizon, keeping its light to itself. A quick check of his phone had his guilt soaring. He'd silenced it before the benefit performance and had never turned it back on. The series of concerned texts from both kids derailed the assumption he'd made about them being asleep last night.

He should've texted, but he'd told them he'd be late. And what would he have said? I'm getting laid, don't wait up?

A harsh scrub of his face didn't dislodge the confusion or the guilt, but he wasn't sorry about spending the night with Kennedy. There was something good there, something he couldn't pass off.

He sent a quick text to let them know he was fine even though they'd clearly be in bed now. They never rose before ten on weekends and that was considered early to them.

The highway was basically empty, thankfully. It allowed him to make the drive on autopilot while he sorted through the change in his life. He hadn't expected Kennedy. Hell, he hadn't expected most of the major changes in his life—not that Kennedy necessarily classified as major. But she was something different.

And that was good.

That nugget of happiness spread with each mile that passed. No regrets. No dread. No doubts or what-ifs? And they had a lunch date this week.

Like that was a major accomplishment or something. *Fuck.* He was acting like a teen with his first crush. Twenty years was a long time between first dates, though. He'd been a college student the last time he'd dated. And the last woman he'd called a girlfriend had become his wife after she'd become pregnant.

Honor was a lost trait that'd somehow been ingrained in him. Not somehow. His father had fled, leaving his mother to raise him on her own. He'd refused to do that to his kid.

He frowned when he pulled up to his home. The lights were on in the kitchen, the house lit up inside like there was a party going on. Did they forget to turn them off? Had something happened?

He hung his head when his daughter appeared in the window. She was up. That probably meant Ben was too. He had a welcome party he really didn't want.

The cool morning air offered little in the way of relief from the embarrassment that was trying to edge its way up his neck. His tie was shoved in his pocket, his shirt open at the collar, his coat and pants wrinkled.

The walk of shame in front of his kids was not on his To Do list.

He blew out a breath, hitting the garage door button a little too hard before he entered the house. Three sets of eyes held him pinned to his spot. *Damn.* At what point had his mother joined the party?

They were seated around the dining table directly adjacent to the kitchen. The entire space was best described as efficient. The updates he'd made kept it from being old, but there was no way anything in his home would be described as luxurious. It fit them, though, this home he'd worked so hard to make for his family.

He closed the door with precise care, set his keys on the counter before turning to face them. It didn't matter that he was over forty, in that moment he felt like the kid instead of the parent.

"Morning?" he ventured, leaning back against the counter. His attempt at casual landed with a solid fizzle. Excellent. "Can I ask why you're all up?"

"What?" Dawn's aghast expression smacked of the same overexaggeration she applied to most things. "Are you serious? Have you not checked your phone? We've been worried about you!"

He made a pointed movement of pulling his phone out of his pocket and checking his texts. "I sent you a response. I said I was fine."

"Twenty minutes ago!"

Ben sat back, his smirk released behind Dawn's back. He raised his brows, speculation clear. Yeah, he knew exactly where his dad had been—or what he'd been doing. It was probable they all did. How fucking wonderful was that?

"I'm sorry," he said, meaning it. "I assumed you'd be in bed. I told you I'd be home late."

"But you never go out."

Accusation rang from his daughter with a hint of something he couldn't identify. Anger? Worry? Concern? Jealousy?

He grabbed a mug from the cupboard and poured

himself a cup of coffee from the pot his mother must've brewed at some point.

"When did they call you?" he asked, looking to her.

"I believe the first text was around one."

He scowled at his kids, but his daughter glared back, defiant. Ben on the other hand shrugged in casual dismissal. More like himself than Matt liked to admit, Ben tackled the world with a practical calm that often masked his true feelings. At close to six feet with growing years still left in him, his son already had a commanding presence. Matt's concern lay in what Ben chose to do with the authority he seemed at once aware of and blind to.

The first hit of caffeine sped down Matt's throat and brought the rush of patience he clearly needed. He took in his family and saw the love behind their overprotective watch. He was lucky they cared so much. He would've done the same thing for any of them if they'd acted out of character.

"I'm sorry, Sunshine." He pressed a kiss to the top of Dawn's head, pulling her in for a hug against his hip. "I didn't mean to worry you." He looked to his mom and son. "I didn't mean to worry any of you. I apologize for not responding."

His daughter softened into his side. "Where were you?"

And there was the question he'd hoped to avoid. He held in his wince, but he didn't miss the smile behind his mother's strategic sip of coffee or the smirk on his son's face.

He blew out another breath, slung his tux coat over the back of the chair and took the last seat at the table as he rolled up his sleeves. His seat. The four of them had consumed hundreds of meals there together. Every scratch, marker stain, scuff and worn spot on the wood came with memories of projects, conversations, games and arguments that'd taken place around it. It only seemed fitting that they'd be having this discussion here.

Not that he'd expected to have it so soon or so early in the morning. And that was his own damn fault.

He stalled by taking another drink from his mug. He let the formality bleed from his posture and mindset now that his dress uniform was removed. How much detail did he give?

"I went to a benefit in the city. A very upscale affair with a lot of potential business contacts." He'd told them that when they'd joked about his tux before he'd left last night.

"And you were connecting with them until five in the morning?" Dawn asked.

Ben snorted, but his mother only lifted her brows, her amusement uncontained. Dawn's persistent attack under presumed naivety was bordering on annoying.

Matt studied his daughter, seeing beneath the messy bun and sloppy pj's to the little girl scared of her world changing. And he couldn't blame her. His choice in women hadn't worked out so well for her last time.

His ex-wife had given up all rights to her children at the order of her Master. He'd wanted her full loyalty without distraction, and in return, he provided the security and structure she craved. Matt would never understand how she could abandon her kids, but in many ways, he was grateful that she'd ended the harm at that.

He grabbed Dawn's hand, giving it the reassuring squeeze she still needed even at eighteen. He'd always tackled the tough questions head on. From their mother to where babies came from to safe sex. There was no point in changing a path that'd worked well to date.

"No, Dawn." He held her gaze, waiting for acceptance to take hold. It didn't. She drew her hand from his, crossing her arms in a show of stubbornness as her eyes narrowed. She was going to force him to say it. To what point?

Ben watched them like a man calculating the odds and taking internal bets on the outcome. But he didn't cut down his sister or smack talk when the topic was ripe for both. Maybe his mother was right, and he worried too much about Ben.

"I was with a woman," he finally said, laying his personal life out for his family to inspect. "We left the benefit together, and I went back to her place."

He let that digest. That was as far as he was going when it came to details. Describing how he'd lost himself in her stunning beauty as he slid into her, or how deep their connection had run when she'd given herself to him, wasn't going to happen.

Dawn looked away, her face crumbling. Her sniff was a jab to his heart. *Fuck.* He glanced to his mother, who only offered a shrug. Yeah, this was his mess to clean up.

Ben sat forward, his scowl darkening his features. He kept the black curls he'd inherited from his mother buzzed short. The effect added an edge to the boy on the verge of becoming a man.

"Why are you upset?" Ben asked his sister, annoyance clear. "He's allowed to have a life. Do you really think he's been celibate since Mom?"

"Ben!" Dawn berated before Matt could. Her open

shock said she might've thought exactly that or had wanted to think that.

"What?" Ben shot right back. "He's allowed to get laid."

"Ben!" This time it was Matt who brought down the hammer. "That's enough."

Ben slumped back in full disgruntled teen mode. His glare transferred his frustration without the need of the added scowl. "I was defending you," he mumbled, holding his own against Matt's stare.

"I understand," he conceded. "But you don't need to be crude. Sex is about more than getting laid, or it should be. I thought we'd talked about that." How did he convince hormonal teens that all sex had an impact? Even mutually casual sex.

"Did you use a condom?" Dawn quipped, her sulk in full defiant mode.

No. He hadn't. And that had been careless of him.

They'd jumped that discussion under the unspoken understanding of safety standards established by the Boardroom. Regular testing and pregnancy precautions were required for all members. That didn't excuse his negligence.

"I'm going to go," his mother said, standing. "There are some things a mother and grandmother doesn't need details about." She winked at Matt, squeezing his shoulder as she passed his seat. He started to rise, but she waved him back. "I can walk home by myself."

He looked to Ben who was already moving. "I'll walk you, Grandma."

"I'm fine," she sputtered. Even at this early hour with little to no sleep, she was the picture of collected efficiency. Her cardigan was years old, yet still looked new, as did the cotton pants that were an in-house staple but rarely worn out of it.

"I've got you," Ben said, sweeping in to plant a kiss on her cheek. "Unless you're afraid you can't keep up." He grabbed his sweatshirt and was out the front door before she could say more.

She shook her head. "Keep up," she muttered before shutting the door behind her.

Silence fell once they were gone. It swirled around Matt in a mess of reprimand and understanding. He ached for his daughter, but he wasn't willing to give up the possibilities with Kennedy. Not even now.

"Dawn," he ventured. She shot him a side-glance, sniffed again. Both kids had inherited his stubborn streak. "You and Ben are always my priority. It was wrong of me to ignore my phone. I regret the worry I caused you all." He spoke every word with the measured honesty they required. He'd been selfish, and it'd hurt them.

"You've never done this before," she accused.

He hadn't. He'd never gone on a date or been missing for most of the night. He was just their dad. The stable one who'd kept them safe after their mother had failed so miserably.

"Her name is Kennedy," he offered. "She's a strong, independent woman who happened into my life when I wasn't expecting it." She gave him a doubtful eye roll. What was it with eye rolls and teenagers? Did they teach it in school?

"Why haven't you mentioned her before now?" she challenged.

"Because I didn't want to have this discussion until I was certain there was something to discuss."

"So your stance on casual sex doesn't apply to you?"

He resisted the urge to bang his head on the table and scrub his face until the nightmare of a morning was washed from existence. Neither of those actions would help him.

"Don't play this game," he called her out. "You're better than that." He waited a beat, almost daring her to prove him right. "I'm an adult, as are you. My love and commitment to you is guaranteed. My relationship with Kennedy—or anyone—will never jeopardize that. Ever. I'm capable of having a girlfriend and being a father too."

Her eyes bugged out. "She's your girlfriend?"

He shrugged, letting a bit of uncertainty show. "We're still in the undefined stage. But...I'm open to it." How that'd work exactly, he didn't know. Just admitting it aloud defined the possibilities while mudding the path.

"Wow." Dawn studied him for a long moment, understanding finally chasing away some of her defensive fear. "I..." She glanced away, picking at her cuticles in a telling display of insecurity. But her sigh when it came held acceptance and eased the worry in his heart. "I know," she started again. "I know all of that. I guess I just wasn't ready to share you."

"I get it." He still wasn't too keen on her bringing home a boyfriend. None of the ones to date had been serious, but the time was coming when one would be. She was growing up, which also meant she was growing away—as she should. "Come here."

He stood, holding his arms open in an invitation she still accepted. Her hug soothed more of his concern and dislodged a bit of his guilt. "I love you, Sunshine."

"I love you too, Dad." She stepped back, her smile a little wobbly. "I'm going to get some sleep. I'll see you this afternoon." He was relieved her parting wink had a bit of that sauce that so defined her.

He dumped his coffee in the sink and poured himself a fresh cup. He drank it staring out the front window. The sky was lightening with the rise of the sun, but the neighborhood was still asleep. He usually had his morning jog done by now and was already started on house chores or at his computer working. He should go into work this morning since both kids would crash. The downside of owning a trucking company was it never stopped running, not completely. Especially as he expanded into longer hauls with higher volume.

Ben strolled up the sidewalk, hands tucked into the front pocket of his hoodie, his size overemphasized beneath the covering. But he was still just a kid no matter how grown-up he appeared.

"Hey," he said when Ben stepped into the kitchen. "Thanks for that."

He brushed him off. "It's the least I could do after Dawn dragged her down here in the middle of the night." He leaned against the fridge, eyeing him. "Is she okay now?"

Matt shrugged. "I think so. How about you? Do you have questions for me?"

Ben's smirk held the teasing light of a smartass kid. "I don't think sex tips from my dad are appropriate." He scrunched up his face. "Not to mention gross."

Matt hung his head, partly in defeat and partly to hide his grin. He let his own sarcastic remark slide. "You're okay with me dating?"

The smile faded from his son's face. He glanced

down. "Yeah. I mean, I'm kind of surprised you haven't before."

He didn't address that. His past actions weren't in question now. "You and Dawn will always be my priority."

Ben jerked his head back, frowning. "Is that what Dawn was worried about?" His eye roll was epic disgust. "College must be affecting her brain because that's obvious."

Matt tried not to laugh but failed. His chuckle trickled out before he swiped it away with his hand. "You're a good kid, Ben." He probably didn't tell him that enough.

He sobered. "I try."

The gravity behind his words triggered a series of questions, but also a big heaping of pride. Matt drew him in for a quick hug before he could object. "I love you, Ben."

"Yeah. Love you too." Ben left with a quick salute and a half-smile.

Matt stood in the silence of his kitchen, a little amazed and humbled at once. He was doing okay. His family was solid, his company was growing, and for the first time in years, he had something else to look forward to.

And he had no idea what to think about all of it.

Chapter Nineteen

"There's a Mr. Hamilton here to see you."

Kennedy scowled at her computer, her eyes darting to the time in the corner of the screen. He was here? Her stomach did a small flip before she pushed the intercom button on her phone. "Tell him I'll be right down."

She grabbed her purse, straightening her suit when she stood. It was just lunch. Nothing big. And the more she tried to tell herself that, the more her subconscious laughed at her. She'd never looked this forward to any date, let alone a simple lunch one.

"Kennedy," her dad bellowed. She bit back her wince when he stepped into her office. His scowl deepened when he took her in. "Are you going somewhere?"

"I have a lunch…meeting," she finished. "Did you want something?"

"Who are you meeting with?"

Of course he'd grill her. That familiar kernel of irritation clawed up her throat, carrying every word she didn't dare spew. She gritted her teeth to hold it in, like she always did. Her smile stretched her cheeks in the automatic position of mild sincerity.

"Matt Hamilton," she told him. "From McPherson Trucking. I introduced you to him the other night."

"Why?" Suspicion lined his brow and tone. "Should I come along?"

"It's fine, Dad." She waved off his concern. "It's a simple get-to-know-you lunch. With the Calloway deal in the pipeline, I thought it'd be good to have some shipping options laid out in case it came through." She bluffed her way through that, but her response was valid.

Her father puffed out his chest, hitching his pants up in that disgruntled affront he wielded to ensure his irritation was known. "You should've spoken to me about this."

"I was planning to after I'd gathered my facts." She drew her brows in a touch to show her concern. "I know you're busy. I'll have all the data together when we do talk about it." He would've demanded that if he'd thought far enough down the pipe to see that they wouldn't have the trucking capacity to meet demand if the sales forecast was accurate.

"I'll expect that soon," he relented, turning to leave. "We'll need to look at inventory and manpower too."

"Agreed." She followed him out of her office. "I'll get on that as well."

He paused, assessing her. His expression softened slightly. "Thank you."

Her eyes widened a fraction before she could stop her reaction. "No problem," she reassured him, prepped for the next stinging barb.

His lips twitched like he was going to say something more, but he turned and strode down the hall without another word.

She stared after him, a little dumbfounded. Her dad

wasn't known for his compliments, so she had no idea what to do with that.

Kennedy breezed into the lobby, her smile in place and greeting prepared only to pause when she saw Matt. He stood by the door in jeans and a black T-shirt with the McPherson Trucking logo on the left breast. His beard was fuller again, darkening his cheeks, and his hair appeared newly shorn, adding a neatness to his appearance that countered his casual attire.

Her stomach clenched in time with that little hitch in her heart. Suits might be her fetish, but he didn't need the clothing to emanate the power he inherently owned. He took her in just as greedily, the hunger in his eyes apparent—at least to her.

They were so screwed. She let that realization lighten her thoughts. They were in it together, whatever it was.

"Matt," she said as she approached. "I thought we were meeting there." He was supposed to text her the location.

"I changed my mind." He held the door open for her. "I hope that's okay."

She shot him a speculative side-eye as she passed him, fully aware of their receptionist taking in every detail of their exchange. "You're lucky I wasn't at another meeting."

"I guess I am," he agreed when she'd expected a comeback.

Her low chuckle mellowed the nerves fluttering in her stomach. His smile spoke of secrets and wants she was completely onboard with. But with it was something warmer. A gentle appreciation and simple enjoyment.

A lot of men wanted her, but few actually valued

her, and even fewer made the effort to see beneath the shields she presented.

But Matt had. And he'd done it with seemingly little effort or false narrative.

"Where are we going?" she asked once they were in the car. Traffic would be nuts no matter where they went given it was the day before Thanksgiving.

"I hope you weren't expecting upscale." His wink could've been a derogatory tease, but she didn't take it that way. No, he was mocking his own appearance. Her customary pantsuit could blend into most situations, which was why she favored them.

"Well…" She waited a beat for him to glance at her. "I only eat at Michelin-approved locations and that's only after it's been referred by a friend."

Matt grinned, catching her joke. "In that case, you are in for a big surprise."

"Oh?" Her smile slipped out. "I can't wait, then."

He navigated the side streets like a pro, taking roads she'd never been down even though she'd thought herself fairly knowledgeable about the area. "I trust you know where you're going," she commented when the graffiti increased in proportion to the bars on the windows.

"Of course." He made another turn, and her concern increased as he wound deeper into a neighborhood she normally avoided. "How's your week been?"

"Fine." She dragged the word out, letting her confusion show. "It'll be great if we both make it past lunch. Are you *sure* you know where you're going?"

"Yes." The laughter in his voice didn't ease her worry. "I would never let anything happen to you." There was nothing but serious intent in his tone and eyes when he said that. He held at a stop sign until the importance of his statement sank in. He meant what he said and not just now.

Her heart did the flutter thing that spoke to the longing for something she'd given up on ever attaining. Could he really be that good? And want her?

Her internal kick knocked that thought aside. Self-doubt had no place in her life. If she'd listened to even half the garbage spewed at her or the bevy of self-doubt cultivated in her own moments of weakness, then she wouldn't be the business woman she was today.

Kennedy controlled her own destiny, and she wasn't relinquishing that power—except with Matt, sexually, on occasion.

He pulled in behind a little store tucked into a row of ramshackle buildings that included a tattoo parlor and a sex shop. Her skepticism must've been plastered on her face based on the amusement he didn't try to hide.

He leaned over the center console to draw her in for a quick kiss. His lips grazed hers too fast to satisfy her craving for him. She frowned, but the laughter in his eyes muted her displeasure.

"You've got this," he confirmed.

"Of course I do." She wasn't about to deny him even though she had no clue what she had or if he was referring to them or the rickety screen door he was staring at. She exited the car and was waiting for him by the hood when he came around. "Lead the way." There was no way she was walking in ahead of him.

He paused, head tilting. "I was thinking a dragon." His eyes narrowed. "Or maybe a phoenix. Between your shoulder blades."

A slither of recognition tingled up her spine at his

subtle movements. She responded to them, going soft and warm with the desire to give him what he wanted before she cut the unexpected reaction down.

A smirk hid beneath his facade of seriousness. It flashed in his eyes and dragged a reluctant smile from her.

She snapped her chin up. "You come anywhere near me with a buzzing needle full of ink, and I'll have no problem drop-kicking you in the nuts. So be warned."

She turned away and marched to the door where a tempting, spicy aroma escaped through the dirty screen. His laugh boomed behind her, but she only raised a brow and motioned for him to go ahead, certain he had no idea the effect his subtle actions had just had on her.

"I'll be sure to keep all needles away from you," he joked as he passed, pausing to lay another kiss on her lips. This one deeper with a hit of passion and tongue, but still way too short. "But not my teeth." He snagged a finger under her collar and tugged it back to rub the bruise that was a dark blob of purple and black.

Desire buzzed in a mellow way that built anticipation yet scrambled her normal expectations of sex and relationships. The two were usually mutually exclusive. One did not depend on or require the other. Things worked better that way. Yet now...

"Hector, my man." Matt's warm greeting was met with an equally big grin from the man behind the counter.

"Matthew." He grabbed Matt's hand in a fist grip that was more of a bond statement than hand shake. "I'd thought you'd died or something." The man's accented English contained a joking tone that also spoke of concern.

"Nah. Just busy."

"I hear you took over that company." Hector gave him an appreciative nod. "Big move."

Matt shrugged his comment off. "Someone had to, right? I figured why not." His casual acceptance of a major investment and risk had her smiling again.

"Better you than me," Hector joked. "Jose tells me you got big plans." He crossed his arms, assessing Matt but also challenging him. "You gonna keep it open, right?"

Situated somewhere near middle age, his round face lined with creases that spoke to his upbeat personality, Hector appeared to be the gossip wrangler of the neighborhood.

"That's my intent," Matt said. "What's your special today?"

"Oh, man. You hit the right day." Hector launched into Spanish, complete with hand gestures and facial expressions, that communicated his belief of the burrito's perfection.

Matt's quick response and equally speedy use of the foreign language had her assessing him yet again. He was full of surprises. Even here, in a deli-style store that, although clean, was worn by time. Scratched shelves, nicked flooring and random clutter combined with that general sense of modest means underscored how out of her realm she was. But Matt seemed to not only belong, but truly connect.

She knew of few men who could transition so easily between social classes. Did he appreciate how valuable that skill set could be? It didn't show if he did.

"You talked me into it," Matt said, grinning. He turned to Kennedy, drawing her forward. "What about you? I can vouch for almost everything on the menu. Hector's food is amazing."

"Aw, man," Hector blushed. "You're embarrassing me in front of this beautiful lady." He aimed his warm smile at her, his brown eyes twinkling with humor. "He's a charmer, this one." He nodded at Matt. "But he's solid, you know?"

She eyed up Matt, agreeing with Hector, but there was no way she was giving him that kind of advantage. "You think so?" She narrowed her eyes before refocusing on Hector. "He always seems a little uptight to me."

Hector's full boom of a laugh bounced off the walls and filled the space with a contagious joy. Any doubts she'd had about this place were erased beneath the kindness and wit of its apparent owner. She knew some upscale store owners who could learn a few things from him.

"What do you recommend?" she asked both men. "Something with chicken."

She narrowed down her choices before deciding on the enchiladas. "With a side of sour cream, please."

"And guacamole," Matt added. "It's a must."

"Is it?"

"More so than sour cream." His expression said what he thought of that addition.

"Let me guess," she said as he led her out another door to a packed fenced-in eating area. "You're a no-pineapple-on-pizza guy too." He found a free table and held her chair out for her in the same casual manner that infused most of his actions.

"I have no problem eating it like that." He took the seat across from her. "But I'd prefer a basic pepperoni any day."

"No everything combo?"

"It's fine." His expression said differently. "But there's something nice about a simple slice of basic pizza." His depth over something so mundane as pizza had her smiling again. Maybe she hadn't stopped.

"There is," she agreed. Especially when surrounded by the watchful demands of a social circle focused on calories, perception and that hunt for the perfect Californian impersonation of what was supposed to be a greasy, cheesy experience.

He sat back, glanced around. The little patio was stuffed with tables and chairs to maximize every available space. The assumption of privacy could never be made when there were strangers sitting three feet away. But in typical Bay Area fashion, people talked and acted as if no one was listening.

"I take it you come here often?" she ventured.

"Not so much anymore." He waved to a man a few tables down, regret showing. "I used to come here with some of the guys before I bought the company. But…" He shrugged. "The dynamics have changed. They look at me differently now that I'm the one who cuts their paychecks."

She could relate to that, only she'd never been in his position. As the daughter of the owner, she'd always been on a different level, even when she'd worked the reception desk in her teens.

"You are different now," she told him, not bothering to sugarcoat the truth.

He flashed a smile. "Maybe." His gaze drifted over the patio again. "Is it bad to say I miss the friendships?"

"No." She couldn't relate, but she could understand. "It's hard to remain buddy-buddy with people who you may have to fire or discipline or layoff at some point. Being in charge requires professional distance."

"But you also have to garner trust."

She nodded. "Which is why being in management sometimes sucks."

"Yet so many aspire to be at that level."

"Mostly for the paycheck." The sun warmed her back and brought a softness she settled into. "Few are really prepared for or enjoy the people part of the job."

"True." He rested his forearms on the table, the muscles flexing when he clasped his hands. "Do you? Enjoy it?"

Her smile was automatic. "I do. But, I've never really known anything else."

"No?"

She shook her head. "I started working in the office when I was a teenager, but no one ever treated me like the receptionist or general admin that I was." And she'd never acted like it either, really. She did her job, but she also strove to do more, learn more. "My father tried to… protect me, which resulted in my exclusion from most of the company social circles, even now."

"How do you feel about that?"

"It is what it is," she answered honestly. "It's hard to want something different when you've never known it." The company was a part of her family, and she'd do her best to see that it succeeded. "What about you?"

He studied her for a moment, his thoughts hidden. "The military has a very structured protocol between officers and enlisted. I understand their reasoning, but I also believe respect is earned, not given."

Of course he would. "You, Mr. Hamilton, are a rare man in the world of corporate arrogance."

She made the statement as a joke, but his expression remained serious. "There's no room for arrogance when people's lives are at stake—or their livelihood."

Okay. Wow. "And that right there is what so many overlooked in their hunt for personal wealth and success." Most probably classified her as one of the arrogant based on her social circle, but they'd be wrong. She cared very deeply about the people they employed, even if they didn't know it.

Their food arrived, the tantalizing scents wiping out any thoughts of expectation and perceptions that never quite aligned.

"This smells delicious," she said, meaning it. Her usual salad with a side of dressing didn't stand a chance against the plate of goodness before her.

"Would I steer you wrong?"

No. He wouldn't. And that was where he beat out every man she'd even briefly dated.

Matt dug into his burrito with the gusto of a man used to enjoying his food. He moaned his appreciation in a lust-filled tone that triggered every erotic memory he starred in. Her nipples tightened with the shot of arousal he'd launched on nothing more than a rumbled sound.

He froze mid-chew, his eyes darkening. He swallowed. "What are you thinking?" The rough edge to his voice said he knew exactly what she was thinking.

She bit her lip in a calculated tease before she glanced to the two men seated next to them. "I'll tell you later."

His brows rose on a slow hike of speculation. "How later?"

She took a bite of her food in a coy play of deflection. The enchilada melted over her taste buds in a burst of flavor that almost pulled a moan from her. Now she understood his love for this little place.

"Wow," she said after she swallowed. "This is really good."

"You'll have to share that with Hector before we leave."

"I will." It was doubtful she'd ever find her way back alone—or dare to come on her own—but Matt could bring her back any time.

"Do you have plans this weekend?" he asked between bites of food. His casual tone failed to calm the flash of hope in her chest.

"Just tomorrow."

"Family dinner?"

"Not so much," she hedged. That was the holiday expectation, but her parents had never been big on following traditions. The nice thing about the country club's Thanksgiving dinner was the abundance of other people who were also there. "You?"

"Yeah." The warmth in his expression said he actually enjoyed it. "Dawn's home from school—that's my daughter. Her and my mom do the sides. Me and the boy are the bird cookers in our house."

"The men?" Her shock was real. She'd never seen her father turn the stove on, let alone cook a turkey.

"Hey," he chided. "Men can cook."

"I'm sure they can." As a single dad, he'd probably mastered that skill better than her. "I've just never experienced it."

"We'll have to change that."

And the thought of him in the kitchen cooking for her touched her in a way she didn't want to analyze.

But that was true about so much of what was growing between them.

She shifted the conversation to business if only to keep herself from diving too deeply into the land of hearts, flowers and heartbreak. Plus, she was serious about the company's potential need for added transportation.

They were almost back to her office, her thoughts mellowed from the food, her body relaxed when he broached the topic she should've brought up earlier.

"The other night," he started, glancing to her. "We, ah, skipped over the condom conversation."

"Yeah." They had. And she'd only thought about it the next day. "We're fine, though, if you're concerned. I have an IUD. Pregnancy isn't a worry." But she'd still been lax when she knew better.

"I wasn't worried about that."

"No?" The firmness in his tone had her eyes narrowing. "Because most men usually are."

"No." He pulled into their lot and parked in an open spot at the back. He shifted the car into Park and turned to her. The serious edge in his expression had her bracing. "I had a vasectomy years ago. I love my kids, but I have no interest in having more." He took a breath. "You should know that."

He'd had a vasectomy. She digested that for a second, just one. A grin broke across her face that must've had a maniacal bent to it, based on his wary reaction, but she couldn't contain it. He just kept getting more perfect.

"What's that for?" He motioned to her face, clearly confused.

"I don't want babies either."

He sat back. "Really?"

"Nope. Not even a little bit." She made sure her conviction came through in her tone. There wasn't a drop of maternal instinct in her, and she had no desire to have a baby simply because it was expected. She'd lived through that herself and would never inflict it on another. But this was usually where people doubted her, especially women.

He eyed her for another long moment before a smile eased over his lips. "Okay."

It was her turn to be surprised. "That's it?"

"Am I supposed to say something else?" He leaned in, cupping her neck to draw her closer. His eyes dropped to her lips before they lifted to hers.

"No," she whispered. "We're good."

"We are," he agreed before he closed his mouth over hers.

Her sigh seemed to come from the deepest part of her. How could she miss this so much? His tongue met hers in a familiar caress that hinted at the dark heat he could unleash with a simple touch. Want burst to life on the flames that never went out with him.

He brushed his lips over hers, backing off when she wanted to dive deeper. He ended the kiss with a series of little pecks broken by a few more swipes of his tongue that left her aching for things she couldn't define.

But there was no need to, right? She just had to be with him. That was it. And somehow, he'd made that okay.

Chapter Twenty

The quick buzz of Matt's phone vibrated on the counter, but it was too far away for him to see the text message. He glanced at his wet hands and the pan he was currently scrubbing. The text could wait. He'd never jumped to his phone like his kids did whenever theirs made a sound.

The follow-up buzz had him reaching for the towel. Damn it. And no, his heart did not do a little jig when he saw Kennedy's name. *I never told you what I was thinking…*

His momentary confusion fled when he remembered her tease at lunch yesterday. His stomach did a twist that sunk to his groin and perked up his dick. That was all it took with her. Just a thought and he was two steps down the road toward a full hard-on. Because, yeah, that was mature.

You didn't. He kept his response short, having zero clue how to play the sexting game.

Should I tell you now?

His groan tumbled into the kitchen.

"You okay, Dad?" The call from Dawn killed his inappropriate semi—as it should.

"I'm fine." The wide archway into the family room provided a side view of the football game playing on the TV. Thankfully, the couch and chairs weren't visible.

Dawn came around the corner, concern in place. "Do you need help?"

He lowered his phone. "I'm good, but thanks." He didn't mind doing the dishes. It gave him time to think in peace.

She looked pointedly at his phone, concern slipping to understanding. "Are you going to see her this weekend?"

"I don't know." They hadn't made plans, yet. "But I would like to, yes." He held firm on his commitment to Kennedy, just like he did for his kids.

She crossed her arms, a weak smile forming. "She makes you happy, doesn't she?"

"She does." He couldn't explain it or understand it, but he didn't have to think about his answer. "That doesn't mean I was unhappy before. It's just an added dynamic to my life."

"I know." She might've agreed, but her tone was far from upbeat. "I'm happy for you, really."

And that sounded convincing. Sure. "Would you like to meet her?" He ignored the pile of concerns that stacked up in his chest. Would Kennedy be on board? It was better to know now if she wasn't.

She bit her lip, her finger working over her thumb cuticle. Any admonishment from him on the habit only resulted in a scowl from her. "I'm heading back to school on Saturday. I want an extra day to get settled before classes start."

"Okay. Who are you riding with?"

"Karen." The volleyball teammate she'd ridden home

with. Again, he was grateful for the family she'd found within the sport. It made letting her go a little easier.

"I'll see what I can do," he told her, reading between the lines. If meeting Kennedy eased her mind, then he'd make that step for her, even if he wasn't quite ready himself.

She left on a nod, her quiet state nailing his heart. He hung his head, trapped between responsibility and possibilities. He lifted his phone to stare at Kennedy's text. How did he navigate the most important relationships in his life without hurting anyone?

A cheer went up from the TV, which was overridden by a complaint from Ben. Their Thanksgiving dinner had been a routine of habits established over the years that exemplified their family. They hadn't expanded their unit or accepted any invites of inclusion. No, they'd been happy as is, just the four of them. And now?

How would Kennedy fit? Did she want to?

There was only one way to find out.

Can you talk? He sent the text and waited. He might've been out of the dating pool for two decades, but he hadn't digressed so far that he needed an app to shield his ego if she declined.

His phone rang, sending his pulse up a notch, but he couldn't withhold his smile when he answered. "Hey."

"You wanted to *hear* the details instead of read them?" Kennedy's low purr took him straight to the bedroom.

He squeezed his eyes closed and shoved back the initial hit of lust before making his way to the garage. The door was securely closed behind him before he responded. "I'd rather see the details in person."

"Oooh. I like your way of thinking."

Yeah, so did he. But... "I actually need to ask you something." *Way to douse the fire. Good job, Matt.* His insecurities were crashing in when he'd thought he had most of them conquered.

"And that sounds serious." Gone was the sexy purr. In was the business tone. "What's up?"

He scrubbed a hand over his cheek, his beard scratching his palm in a manner that was somehow comforting. He needed to know her answer, but he didn't want to throw down a gantlet and declare an ultimatum.

"How would you feel about meeting my kids?" *Way to dump the decision in her court.* "I mean," he interjected before she could answer. He blew out a silent breath. "Let me clarify. My family was waiting for me when I came home on Sunday morning."

Her snorted laugh dragged a reluctant smile from him. Yeah, he could see the humor in it now.

"I would've paid to see that," she said.

"I bet you would've."

"What happened?"

"Well..." *Here it goes.* "I got grilled, as you would expect. And appropriately reprimanded for not responding to their texts."

"That's...nice."

He hadn't expected that or the hint of envy in her voice. "In some ways, yes. They care. I would've run them through the same ringer if they'd done it. Anyway," he rushed on before he lost focus, "now that they know about you, they're interested in meeting you."

Silence met his statement. He dropped down to sit on the doorstep, rubbing his jaw as he scrambled to salvage the mess he was making. Yet, this was who they were. They might rock in the sex department, but that didn't mean their lives were compatible.

"You've said that you don't want kids," he ventured. "And I get that. There are reasons why I chose to end any possibility of having more myself. But I do have two and they're mine full time. Their mother gave up all rights and basically walked out of their lives on a kiss and be good." It'd taken years of therapy and consistency from him and his mother to undo the harm she'd done. "Ben's sixteen. He's going to be around for a few years. I don't have the freedom a bachelor has. I want to see where this thing with us is heading, but I'll under—"

"Matt."

That single word, said in a tender tone, was all it took to stop his rambling. He squeezed his eyes closed despite the darkness that already surrounded him. Every sound seemed muffled within the walls of the garage, which overamplified the pounding of his pulse in his ears.

"Yeah?" he said when she didn't go on.

"I'd love to meet them."

He jerked up, unsure when he'd hunched over so far. Relief poured in on a wave of hope he resisted riding too high. He swallowed hard, blew out another breath. "Good. Thank you."

"You sound surprised."

He wished he could see her expression, yet there was a blessing in her not seeing his. He was certain it showed every twisting, knotted emotion within him. "I am, a bit."

"Why?" Now she sounded surprised.

He dropped his head on the door, still riding his

relief. "Kids complicate things. I wasn't sure if you wanted that."

"I'll admit to not wanting my own for that reason—among others." The last was mumbled. "But…your devotion to them is…a reflection of how you'd treat anyone important to you."

His swallow was a little thick that time, but he had no words to express how much her understanding touched him. Few took the time to look past his single-dad status to see the man beneath. To see what drove him beyond obligation.

"I'd be foolish to walk away from that possibility." Her words whispered through the line on an offer that extended his hope and opened dreams he'd thought long dead.

"Yeah?" His grin lifted his voice. His kids would probably laugh if they saw him now, but he didn't care. A weight had been lifted, and he was ready to see what was next.

"Yeah," she confirmed, her smile coming through the line. "I have to go, but let me know what you're thinking. We can make it work."

They could make it work, or at least they were going to give it a try. "Thank you, Kennedy."

"Goodbye, Matt."

He sat in the darkness for a long time after he hung up, too content to move. He savored the fresh sense of possibility lightening his every commitment. He didn't regret a single one of them, but it was nice to have something else in his life.

Something…good.

His expectations were still muted. There were a lot of unknowns and a long way to go before what they had could become more. But for now, he was going to enjoy every damn moment of just being with her.

The phone was a weight in Kennedy's hand that seemed to pull her doubts and worries out. *What did I just agree to?*

"Who was that?"

She snapped her head up, shoving away from the wall and thrusting her phone into her purse as she did. Her auto-smile locked in almost instantly. "Dani! I didn't see you there."

Her longtime friend crossed her arms, not buying an ounce of the crap she was dishing. Dani flicked her chin, looking to Kennedy's purse. "What are you hiding?"

"I'm not hiding anything." Not really.

"Riiiight." Dani dropped her disgruntled pose, which didn't go well with her outfit anyway. The dress hugged her figure without being blatantly sexy. But it was on her, like almost everything she wore. She was one of those women who could make a garbage bag glamorous.

Kennedy glanced down the hallway. It'd been empty when she'd hunted out a place to call Matt. "Did you follow me?"

"Yes." She didn't even try to deny it.

"Why?"

Her shrug tried to be dismissive, but the concern in her eyes said otherwise. "Curious, I guess."

"Curious?" Kennedy stared at her, lost. "About what?" This wasn't like her friend, at all. They didn't dig into each other's business unless they were invited. That's just how they worked.

A little smile lifted the corner of Dani's mouth.

"About what put that happy look on your face. Or should I say who?" Her smile spread. "Was it Matt?"

Kennedy looked away, embarrassed and happy at once. How had things progressed so quickly? "Maybe," she hedged, but her grin confirmed Dani's assumption.

"That's good, right?"

Was it? "Yes." And no, but she wasn't going to think about the downfalls. Not when that flutter was still going on in her chest.

Dani looped her arm through Kennedy's and started a slow stroll back to the dining room. A good six inches taller than her, Dani had an intimidation factor that her beauty only added to. Where women became jealous, men reacted with a need to conquer. Dani wanted none of it but handled all of it with a reserved grace.

"He seemed like a very nice guy," Dani offered. "Good manners. Charming if quiet. Trevor likes him."

Kennedy stopped. "Trevor?"

"Yes." Dani started walking again, forcing her to do the same. "He wouldn't have sat Matt at my table if he didn't."

"And what am I supposed to do with that?" What did Trevor have to do with anything—except everything. The man could be infuriating, but he took care of his people, and she'd been lucky enough to become one of them many years ago.

The din of the dining room stretched around the corner to reach them. That was her world. Matt had showed that he could blend into hers, but how would she do in his? What if his kids didn't like her? What if she didn't like them? Was this all a big mistake that should've ended after a single night of great sex?

"Hey." Dani nudged her. "Why the sad face? You were happy a minute ago."

"Do you ever have doubts?" she asked instead of answering.

Dani's self-deprecating laugh said it all. "Of course. Who doesn't?" She drew to a stop, turning to face Kennedy. "Take a chance, Ken. What will it hurt?"

Everything? Nothing? "Oh, my God." She dropped her head back, squeezing her eyes closed on a huff. "I'm thirty-six years old, yet I'm acting like a teenager." The prolonged silence that followed forced Kennedy to drag her eyes open to look at her friend.

"You were never like this in your teens," Dani stated.

Kennedy snorted her agreement. "Right?" She'd thought the world was hers back then and had treated it as such. She'd never been tempted by romance or the false promises it brought. Not back then. "What happened?"

"You grew up." Dani smiled at her scowl. "Sex is easy. It's the relationships that are hard."

"Which was why I stuck to sex." Her quip landed flat before it crashed. Dani wasn't letting her off that easy. She didn't know if she should be mad or grateful for that.

"You deserve more than that, Kennedy."

Did she? Sometimes she wondered. "So do you."

Dani looked away, her puff of laughter containing a dose of sarcasm. "Yeah, well, maybe that'll happen someday." Her one marriage had ended almost before it'd started, and she'd shared little on why.

They returned to the dining room on that somber note. The room was filled with people she'd known for most of her life. There were newer faces, but her mother had the details on everyone, which she updated Kennedy on regularly. She smiled and chatted and laughed when she was supposed to, but the fakeness seemed more pronounced than ever before.

When had she started to see it as fake? Maybe it wasn't. Maybe this was who they all were. She watched her mother work the room, her smile never faltering as she listened intently before commenting on whatever was said. This was her domain, and she loved it. Society was her life, and it worked for her.

Kennedy didn't begrudge her that. Not really. But tonight it highlighted what she'd worked so hard to avoid, only to wind up being a different version of the same mold. Her job in the company hadn't changed her status here. Nor had her years of uninhibited sex or defiant exhibitionism.

She was still seen as a society girl, playing in the family business until she settled down and popped out kids. Would the company ever be hers or was her dad just waiting to hand it over to her husband? And who would she hand it down to without kids of her own?

Her laugh held the dry grit of lost dreams and thoughts that had no value. She couldn't change the past or who she was, but she could manage her future. And for the first time there was a path she hadn't anticipated.

Matt was more than she'd expected and everything she'd never wanted—or was it that she thought she *couldn't* have it? But now...

Now she'd see where he led her, and maybe, just maybe, it'd turn out okay.

Chapter Twenty-One

Each step up the walkway to Kennedy's door brought a hit of nerves, worry and excitement at once. They were just having dinner—after swinging by his house for a brief introduction.

His knock on her door echoed over the small patio. Matt tucked his hands behind his back, exhaled. The door opened, Kennedy's smile confirming what he'd already known to be true. She was worth it.

"Come in." She swung the door wide. "I just need to get my coat."

"Hey," he grabbed her hand before she could run off. "Just a minute."

She turned around as he closed the door. He doubted he'd ever get over how beautiful she was. Her skirt and sweater were casually nice, her legs long and sexy. But he barely saw them. His focus was stuck on the warmth in her expression that didn't quite mask the worry beneath.

"Come here." He brought her around on a slow tug until she was in his arms. He was taken in by the vulnerability she didn't try to hide from him. It flared in her eyes and softened her in ways he couldn't pinpoint as much as sense.

He tilted his head, eyes narrowing as he brushed the backs of his fingers down her jaw, loving how her chin tilted into his touch. "It's going to be fine." She relaxed in his arms, the slight tension fleeing from her muscles.

"Is it?" She teased his hair with little strokes at the base of his skull.

He couldn't promise anything, but he hoped his words were true. They'd figure it out. God, he really hoped they'd figure it out.

His senses were alive with her sultry scent and addictive touch. Just having her in his arms was an overload of comfort and want. How could those two things mix so well? He wanted to hold her forever and ravish her at the same time.

He drew her in for the kiss he'd been aching to claim for the last week. The deep, searing one that fed on his longing and filled the need that only grew stronger. He cupped the back of her head, swiping his tongue over hers again and again until his breaths grew short. His heart pounded his desire as his dick grew thick and heavy in his slacks.

"Matt," she whispered. Desire along with that wisp of vulnerable wonder spread through the single word. It stoked his desire while diminishing the empty ache he'd smothered for so damn long. Too long.

She met him on every brush of his lips over hers, giving as much as she received. Always strong, always so damn bold. Fearless despite having fears. Could he ever match her? Be enough for her?

He backed her up to the wall, dragged a hand down her side until he could slide it beneath her sweater. Her abdomen contracted as he ran his palm over the softness that continued to tempt him. Everything about her tempted him.

To dive in. To take. To give. To get lost in all that she was.

She arched into his touch. Her moan trembled over his lips when she drew him closer. "How do you do this?" she mumbled between kisses. A lazy sense of ease permeated the slow exploration, reinforcing the bond that'd drawn them together and continued to tighten.

He kissed up her jaw, reaching the sensitive shell of her ear. "Do what?" Her head tilted to give him the space he needed to follow her neck downward. He drew aside the higher collar on her sweater until the fading bruise from his bite mark was exposed.

He ran his finger over it. Her breath hitched. "Does it hurt?"

"No." That blue that he loved in her eyes added a truth to her answer. "Not too much." Meaning it had, and she'd never said a word.

He brushed a kiss over it, using his tongue to savor both the impression and the salty hint of her skin. That little mark represented so much and nothing at all. But she'd begged for it. Came with it. She wanted something from it, but not everything. Neither did he. They could manage it. Take what they needed and leave the rest.

Her gasp floated over his head when he squatted before her. He watched her through the slow rise of his hands up her thighs until her skirt was bunched around her hips.

"Now?" The arch of her brow was almost a dare. One he couldn't pass up, not that he wanted to.

He leaned in to take a long draw of her musky scent. Still slight, still haunting enough to have him salivating for a taste. A silky swath of pink hid her secrets, but he knew them well. How her lips were a dark shade of rose and her clit a slightly elongated nub that hardened so beautifully beneath his touch.

Her hand settled on his head, not directing, just waiting. He glanced up, drawing a finger along the edge of her panties. Her legs inched wider when he reached between them, her mouth parting on an inhalation.

"I had to scrub my beard three times to get your scent out of it." He ran his finger through her folds, groaning at the wetness that greeted him. "And then I missed it." Those little catches of dark musk that'd sent him straight back to their night.

"Maybe you shouldn't be such a sloppy eater." Her mouth quirked, her smile simmering beneath.

His laugh crashed against his lips. He held it back for a beat before it burst free. "Oh, my God." He laid his forehead on her hip, which jerked from her laughter. This right here, this would've never happened with his ex. She wouldn't have dared to snark, let alone think about such a comeback.

He laid a kiss on the side of her hip. Slid his finger over her clit in a tease that cut her laughter short. The slick folds embraced his finger as he eased it down to dip deep into her heat. Her legs dipped. Her hand tightened on his head.

Desire crashed against logic, but then it'd been doing that since he'd met her. His dick was a hard reminder of why he continued to ignore what he'd once claimed as his greatest asset. Logic had no place in lust or love—

But it did have a place when there were people waiting on them.

He removed his finger, taking a moment to suck it

clean before he settled her skirt back around her legs. His thighs burned and his knees protested when he straightened, providing a distinct reminder of his age—which came with those damn responsibilities.

Her scowl was almost comical. He flicked his brows up.

"You better finish that later." She hauled him in for a hot, quick kiss before she stalked away. "I'm going to fix my lipstick."

His grin stretched his cheeks and eased into his heart. There was the fire he wanted to see. He treasured her softness and the vulnerability that came with it, but she didn't need that now. Not when she was meeting his kids for the first time.

Her confidence was on full display when she stepped from the bathroom. Her posture contained that same bold certainty she'd presented at the benefit. Her freckles provided the only hint to the innocence that lay beneath. She'd probably claim she had none, but she'd be wrong. He'd never counter her belief, but he'd do what he could to show her that love didn't have to hurt.

Did he love her? That was twice now that it'd entered his thoughts.

"Ready?" he asked.

"I was ready before, but somebody had to mess up my makeup." Her scowl was all tease. She grabbed a coat from the closet, and he helped her into it, letting his hands linger on her shoulders.

"I'm having a hard time feeling guilty about that."

She turned her head, her side-glance one of speculation. "Then maybe you shouldn't."

"No?"

He offered her his arm and led her out the door,

that warm sense of belonging filling every corner and crack within him. Kennedy brightened his life simply by being her. Did he love her? It was still too soon to lock into that, but he had enough miles behind him to know he was fortunate to have found her.

And he wasn't going to waste the opportunity.

Chapter Twenty-Two

The semidetached house sat on a street lined with similar yet distinctly different homes. The potential uniformity was offset by the variance in paint colors, roof lines and window décor that made each place unique, unlike her townhome.

Matt pulled into the driveway. A face popped into the front window, but it disappeared just as quickly. Lights blazed from within, giving it a warm feel against the night. The house's yellow color would probably be welcoming during the day, the white trim sharp.

"This is it," Matt said. He turned off the car, the engine ticking in low beats.

"It's cute," she told him honestly. She'd never been to this part of Daly City. Actually, she'd been to very little of it outside of driving past the exit on her way to San Francisco. But she meant what she said. The little house might be smaller than any she'd lived in, but it looked like a home.

She let her honesty show when she smiled at Matt. "I can't wait to see the inside." He'd told her about how he'd slowly remodeled it since he'd purchased it ten years ago. She imagined he'd given it the same focused dedication he applied to everything he did.

He leaned over to give her a quick kiss. "We won't stay long."

"It's fine." Her reassurance seemed to graze off him. "I won't bite them." That got a quirk of his lips. "Or share my sex toys with your daughter. I promise."

His chuckle rumbled through the car as he pulled her in to kiss her temple. "For future reference, the words *sex* and *my daughter* don't belong in the same sentence."

"You do realize—"

"Yes. I do. And we've had all the talks and she's on the pill, but I don't need the images or the details."

She nodded long and slow. "Got it." She certainly didn't want to think about her parents doing—nope. "Should we go in?"

He glanced at the house. "We could still sneak away."

"I think we were spotted before you stopped the car."

"Right." He hung his head in mock defeat. "Then I guess we better go."

She appreciated his attempt at lightness. It helped, just like the kiss, foreplay and quick shot of control at her place had. A large dose of her nerves had vanished beneath his consuming assault that'd ended with her panties wet and lipstick smudged. The excited edge he'd built still lingered beside the steady comfort that flowed from him.

He led her to the front door, his hand on her lower back providing reassurance she hadn't known she needed. She was a pro at meeting new people, but no meeting had ever felt as important as this one.

Her stomach flipped as he opened the door. Her first impression was of cozy comfort. Deep-cushioned sofas, warm tones of browns and beige accented with pops of sage in the pillows. The hardwood gleamed beneath her heels, but a few scuff marks and scratches high-lighted its wear.

Evidence of people was spread throughout the room. Family photos lined one wall. A blanket was tossed randomly on the recliner. A sweatshirt lay across the back of the couch. Shoes were tucked along the wall by the entry. A half-empty glass of soda sat on an end table next to a stack of magazines. There were text books on the coffee table along with an open notebook and calculator.

She'd been right. This was a home. It wrapped around her in a welcoming hold that shoved some of her concerns aside while raising new ones. She had no idea how to fit into this environment.

It didn't take a ton of smarts to understand that the three people standing in the archway leading to the dining room, every one of them openly assessing her, would see straight through a fake smile or blithe come-back. She was being judged and weighed on her accept-ability for their dad. She got that, liked it even. Wealth and connections were the two biggest factors on her family's suitor checklist. Those items wouldn't even make it on the list for Matt's family.

"Hey, guys," Matt said as he took her coat and laid it over the corner of the couch. She set her purse on top of it and let him take her hand as he led her the few steps it took to stand before his family.

"Ben, Dawn, Mom. This is Kennedy." Pride threaded through his voice, not fading a bit on her name. "Ken-nedy, this is my family. My son, Ben. Daughter, Dawn, and my mother, Roselyn."

Each of them greeted her with varying degrees of warmth. She stepped up to Matt's mom, tackling the most welcoming smile first. "Mrs. Hamilton. It's a plea-sure to meet you."

His mother's handshake contained the same effi-ciency she presented, much like her son. Gray hair cut short on the sides and back with a longer side part that complimented her features but wouldn't take work. A blue sweater, cotton pants and minimal makeup com-pleted her look that was simple but nice.

"Likewise," she answered.

Kennedy transitioned to his kids on the next beat. "Matt's told me about you both," she said, taking in the two of them. She could see Matt in them, especially Ben. He had the same strong bearing, square jaw and dark hair of his father. His face still had the freshness of youth, but he was already handsome.

Dawn extended her hand, a stiffness present in her movements. "Hi. Thank you for coming over." The sweetness in her voice brought back memories of free-dom, parties and life before it was loaded with responsi-bilities. Even with her hair pulled into a ponytail and her baggy sweatshirt hiding her figure, she was a beauty. A wide mouth, big eyes, strong features that were also soft, made his daughter stand out.

"Thank you for having me," Kennedy said, putting warmth in her voice. "I was looking forward to meeting all of you." She spoke the truth. She wanted to know these people who meant so much to Matt.

"So where are you headed tonight?" His mother asked before the silence became awkward.

"We have reservations in the city." Matt left it at that. He rubbed a hand over the small of her back. "Don't stay out too late." He spoke to Dawn, but his gaze cov-ered Ben too.

"I won't." Dawn reassured him. "Maybe you shouldn't either."

Kennedy's eyes widened before she could stop her surprise. She didn't even try to hold back her smile.

"I'll be home before you wake up." He leveled a firm eye at his daughter. "And no, you don't have to wait up for me."

Ben barked a sharp laugh. "I told her that last time."

Dawn's glare would've inflicted damage if it'd been possible. "At least I cared enough to be worried."

"I'll text you later," Matt jumped in before Ben could respond. "Are Pat and John still coming over?" He looked to Ben who nodded. "Are they spending the night?"

"Nah. They'll head home."

"Wrap it up before midnight, then."

Ben gave him the thumbs up. "Got it."

"What do you do?" Dawn asked her when Matt had obviously been winding the introductions to an end.

Kennedy gave Dawn her full attention, aware that she was still being appraised. "I'm the VP of Operations at Keller Pallet."

"You are?" Her surprise was clear. "Where'd you go to school?"

"I received my BS and MBA from Stanford." She could've gone anywhere in the country, yet she'd chosen to stay close to home so she could remain connected to the family business. She'd worked her entire way through college, despite her father's insistence that it wasn't necessary.

"Ha!" Ben grinned at his dad. "She's probably smarter than you."

Matt assessed her, his smirk teasing. "I'm pretty sure you're right about that."

She gave him a playful nudge. "We'll have to test that out someday."

"We need to head out if we're going to make our reservation," Matt said. He gave his mother a kiss on the cheek. "Thanks for coming over."

Love glowed from Roselyn even though she only patted him on the arm. "Enjoy yourself tonight."

Ben gave another half-snort that was cut short when Dawn elbowed him in the ribs. He flinched, his grin wide as he rubbed the sore spot. They might spar like siblings, but they obviously cared about each other. The whole family was one big bundle of connection and love that both dragged her in and shoved her out.

"You two be good and have fun." He gave his daughter a hug and Ben an odd arrangement of fist bumps and handgrips that Kennedy had no chance of ever replicating.

"It was nice meeting all of you," she told them, feeling like she was on a reverse prom date, something she never imagined. She said that a lot when it came to Matt.

They left with little fanfare. Ben took off down the hall. His mother went into the kitchen and Dawn slumped onto the couch, flicking the TV on. That was it. The ending was anticlimactic and completely normal, apparently.

Her laughter bubbled free when they stepped outside.

"What?" Matt asked, slowing.

She wrapped an arm around his waist, leaning in. "That was unlike any family meeting I've ever had."

He shot her a look as he opened the car door for her. "Is that good or bad?"

"Good." Very good. No pretenses. No show of formality and manners with drinks and small talk and polite exchanges with the appropriate name-dropping. Nope. Just honest love and concern all around.

Matt still had that curious look on his face when he got in the car. "Are you okay?"

She studied him, the darkness providing a softness broken by the streetlights. He was back in a suit tonight, minus a tie. He'd trimmed his beard down to a shadow. Would it still trap her scent? Would it scratch on her inner thighs?

"Yeah. I'm fine." Better than, actually. "You have a nice family." And he'd introduced her to them. That was big for him—for all of them. She hadn't realized how much until she'd seen their family unit in action.

Love beamed in his gentle smile. He glanced at the house. "Yeah." His easy agreement hid the concerns he'd talked about on the ride up. The ones about Dawn's growing freedom and how he worried about Ben. About letting go when his instinct was to hang on.

"You're doing an excellent job with them." He didn't need her assessment, but she doubted he got a lot of positive reinforcement given that most parents rarely did—or so she'd been told.

His kiss said thank you for more than her compliment. It soothed through her on that ever-growing whisper of trust that freed too many hopes and even more dreams. The flutter in her heart spoke of things she had a hard time accepting but was further from denying.

He held her hand as they drove to the city, his strength a silent promise she was coming to rely on. That should've had her running, but Matt wasn't looking to manipulate or use her, like so many men had thought they could do.

"I was thinking of heading over to Half Moon Bay on Sunday," he said. "I was hoping you'd want to join me."

And just like that, her weekend plans had changed. "That sounds nice."

Being with Matt made her happy in a way she couldn't quite define yet didn't want to lose. Being with him was almost too easy. Why? What about him worked so well with her?

She ran her thumb over his knuckles, letting her worries go. They had the whole night ahead, which would hopefully end in her bedroom again, and now a day at the beach too. And all of it sounded…good. Really, really good.

Chapter Twenty-Three

"You add the cheese next." Matt laid the slices of mozzarella over the cottage cheese layer with a serious precision. His brow was furrowed, that dedication of his applied even to this.

Kennedy leaned into him, amused. "You don't have to teach me how to cook."

"You know how to make lasagna?"

"I can cook." Her defenses went up, but only a little and more as an auto response.

"Such as?"

She propped her hip against the counter, snubbing his doubt. "I'm stellar at warming up meals and mixing bag salads. I can even master a sandwich if needed."

He stopped mid sauce scoop. "That is not cooking."

"Then what is it?" She snagged a small crumble of mozzarella cheese from the cutting board and popped it into her mouth. Their friendly banter had become a normal part of their relationship over the past few weeks. From hiking to shopping to movies, they tackled their differing perspectives with a bit of humor and mock disbelief.

"Surviving." He spread the meat sauce over the cheese layers with quick efficiency before laying more noodles down. "Cooking involves the actual act of combining ingredients to make a dish that is pleasant to eat after it's heated."

She fully agreed with him. She'd just never had the need to do it herself. Her meals were delivered already assembled and ready to pop in the oven. "And you're doing a fabulous job of it."

"Here." He held out the bowl with the cheese mixture in it.

"I'm good," she insisted. "Really." She snagged her glass of wine from the counter, lifting it to him. "My hands are full right now."

He shook his head in an exaggerated fashion, but she caught the smile beneath his bewilderment.

She stole a quick kiss that left a nice tingle on her lips before she wandered to the other side of the peninsula. Matt's kitchen had that same cozy feeling that permeated the entire house. Dark wood cabinets were softened by the quartz countertops and stainless-steel appliances. Apparently, he'd done the work himself, with the help of some friends. That impressed her the most.

"Is there anything you can't do?" she asked, musing.

"I can't give birth." His comeback was quick and given without a hitch in his assembly process.

She stared at him for a moment before her laughter broke free. "Good one."

He shot her a wink as he wiped his hands on a towel. His back muscles flexed beneath his T-shirt when he ripped a sheet of tinfoil off and wrapped it over the finished pan of lasagna. Her smile grew when he bent to put the pan in the oven. His ass was perfection. Round, firm and tucked so nicely into his jeans. The fact that he also looked that good in a suit made him a very dangerous man. He'd be deadly if he had any idea how handsome he was.

"That'll be done in an hour," he said as he came around the peninsula. That predatory thing of his emanated from every pore. He trapped her against the counter and set her wine glass aside.

"What are you doing, Mr. Hamilton?"

He eased a hand around the side of her neck to her nape in a fashion that was now so familiar. She closed her eyes, savoring the odd mix of belonging and comfort that came with that simple touch, one that was both possessive and soft.

"I'm kissing you." His low tone teased her with what was coming.

"Is that so?"

"Yes." Smoky heat filtered from his voice to his eyes and transferred into the kiss. Her knees went weak almost immediately beneath the slow strokes and gentle touch.

She let herself drift in the desire he created with just a look, a touch, a smile. Warmth built in a gentle wave that spread from her chest outward. She'd given up trying to explain it, simply following now.

He lifted her onto the counter in one easy motion. She wrapped her legs around him, the kiss continuing at the same languid pace that had the world spinning out until there was only him. Her breath merged with his on every swirl of his tongue and each little nip, the sting fading beneath the tenderness that flowed with each brush of his lips.

He drew her closer until her crotch rode the hard line of his erection. Their jeans created a barrier that had her cursing her choice of clothing. Yet the lazy build wound its way deeper until her entire body hovered on a slow simmer of anticipation.

"Matt," she whispered, dragging her nails down his nape to chase the line of his spine. He rocked into her, his breaths deepening. She wanted him. She always wanted him. It didn't matter where or when, she wanted to crawl inside him and never leave his side.

"I could take you here," he mumbled along her jaw, his palm scraping over her ribs, his calluses as intriguing as him. He was more than he presented, but then so was she.

And he saw that. He understood that. And he still liked what he found.

As did she.

She dropped her head back, reveling in the swirl of his tongue and hot kisses he trailed down her throat, the ache building in her groin. "What about your neighbors?" She ran the base of her palm down the hard outline of his dick, not at all gentle.

She could still be that way with him. Demanding, teasing, direct when she'd once feared that giving away even an ounce of her control would strip her of all power. But it hadn't. Not sexually or otherwise.

He nipped the tender skin on her neck, but she only hummed as the sting slithered south. He slid the edge of her bra aside, flicked her nipple. Sensation flared in a sharp dig before it spread over her chest in a rush of tingles. She arched into his touch, silently begging for more.

He could fuck her right there and she wouldn't care. She was that gone with him.

"They'd get quite the show." He pulled on her nipple to emphasize his point. Logically, she knew they were both still covered, but she felt totally exposed. More so than she ever had on any boardroom table.

"I thought you didn't like shows."

"I loved yours." He drew back, his hand falling away from her breast. His lids were heavy, eyes dark with hunger. He'd only seen that one show of hers, in the Boardroom. The one that'd changed so much. She hadn't been back since.

She didn't need to go back. Not when Matt gave her so much more.

"I could give you another," she offered, letting her voice fall to a husky purr.

His mouth cocked up at one corner, speculation flaring. He hauled her off the counter and was leading her out of the kitchen almost before she'd processed that they were moving. Her laughter came out in a tumble that lifted her higher, her chest expanding with the joy.

This right here. This light, playful flirting was so much more than she'd expected. Matt had given her a side of romance she hadn't believed in. But here it was, dancing on her heart and lightening her life.

She barely noticed his bedroom before she was wrapped back in his arms, his mouth claiming hers. She moaned into the kiss, hungry for more. Her lust blazed into full need. God, she couldn't get close enough, touch enough, taste enough.

What had he done to her?

She'd been embracing her sexuality since her first forays into sex. But this was deeper than sex, more than simple physical release or power displays.

She was falling for him—*had* fallen for him—with barely a struggle or flinch. Every second thought had been silenced by this crazy, soothing flood of peace. Of joy and exhilaration. Of fear and excitement and love.

Love.

Oh, God.

How did that happen? When? Her instant flash of panic chilled her. She drew back, suddenly uncertain when everything had been so clear just a moment ago.

His eyes narrowed, head tilting. "What?"

She softened the second his look registered, even before he brushed his fingers down her jaw in yet another action she'd grown to treasure. It triggered a response she couldn't fathom, the one that had her opening to him, trusting what he'd never abused.

This was him. This caring, concerned man. But he was also strong, commanding, possessive yet not obsessive. Could she really love him?

Her heart pounded her answer. It beat at that point on her neck and raced up in a wave of warmth that blew past her cheeks to engulf her entire body.

"What's going on?" His worry touched that spot buried deep beneath her layers of self-reliance. He truly cared. He wanted to help. He…what?

He was a man of commitment. She'd known that almost from the start. He'd stated his intent long before she'd accepted it.

"Are you sure Ben is gone for the night?" She took the easy out. Talking about the scrambled swell of emotions balled in her chest wasn't going to happen. She could master them—or ignore them. But spilling them? Not a chance.

Relief dropped over his face, his smirk taking on a darker edge. He drew her shirt up, slipping it over her head with no resistance from her. His gaze dropped to her breasts as he cupped one, lifting it. "I'm very sure."

She let his desire fuel her own. This she could control.

She drew a hand down his chest to the hard line of his dick beneath his jeans. Her slow caress of his erection was meant to tease. "Are you going to fuck me?" There was the power she claimed. The right to own what she wanted. To declare and take it.

Yet…

It'd never been about *just* that with Matt. Not even the first time.

He hitched her forward by the waist of her jeans. Her mouth fell open, but no sound escaped. His eyes were darkened swirls of all things naughty and fun. He fisted her hair in his hand, drew her head back until her mouth was lifted to his.

Yes. Please. This. The words pulsed in her mind, building with the truth. This right here was his to claim. If he wanted it.

"I'm going to do so much more than fuck you." His promise came out with a harshness that was somehow tender too. What did he mean? Could she trust it? Him?

She had so far.

Matt drew a naked Kennedy down, her skin scorching his everywhere they touched. He kissed her with the same passionate wonder that continued to stun him. This woman, this amazingly strong yet tender woman was still with him.

Want powered beside an urgency that had nothing to do with the timer ticking down on the lasagna. It left him scrambling to define what he refused to box in.

This, what they had and were building, altered every belief he'd laid down after his ex-wife.

He rolled until she was trapped beneath him. Her surprise fled on a sigh that rippled down him. His dick ached for her heat. His heart wanted so much more.

The low glow from the hallway provided enough light to catch her expression, one that shifted from cunning to lust-filled to lost in a matter of moments. He rocked his hips, embracing the desire as his dick rode the firm edge of her mound.

"Matt."

The breathy plea in his name had become her calling card. She urged him on, her nails cutting a path across his shoulders, her hips lifting in time with his. He gave her what she wanted, while taking what she gave.

She'd teased him about a show, and damn how he'd enjoyed the one he'd seen. But what she really wanted from him—what she'd always wanted—was to let go. For him to take her where she'd never trusted enough to go before.

And damn how he loved that. Loved her trust. Loved her sexual ownership. Loved her strength and softness. Loved her.

Her. Kennedy Keller.

He loved every goddamn inch of her, inside and out, but she wasn't ready to hear that. Not yet. But he could show her—would show her.

Every nip on her neck, each hard suck on her nipples, the firm holds and silent demands were his declarations to her, her cries his reward. He scraped his teeth down her neck, drew her legs up so he could tease her cunt with his dick. She arched up, begged for more but never took it. Not now.

"You're so damn hot," he murmured against her lips before he swept his tongue in. Her wet folds cradled his dick in a temptation so maddening he barely withheld the urgency building in his groin. It burned so damn hot, yet he let it grow, bringing her higher as he held back his own release.

He could flip her onto her stomach, drive in hard and fast, take what she gave while cherishing every second. But she didn't need the force tonight and neither did he. Not that kind.

He lifted up, his arms shaking with his restraint as he eased himself into her. Her lips parted, eyelids falling with each inch that slid into her. Warmth and softness hugged his dick with the erotic sensation that could never be replicated. Her walls contracted, hips lifting to bring him deeper.

She watched him under hooded lids, the blue of her eyes sparked with dark lust and something he longed for yet couldn't quite believe. He held there, connected in the most physical way possible, but that alone didn't make it intimate. No, it was the tenderness spreading in his heart and the high that hummed their connection and bound them together.

Rightness curled up his spine to snap his control. He rose to his knees, holding her hips up so he could watch his dick slide in and out of her. She gripped the bedding and wrapped her legs around his waist, passion wiping out the innocence her freckles tried to project.

Power raced on a rush of adrenaline and authority. He had no command over her, which made her gift so much more addictive. She was his to have. His to drive wild. His to possess.

The thrill of that tore through him to demolish his

good intentions. He drove into her until his thighs burned and his arms struggled to hold her still as she twisted and arched, lost in her desire.

"Kennedy." Fucking… "Your cunt is so damn tight." Her walls clenched around him, ripping a guttural groan from deep in his chest. "Do it again."

She complied immediately, a devilish gleam in her eyes. That was the fire that drove him.

That underlying strength that never left her. Even now.

He dropped down, wrapping her in his arms. Her breasts pressed against his chest, her legs remained around his hips as she dragged him even closer. Tighter. Until there was nothing between.

Nothing.

His heart thundered its wants and fed his dreams. He nuzzled her neck, hunger darkening his sight. It shattered everything except the unrelenting drive to fulfill her need. To give her what she craved while keeping her his.

His. She was so damn his, even if she was scared to acknowledge it.

Her skin was tender beneath his lips. Salty. Ripe. She tilted her head to the side. He thrust hard. Again. And again. Her muscles convulsed, tensed.

His sweet, sweet Kennedy.

He clamped down on the juncture of her neck and shoulder, holding tight when her cry pierced the air. Her pussy gripped him, stroking his dick in undeniable confirmation of their power. The two of them.

His release tore through him in a savage declaration of trembling muscles and unrelenting relief that threatened to drown him. Her whimpers mellowed into a sigh, bringing him back to the woman in his arms.

He pressed his lips to the spot he'd just marked. That wonderfully tempting spot on her neck that bruised so beautifully. Yeah, he liked that. He liked seeing his claim stated so boldly. Liked knowing that she did too.

That dynamic only strengthened what they had, instead of hurting it. And it stayed within the limits they'd both set. It worked. They worked. He'd withheld that side of himself for years out of fear, now he couldn't imagine their relationship without it.

He drifted in the afterglow, getting lost in the long, lazy kisses that tasted of lethargy and contentment. What they'd just shared had been so much more than a fuck. He honestly didn't know if he'd ever simply fucked her. Not Kennedy.

And he was going to keep showing her how good they could be until she accepted the truth of what they shared. He was just as much hers at this point. Maybe more than was good for him, but he couldn't change who he was. When he gave, he did it wholeheartedly, and Kennedy had his heart.

Now she just needed to claim it.

Chapter Twenty-Four

"I'm here to see Ms. Keller," Matt told the receptionist.

"Hi, Mr. Hamilton." The young woman flashed a smile, a cheekiness underlying her professionalism. "You're looking nice today."

He glanced down at his suit. "I have a meeting."

"Oh!" She straightened, switching into full business decorum. "I'm sorry. I thought you were taking her to lunch again."

"I think coffee would be more appropriate right now." Given it was only nine in the morning. They might've had more than a few lunch dates since that first one, but they were both too busy to take three-hour lunches.

A blush rose up the receptionist's neck in a steady flow that quickly engulfed her cheeks. She ducked her head. "I'll let her know you're here."

Matt placed the woman somewhere in her early twenties. Her first job maybe? Or was she connected to the Kellers somehow? Anyway, he hadn't meant to make her self-conscious. "Thank you, Susan."

She blushed even deeper, and he moved away before the poor girl went up in flames. He stood by the door where he usually waited for Kennedy, the lobby empty except for him. He shifted his briefcase to his other hand and ran through the contract details in his head. The two of them had been floating the idea of how their businesses could help each other, but he hadn't expected a deal to come through so quickly. He wouldn't turn the work down or the opportunities it'd open. However, he wasn't looking forward to the negotiations ahead.

Separating pleasure and business was never fun, but he'd done plenty of work with men he considered friends. They could manage this.

"Matt." Kennedy entered the lobby, a warm but professional smile in place. "Thank you for coming over." She extended her hand.

He fell into business mode with zero effort or affront. "My pleasure." Their handshake was nothing more than the standard efficient pump and release, yet her touch lingered in a reminder of how it could warm his palm when they strolled down the street or beach.

"My father's waiting in the boardroom."

She turned around without a hint of reaction to her words, but his own stomach dipped at the memory of his only trip to the Boardroom. The boardroom in this building. His groin tightened, lust flaring.

He gritted his teeth and slammed a wall down on the images of Kennedy spread naked on the glossy table, of him sliding that lifelike vibrator into her. Yet they didn't diminish as he followed her up the stairs and down the same hall he'd trekked only once before.

He hadn't given a thought to exactly where their meeting would take place. And now…he'd have to pretend he'd never seen Ray Keller's daughter getting off on his fingers precisely where her father sat at the head of the table.

Good fucking chance of that happening.

"Mr. Keller," Matt said, stepping up to greet the man who had the power to tank the contract—and potentially his relationship with Kennedy. "It's a pleasure to see you again."

Ray gave him the same unbending glare his daughter could level. "I'm hoping I'll be able to say the same thing."

Let the games begin. Matt chuckled appropriately, while realigning his tactics.

"I'm sure we'll all be pleased with the outcome," Kennedy interjected, breezing over the tension with grace. "I asked Thad to join us since he closed the Calloway deal and has the best understanding of their expectations." She turned to the older gentleman seated next to Ray. "This is Matt Hamilton, owner of McPherson Trucking."

Matt greeted Thad, who appeared to be close to Ray in age, but his persona was all affable salesman as opposed to hardass owner. He took a seat next to Kennedy, who sat in the free chair next to her father. The three of them presented a cohesive unit Matt had to navigate to land the lucrative contract Kennedy had presented.

This was a prime example of connections landing deals better than any amount of cold calls or convention finagling. A part of him hated this side of his job, but another part of him thrived in the analytical gameplay.

Ray flipped the folder open before him, effectively starting the meeting. "These rates are too damn high." And they were off.

The next hour was spent haggling over mileage, weight, rates, drivers, liability and almost every term in the contract. But the short of it was Keller needed more trucks to deliver the ongoing order of pallets Calloway needed and they didn't have the means to do so. His lawyer had combed through every detail and would do so again before he signed the final agreement, but they were making headway here.

"When is Calloway expecting the first shipment?" Matt asked when Ray continued to lowball the deal, which was already a bargain as far as Matt was concerned.

Ray's scowl said it all. Matt already knew the answer and it didn't give them much time to find a company who could fulfill the deliveries for them. They didn't have the trucks themselves, and their resources were focused on increasing production to meet the new demand.

"You're not the only trucking company in the area," Ray stated, like the fact wasn't common knowledge.

"But I'm the one who's here with the available trucks and the manpower ready to meet your demand."

Ray's scowl deepened. "What kind of business can you have if that's true?"

Matt looked him in the eye, refusing to flinch in the face of the benign insult. "One I've been prepping for an opportunity such as this." He sat back, casting his gaze over the three of them. "We're ready to grow, just like you are. I believe we can do so together, but those numbers are set for me." He was done haggling and playing the game. "I can't go any lower." Not if he wanted to maintain his profit margin.

"All right," Kennedy said into the stalemate. "We're both looking to expand. Calloway is our first venture into the LA area. We negotiated the pallet recycling requirement into the deal so you're not driving back empty trucks."

"And a deal between us wouldn't be possible without that." He nodded to Thad, who'd been basically quiet through the entire meeting.

"Which is why we included it," Kennedy interjected. Her glare held an annoyed flare along with a hint of anger. "I was fully aware that no one can make a profit driving empty trucks around. The cost hike would've blown any benefit we're trying to gain." Irritation bled through her tone and punctuated each word.

His need to help flared up so quickly, Matt didn't even think to halt it. Kennedy was upset and it appeared to be at him. His eyes narrowed, head tilting a notch. He moved his hand without thought, intending to stroke her jaw in that way that soothed her.

She stiffened, her eyes widening before they closed. Briefly. For less than a second. But that was all it took.

"Kennedy." Ray's reprimand crashed through the room to smack his daughter before it ricocheted off her and onto Matt.

He dropped his hand, fisting it so tightly in his lap his knuckles ached. Bile soured in his throat the instant understanding took hold, but it was too late. He'd just shifted into control mode, and she'd responded. Right there. In the middle of the damn meeting.

In front of her father.

Sweat beaded down his back as his mortification took hold. No. Just no. He would never do that to her— yet he had.

Kennedy swallowed, a stiff smile forming. She looked to her father as an icy control took over, making every movement appear stiff. "Did I misspeak?"

Matt could only sit there, thoughts reeling, a clammy sweat coating his back, lost in the turmoil tearing down every belief he'd indulged in over the last few months. He couldn't trust himself. Not with this. Not with that fucking power game. The edge, that damn desire to control, drove him to excel, but it'd also driven his ex-wife to want more.

Kennedy wasn't his ex. But…

Ray sniffed, his disapproval radiating so clearly, he didn't need to clarify it. Thad leaned forward, his gentle manner sliding in to interrupt the silent standoff taking place between father and daughter.

"I believe the terms of our agreement with Calloway, as well as the ones we're currently discussing with McPherson, are beneficial to *all* parties." His smile appeared calm, yet the lines around his mouth were tenser than they'd been before. "No one is stating otherwise. So how about we let this breathe for a day and we'll get back to you, Matt?"

"We don't need to let it breathe," Ray countered. "At least I don't." He flipped his folder closed before he stood. His curt demeanor would've been abrasive to most, but Matt had experienced worse in the military. Ray was the top of the Keller enterprise, and he held his power over every aspect of the company.

Matt had just demoted Kennedy in the eyes of her father.

His stomach heaved. His tie seemed to constrict around his throat. The strength he'd gleaned from this faux uniform, that sense of authority and position, threatened to choke him now. What had he done?

"I'll have legal fix what we agreed to and send over the amended contract to you ASAP. We'll give this a six-month trial. Hopefully, with good results." Ray nodded to Matt, which was clearly his signal to respond.

Matt slowly stood, his composure falling into place on pure habit. *Never flinch. Never buckle under a direct attack—no matter how messed up you are inside.*

"I look forward to doing business with you." His voice sounded flat in his ears, but he couldn't inject an ounce of pleasure into it. Not when Kennedy refused to look at him. Her eyes were focused out the window, that stiff smile barely hanging on.

He'd done that to her.

Ray came around Kennedy's chair to shake Matt's hand. He landed a hard slap to Matt's arm in an attempt at camaraderie that fell flat. "Good. Let's make this work for both of us." He strode from the room, completely unware or uncaring of the wreckage he'd left behind.

Kennedy slowly shoved her chair back before she rose. "I'm glad we worked that out." She picked up her folders, clutching them a bit too firmly. "I have another meeting to get to." Her apology was flashed to Matt in the form of a false smile. "Thad, do you mind seeing Matt out for me?"

"Sure."

Thad had barely responded before Kennedy was passing Matt on her way to the door.

Guilt tore at him, and he tried to apologize. "Kenne—"

"Thank you." She cut him off, her words sent to Thad before she left.

Her dismissal was as harsh and cold as the one her father had flung at her. The chill built in his chest and spread outward until everything was numb. His heart. His thoughts. His emotions. Responding was impossible and inappropriate in the moment, so he simply moved forward.

Thad came around the table as Matt placed his notes in his briefcase. "I, ah—"

"Don't worry about it." He didn't want Thad to explain or apologize for a situation he hadn't created. Matt strode from the room, unable to engage in small talk and pleasantries. He didn't need an escort to find his way out, but Thad still trudged behind him.

"Matt."

The question in Thad's voice caught him in the stairwell. *Fuck.* His urgency to get the hell out was overridden by the manners hounded into him by his mother. The salesman had nothing to do with anything that'd gone down. He'd tried to keep the peace and had quite possibly salvaged the deal with his one mediation.

Matt stopped on the landing, choking back the anger he could only point at himself. That strangling sensation returned with a force, clenching down on his throat until he wanted to tear off his tie along with his coat and shirt and every piece of clothing that declared the authority he had no right to have.

He forced himself to turn to Thad. His slower pace and wince highlighted his age and dropped another nail into Matt's guilt coffin. Thad leaned on the railing as he took the last steps down to the landing.

"Sorry about that," he said with a grimace. "My knees aren't as agile as they once were."

Matt hadn't even thought about the elevator since Kennedy had never taken it. "Sorry. I wasn't aware." Or thinking of anything except getting the hell out.

"I'm fine." He waved off Matt's piss-poor apology.

"I just wanted to check if everything was good on your side."

Matt almost snorted at that. Right. "I'm good," he managed to say without scoffing. "We'll sign the contract if the terms come back as we agreed to in the meeting."

"Good." His smile should've been pleased, yet it lacked the warmth required to make it so. He shoved his hands into his pockets, his suit coat tucked behind his arms. The whole kindly elder vibe of his cracked slightly. He glanced up the stairwell. "I probably shouldn't say this, but Kennedy is the true backbone of the company. She outlined and fought for every item in the Calloway deal, including the recycling item."

He looked away, unable to meet the eyes of the far-too-astute man. "I don't doubt it. She's an intelligent woman." And he'd ripped that away from her when he'd directed his praise to Thad.

"She is. Strong too." Thad went silent, forcing Matt to look at him. Understanding was layered in eyes aged by time and wisdom. "The rumor mill's been working overtime about you and Kennedy. I don't know the details, but I do know she's been happier since you started taking her to lunch."

Excellent. And he'd just burned her before the one person she tried to impress the most. "Your point is?" Matt asked, voice flat. Shame at being lectured by a man he didn't know stung his pride and soured his stomach even more, but he'd earned every word.

"My point is…" Thad's tone hardened. "Her father rides her hard because he wants to see her succeed in an industry that has little respect for women in it. And she spends every damn second of her day trying to earn what is freely given to most men. I'd hoped that you understood that. Just like I hope you'll think about what happened back there and then fix it."

Matt studied him, wanting to be annoyed at his overstep, yet humbled by the truth, and by Thad's concern for Kennedy. "And who are you, exactly?"

Thad's shrug was a nod to casual that didn't quite make it. "Just a guy who's been working here since Kennedy started showing up with her father, asking questions no ten-year-old should be concerned about. Like how the production line worked, and pallet sizes, wood and sales channels, you name it. Her curiosity only increased as she grew. She loves this company, and most of the people here feel the same about her."

He turned around, starting up the stairs before he paused. "I assume you can find your way out. You appear to know your way around."

Matt stared at his retreating back, too floored to do more. Shame was now a close intimate friend that burned in his throat and ate at his honor. It'd been a long time since he'd been so properly schooled. It didn't help the emotions tearing apart his heart, but he appreciated the message, even if it hadn't been necessary.

He'd just fucked up the best relationship he'd ever had. He'd hurt Kennedy and undercut her in front of her father. But worst of all, he'd lost her trust.

And he didn't know if he had any right to it again. How could he, when he no longer trusted himself?

Chapter Twenty-Five

Kennedy stared out her office window, numb after cycling through rounds of anger, shame, disappointment and embarrassment. She'd already berated herself for her reaction in the meeting, yet the self-flagellation continued.

How had that happened? Why had she responded? Why?

She squeezed her eyes closed, head bowing as she swallowed back the doubts threatening to pour out. She'd never flinched like that before, especially in a meeting with her father. Never.

And she'd never had that softened rush of warmth flood her in the middle of a tense negotiation. That instant desire to give herself to Matt had burst forward before she'd had a chance to check it. Again, how?

That single question refused to go away even though she had no answer for it. Not one. Not for why her nipples had pebbled or her chest had tightened. Or how her thoughts had fled to the last time they'd been in that room together. When he'd mastered her without taking away her power.

The dichotomy of the situation pulled a sarcastic

scoff from her. He'd done the exact opposite today with one little move.

She rubbed her temples, yet the throbbing behind them remained. She had a stack of work to do, which included getting the revised contract to legal. The task was hers even though her father had taken ownership of it in the meeting.

Resentment built in a steady stream she had no will to contain. Was it worth it? The daily struggle and fight to meet a standard she had zero chance of ever reaching? Not her father's, at least.

A weight pulled on her shoulders, and her eyes stung with the tears she refused to let fall. The urge to curl up in a ball and cry was overruled by the same determination that'd gotten her to this point.

She couldn't remain shut in her office forever. No. Hiding never fixed anything, especially with her father. He respected a solid confrontation more than meek acceptance. She'd learned that the first time she'd challenged his bedtime rule when he'd never been home to enforce it. She'd been six. He'd relented, and she'd discovered his path to acceptance.

She could deal with her father. Matt, however... The sense of betrayal struck too deeply to reject. At least not yet. She wasn't ready to face him. How could she when she couldn't face herself?

She'd thought her little desire had been limited to the bedroom. It was just an escape, and she'd trusted Matt to keep it there.

But she'd apparently forgotten to inform herself of that.

Disgust swelled until she wanted to choke on every

promise, every lie, every excuse she'd made for giving her power to another for even a moment.

She thrust up, rolled her shoulders back, stretching the kinks that'd locked into the muscles. Beating herself up for what was already done wouldn't accomplish anything. It was up to her to take her power back. Wallowing only gave away more.

She checked her dad's calendar and headed to his office when she saw it was open. His assistant barely raised her head before Kennedy swept past, a brief smile given in exchange for her abruptness. Her quick rap on his door fired off her warning before she entered, closing the door behind her.

Her dad sat back, frown already in place. "What's going on?"

"We need to talk," she told him. "About what happened in the meeting." They'd only had one this morning, so there was no need to clarify.

He set his pen aside before he crossed his arms over his chest. His suit coat was slung over the back of his chair, his shirt sleeves rolled up in his preferred mode of work. "What about it?"

Two visitor chairs sat empty before his desk, but she didn't even think about sitting. Fire burned in her chest to counter the roll of her stomach. She met his gaze straight on, resolve clear.

"I didn't appreciate you cutting me down in the meeting like that." She held her ground when he didn't respond, not even a raised brow or scowl. "It undermined my power and set a bad precedence for future negotiations with McPherson."

Here came the scowl. Hard, drawn and not at all welcoming. "How do you figure?"

"That was *my* deal." She let her anger fly, uncaring of the potential fallout. "Yes, Thad is the salesman on record, but *I* was there for every step of the negotiations. *I* brought in the business. *I* brought in McPherson. *I* had the vision and executed it. And you ripped that all away with your condescending reprimand." Her nerves trembled in small quakes she smothered behind the knowledge that she was right. She might be his daughter, but she was also the VP of Operations. "Would you have done that to anyone else?"

Her father could be a cagey old bastard who growled more than smiled, but he'd never been tagged as intentionally cruel. Most respected him, and just as many liked him. Her mother said she loved him, but Kennedy had spent her entire life trying to please him. Maybe that was her problem.

Ray Keller didn't want to be pleased.

He lowered his arms, his expression flattening out. Something softened on him. Something she couldn't quite define. Something that took her back to the years before she'd started working in the company. To when she was just his little girl.

"Ken…" He clasped his hands on his desk, his shoulders falling. "You showed a weakness right there for all of us to see. That's not you."

She inhaled through her acceptance. He was right. That wasn't her. Not usually. "You didn't need to scold me like a child." Especially in front of Matt. What was he thinking of her now?

She scratched that thought as soon as it appeared. Worrying about Matt's thoughts—especially about her—had no place in her world right now.

Her father stared at her for a long moment. Tension

strung between them on a tenuous balance that matched their status. Were they father and daughter, boss and employee or some mix of the two?

"You're right." His agreement shocked her more than a terse denial would have. "I'm sorry."

He was sorry—and he'd actually said it. She'd heard it with her own ears, yet she still didn't trust it. "You are?"

His puff of sarcastic laughter reminded her too much of herself. "Yes. I am." He came around his desk, no hint of authority displayed. For once, he was just her dad. "I just…" He glanced away. His expression was sterner when he looked back. "I'm aware that you have a relationship with Matt, even though you haven't seen it as important enough to inform me or your mother."

Guilt took a strange hold at her father's accusation, which was again true. She hadn't told either of them about Matt, but there was very little she did share about her life with them. Why should she when neither one of them seemed to care that deeply?

"What does that have to do with today?" She wasn't going to deny or confirm her father's statement.

"You're my daughter."

She waited for him to expand but he didn't. "Yes. I am."

He propped his hands on his hips, leaning in. "A connection between our companies would be advantageous for both of us. He's not going to respect a woman who hesitates when he looks at her."

Disappointment swept in when she'd thought she was beyond that. His reprimand had been over a hesitation. That was all he'd seen. Her years of diligence, commitment and determination had been dismissed by a blink. If he'd known how deeply she'd responded to Matt's look, how she'd instinctively yielded, what then?

She focused on the man who didn't know her or really see her at all. Was she just a tool for him to use? Had she always been?

Would it ever change?

Or was this just another version of her father's gruff way of caring?

Her throat burned with the hurt threatening to spill out. She wouldn't let it, though. Not in front of him.

She hunted for a response, coming up blank. In the end, she gave him the only thing she had left. "Thank you for your apology." He was still her father, no matter how much he'd just hurt her.

She turned to leave, but swung back around when he started to speak, cutting him off. "I'll be on vacation, effective now. I have months stored up, and I have a sudden desire to drink margaritas on the beach. I'll let mother know that I won't be around for Christmas."

She left after that, her back straight, her dignity wrapped up tight. There was so much she wanted to say. So much she wanted to yell and demand. She didn't, though. She wouldn't lower herself to that level.

"Cancel all of my meetings for the next two weeks," she told her assistant as she passed. "I'll be on vacation." She didn't bother to expand. Nor did she respond to the startled round of questions when she left her office five minutes later, laptop packed up, car keys in hand. "Enjoy your holiday."

She avoided all eye contact as she left the building, not that anyone tried to stop her. The few people she encountered all stepped aside to let her pass. Was she being unprofessional? Maybe, but she couldn't get herself to care. Not when she'd followed the rules, maintained every protocol, smiled, coddled, bit her tongue and played the damn game just to be shut down because she'd blinked. Literally.

One damn blink.

She tossed her briefcase in the passenger seat, heedless of her laptop tucked inside. If it broke, then she wouldn't be compelled to respond to the emails that were going to stack up. Why did she still care about them? Why was she worrying about the work that'd be dumped on others?

Because she cared too much. Because she was responsible and professional and…still a woman.

A proud, strong woman who was…tired.

The weight of that pressed on her, reinforcing every slight, comment, dismissal and assumption that'd been directed at her. No matter how strong she tried to be, she would never overcome her one fatal flaw of being born a girl.

She drove out of the parking lot only to stop at the curb when she was out of sight of the building. The interior of her car echoed in the silence. It insulated while weakening her at once. *Just breathe.* That's all she needed to do. Just breathe.

This wasn't her. She didn't blink back tears or struggle with who she was. She knew exactly who she was. Or at least she had—until Matt had showed her something different. Something softer. Something…just as strong but infinitely more vulnerable.

Her gaze wandered in the general direction of his office. It was south of there, not more than five minutes away. She could go talk to him or even call him. And say what? "Fuck you" probably wouldn't go over very well when the situation was mostly on her.

She shouldn't have responded. She never would've with any other man. Right? She never had before. Yet that one incident had her doubting everything about herself.

She didn't flinch—but she had. For Matt.

What did that mean? She had no clue, but she knew what it couldn't mean—what she wouldn't let it mean.

She had the app open and a scene arranged a minute later. The Boardroom was her domain. No one judged her there. No one looked down on her. No one tried to alter her or diminish her wants. No one made her feel badly about who she was.

Had Matt really done that? No. But here she sat feeling all of those things. She had her father to thank—for most of it anyway. The rest was her own doing, and she was fixing it the only way she knew how.

She sent a quick message to Trevor before she posted her scene. She was being impetuous, yet the demand clawing inside her wouldn't let her be cautious. She needed her power back, now.

Her fingers did a jittery tap on her thigh as she waited for Trevor to respond. What if he was busy tonight? She'd do it anyway.

Forget this. Why was she waiting?

She left the location open and hit Post. Someone would likely offer up a boardroom. That was all she needed. The thought of getting off on her father's boardroom table wasn't so appealing right now, even though it'd be the perfect clichéd FU.

She drove home on autopilot, thoughts swirling in the muck of emotions that left her drained and even more focused by the time she reached home. She studiously dismissed every hint of guilt that tried to emerge. Matt didn't control her. He had no ownership over her or her actions.

Her phone buzzed with an app message when she stepped into her house. She set her briefcase and purse on the counter before she opened the message. Is there something I should know about? Trevor was still playing the protector role, which she wanted but didn't.

No. He'd never required details or an explanation before.

She slumped into the couch as she waited for his response. You can use my boardroom. I'm not free until ten.

Thank you. She switched over to add the location only to see that Trevor had updated it along with the time change. Her breath hitched when she saw the list of attendees already signed up.

She waited for that rush to fill her. The one that came with owning her sexuality, with feeling the lust directed at her and the want she denied them. She waited, but it didn't come. Not yet, at least.

That was all the proof she needed to confirm that this scene was long overdue.

Chapter Twenty-Six

The view hadn't changed in the last hour that Matt had stared at it. The warehouse across the parking lot was still white beneath the building lights. Not even a car or person had passed by to change the picture.

Yet he still sat there, staring at nothing when the rest of the office had emptied hours ago. Kennedy's reaction circled his thoughts on an almost continuous loop now that he'd given up all pretenses of working. The shock and hurt. The disappointment. And lastly the resentment.

The day had slipped by, but he had little memory of what he'd accomplished. He'd responded automatically to everything thrown at him without absorbing any of it. The company was starting to thrive after years of getting by. He should be proud of that. The Keller deal would be another giant leap into the expansion he'd been working on since taking over.

And he'd walk away if it meant losing Kennedy.

He'd come to that conclusion not long after he'd returned to the office. There would be other business opportunities. There was only one of her.

He dragged his gaze away from the window to call

up the Boardroom message he'd received from Trevor around noon.

Thought you'd be interested in this. The link opened to the scene set up by Kennedy less than two hours after he'd left her office. Six—make that seven—men were signed up to attend.

His hand tightened around his phone, a shot of pain nailing his chest. Yet he wasn't mad at her. This was his doing. He took full responsibility for it. How he'd hurt her. How he'd taken her power without her consent. How she was taking it back the only way she knew how.

This was all on him.

"Fuck." His anger shot through the room, solving nothing. He didn't know if he deserved to have her back, but he owed her an apology—at the very least.

He typed out a response to Trevor. I'll be there. He wasn't adding his name to the scene. Nope. He wouldn't take the moment from Kennedy. She obviously need it, and he wouldn't undercut that. But he'd ensure she was okay. That she was safe.

That she got what she needed—whatever it was.

He could do no less. He loved her too damn much to see her hurting. *Fuck.* This was why he'd stayed away from relationships, why he'd shut down his dominant desires. And yet, he didn't regret a single moment with Kennedy—until the meeting today.

His phone buzzed. Trevor. You cause any trouble and your ass is gone.

A weak smile formed. He respected the guy's commitment to everyone in the group, but he was grateful for the protection he extended to Kennedy. Her family was closing around her even if she didn't share her blood with any of them. Did she know that? Was she aware of how many cared for her?

His heart gave another heavy lurch when he typed back his response. I'm not going to cause trouble. It killed him that Trevor thought, even for a moment, that he'd do anything to hurt her.

See that you don't.

He wouldn't. He'd leave before that happened.

He'd already texted Ben to let him know he'd be home late—again. He owed his son an apology too. He'd been around more when Dawn was his age. Always home by seven—or his mother had been there. He just seemed to expect more of Ben and from him, which was unfair.

And listing out his failures wouldn't solve a thing.

He scrubbed a hand over his face, thrusting up as he snatched his tie off his desk and quickly redid the knot around his neck. He replaced his business uniform with more precision than when he'd torn it off. The relief after he'd slung his suit coat into the visitor's chair had also provided clarity.

The fucking suit had been his trigger from the very start.

The formality and decorum expected within it bled too closely to the expectations of his officer's uniform. That same sense of command, of order and control, settled into him as he slipped the suit coat on. It triggered something in his head he couldn't pinpoint, but it wove through his awareness on a trail of authority so comfortable and familiar he'd failed to heed the warning signs.

But he couldn't blame his overstep on the damn suit.

Just like he couldn't blame his military uniform for what had happened with his ex-wife.

His actions were his to own.

The office was empty, the truck bays locked up and silent. His ride into the city was executed with little thought. He made the turns to Trevor's building with equal efficiency, having made the trip multiple times but for much different reasons.

The parking garage beneath the building was mostly empty. He had the elevator to himself, which wasn't a surprise. It opened to a lighted exterior lobby. Trevor stood behind the glass doors that marked the Faulkner Investment Group entrance. The grandness of both the building and the offices themselves were a statement to the money that flowed within it.

Trevor met him with a cold glance and even harder stare. "I don't know what happened, but I hope you fix it." Trevor's tone wasn't as harsh as his expression.

Matt found only honesty projected at him, so he gave back the same. "You and me both."

"To be clear, though. I will bust your ass if you step out of line in the scene—or anytime with her."

He'd do the same damn thing if their positions were reversed. "Understood."

Trevor led him up the main staircase off the lobby and down a hall to a smaller conference room. The other men were already in it, but Matt barely saw them. He didn't care who else was there to watch, and he had little interest in what they might think of him. He was here for one reason only: Kennedy.

Trevor ran through the same spiel as before regarding scene rules. None of them had changed. This was voyeurism only, unless she granted specific permission for more. That landed like a sucker punch to his gut. He wouldn't stop anything but watching another man please her would be pure torture.

But he'd lost any right he might've had to object to anything she did.

His mouth was dry, his pulse thumping so hard he counted the beats where they throbbed in his neck as he followed the men down the hall. Each step was made with force and restraint as he battled the urge to run into the room and away at once.

The boardroom was lit by a sole lamp on the credenza that ran the length of the far wall. Windows lined the exterior, displaying a skyline of buildings and lights. And Kennedy sat on the end of the table, her bare back to the door, feet propped on the edge.

The sight stole his breath. Pain sliced through him in a combined twist of want and regret. The line of her spine was graceful, her hair soft as it flowed over her shoulders. One hand was between her legs, the other braced on the table as she pleasured herself.

She was so damn beautiful. That was his Kennedy. Strong. Confident. Sure of herself and her sexuality. She owned the room and every man in it right now.

Pride lifted his shoulders as it blazed a path to his heart, but it was quickly followed by shame. He'd taken all of that from her today with one thoughtless move.

The other men edged around the table to gain a better view, but Matt stayed at the back. He didn't need the visual when he already knew every inch of her. Her mouth would be parted, her cheeks flushed, her freckles dark marks of temptation. Her breasts were slightly fuller on the underside, her nipples a deep rose that peaked with the slightest touch.

But who would pull on them? Bite them until she arched into the pain?

He choked back his groan, hands fisting before he slid them behind his back. A sliver of calm cut through his mounting torment. She had this. She didn't need him. She'd never needed him. And that was precisely why he'd fallen so hard for her.

Her low moan rumbled through the air to caress him with its heady notes of arousal. Her head fell back, her throat exposed in a lovely request he would accept. The bruise on her neck had faded to a faint dark mark, but he was the only man in the room who knew what it was, what it meant and how it'd gotten there. Only him.

His possessive streak blazed to life on a pulse of his dick and a rush of longing he embraced. She was everything he never dreamed he could have. He could only hope that he hadn't crushed his chance of having even more with her.

Of holding her again. Of loving her. Of cherishing every damn thing she gave him.

Lust reigned on the faces of the other men, and Matt didn't begrudge them for it. One glanced to him, frowned, but his attention quickly returned to Kennedy.

She lay back, her chest rising as she rolled her hips. Her eyes were closed, passion stamped on every feature. Her hand moved in a steady motion between her legs, her breaths short.

There were no toys on the table, no condom either. This was simply Kennedy: pure, exposed and…alone.

His heart broke as understanding took hold.

Her bold statement was a mask for what Trevor had obviously seen long ago. Beneath the strength and power was a woman alone on a cold table. Untouchable or afraid to be touched? She'd claim the first, but how close was the second?

His throat burned as he blinked back the rush of emotions that threatened to choke him. How did he help? What could he do? His arms ached to scoop her up and never let her go—but she wouldn't want that. Not Kennedy.

He blew out a long, slow breath, took another. He couldn't hold onto love, just like he couldn't force it. He could only show her what she meant to him and hope it was enough.

Her hips bucked, lifted. She slid her other hand down, a moan falling free. One of the men undid his pants and fisted his erection. They were relegated to the edges of the room, but Matt struggled with their proximity. They were all too close to her—and he wasn't close enough.

Trevor was in the back corner just a few feet away from him. He appeared to study the scene with a detachment Matt was incapable of. What did he see? More importantly, what did he know?

Trevor's mask didn't crack when he looked to him, but his brow rose with a question that could've been one of many. There were a few dozen racing through Matt's head.

A low grunt pulled him back to the scene. A second guy was jacking off to the increased rate of Kennedy's movements. Her eyes were squeezed tightly closed, her face turned to the side. Her lower lip was trapped between her teeth, the tendons straining in her arm. A soft but distinctive slurp burned the picture of her fingering herself into his mind.

Lust built in his groin. His dick was hard, desire

present like it always was around her. But their connection was just a faint buzz over his skin. She didn't
know he was there. None of this was for him. It was
most likely about him, though.

And there came the kick to his nuts.

His suit was suddenly claustrophobic, threatening
to suffocate all he'd strode to achieve. He wanted to go
to her, to touch her and drive her wild. He wanted to
tease and sooth and watch her come undone beneath
his tongue. Her musky flavor flooded his mouth, her
cry coinciding with the one in his mind.

And he was stuck there watching what he'd caused
and unable to do anything about it—except to let this
play out. He wanted this for her because she wanted it.
He'd never judge her for taking what she needed.

Relationships were built on understanding, and he'd
failed on that with his ex-wife. That old guilt rose to
the top of the pile he carried with him. His lack of observation and understanding had hurt them all, but especially his children.

And now?

He'd thought he'd had it all under control—and that
had been his downfall.

Chapter Twenty-Seven

Kennedy squeezed her eyes closed, her finger moving in hard circles over her clit, two fingers thrust into her vagina. Every muscle strained for the ending she'd built. Her orgasm hung on the edge but wouldn't crest. It was right there...holding in her core...teasing her with the release she...wanted...so...badly...

Her cry was one of frustration more than desire. She pried her eyes open, finger slowing on her clit, which teetered between numb and oversensitive. She flicked it softly as she sought the gaze of the first man she saw. His eyes were heavy, lust openly displayed. He stroked his palm down the outline of his erection in his pants, licked his lips.

Yeah, he wanted her. She hunted for the rush of power that usually came with that knowledge. It simmered in her chest but didn't spread. It didn't fill her with strength or give her the high like it normally did.

The table dug into her shoulder, and she shifted, letting her hips fall back to the hard surface. Her breaths were labored, skin heated. Everything should've been right. The situation was one she loved. Men in suits, all that authority watching her, wanting her, longing to have her when they couldn't. She held them all suspended beneath her desire—and all she could think about was Matt.

How he'd touched her that last time in the Boardroom. How he'd known what she'd wanted and given it to her and more. He hadn't judged her then or ever. Not once.

Her eyes fell closed, her memories dragging her pleasure forward. She imagined him between her legs, his tongue teasing her clit instead of her finger. Heat swelled over her pussy, her walls clenching on the thought of his fingers plunging into her. She mimicked the image, riding her own fingers when she longed for Matt's.

A low grunt urged her on, but it wasn't the husky rumble she knew by heart. The one that sunk deep and turned her to mush. That was the one that fed her now, that said she was strong and beautiful and his.

She cursed her thoughts right along with her heart that denied her wishes and hungered for his touch. She didn't need a man. She didn't need someone to confirm everything she knew about herself. She didn't need to be coddled and reassured. She didn't need…

But she wanted it. She wanted all of it. And now that she'd had it, she wanted it even more.

To have Matt here in the room with her, doing to her what every other man wished he could do. That… would be…

She stretched for her orgasm, increasing the pressure on her clit as she rode that one spot, that one place that buzzed beneath her skin and bunched her release into a tight little knot…right…below… There!

Her cry sprang free on the crash of ecstasy that finally broke. She curled up, straining for every last drop of pleasure that spread to her toes and scorched her skin. Her breath held in her lungs, her muscles tense, her pussy hugging her fingers. Her walls pulsed, looking for something bigger, something thicker and harder to grab.

She fell back on an anguished sob. Her chest rose and fell with each quick intake of breath, her head spinning as the brief intensity faded to a dull afterglow. A man grunted through his own orgasm, his sounds distinctive enough to visualize the event. She didn't look, though, when she would've before.

Yeah, she'd done that to him. She'd driven him to that state. He probably wanted to sink into her and fuck her until she cried out again. He couldn't, though. Not here. Not without her permission.

And that knowledge gave her nothing tonight.

She closed her legs, resting her hands on her stomach. The quakes started deep within her chest as little ripples. They spread over her heart and dipped into the emptiness she'd refused to acknowledge for so damn long. She tried to smother them, tried to find the strength she relied on to hold her steady. Yet they raced beneath her skin in uncontrolled waves that never quite expanded into a full shudder.

"The scene is over, gentlemen."

She bit back the sob holding on her tongue. It gouged at her throat and bled into her sinuses until everything burned. *No. No. No.* She wouldn't break here. Not yet. Not in front of the very men she'd just mastered. Or had she?

Were her displays just an illusion of her creation?

Of course they were.

Her response came so quickly she couldn't reject it. They were always for her. Always. Since that very first time. She'd done the scenes because she'd wanted to. They'd given her the feedback she'd craved without the risk of anyone getting too close.

But everything was different now. She was different.

She blew out a quiet breath and tracked the men as they left the room. A mumbled thank you came along with words of praise. They floated past her, barely hitting her consciousness before they were gone. They were meaningless now.

She sensed Trevor as he came around the table, tapping a warning on the surface. He was always courteous like that. Aware of her headspace often before she was. His suit crinkled as he leaned over her. She tensed slightly but kept her eyes closed.

"Matt is here." He whispered the words in her ear, his breath a shock of warmth before the chill hit.

Dread sped down her spine in a flash of denial. She tensed, thoughts spinning random chaos. Why? How? How long had he been there? But they were gone in the next instant, washed away beneath acceptance. Just like that, her muscles relaxed, and her thoughts emptied.

Matt is here.

He. Was. Here. And he'd stayed hidden. He'd let her do her thing without interfering. And now?

The low click of the door signaled Trevor's departure. He'd left her there with Matt, which meant he wasn't worried. For whatever reason, Trevor approved of Matt. It shouldn't mean anything, yet it did. Two decades of friendship, along with Trevor's unwavering loyalty, raised his opinion far above her parents'.

She sat up and wrapped her arms around her legs, hugging them to her chest. The position probably gave away too much, but she didn't care. Her clothes were on the chair in the corner. She could get them, but that would require standing.

She laid her cheek on her knee, a shiver trembling through her. Awareness tingled over her back, but Matt remained silent. Why? Was this the end for them?

That thought had another shot of regret twisting hard and deep. She wasn't sorry about doing the scene. It'd been her choice. But she honestly wasn't ready to let Matt go. Not when she still loved him.

She loved him.

She wasn't certain how or when that'd happened, but it had.

Material rustled, the whisper of silk on cotton. She squeezed her eyes closed. Out of fear? Yes. It balled beside the regret and clawed open the insecurities she'd thought long trampled.

And today had proven exactly how wrong she'd been.

His scent rushed up to cut and comfort as he settled his suit coat around her shoulders. Warmth eased into her and chased away the cold. Her hold on her legs tightened as she tried to squeeze back the ache that continued to grow. It spread up her throat, dug at her heart and tried to swell from her eyes.

"Kennedy."

Oh, God. The softness in his tone was almost her undoing. She'd started rocking at some point, short little movements that kept the grief at bay. She focused on that, keeping the rhythm that somehow prevented her from crumbling. *Breathe. Just. Breathe.*

"Kennedy," Matt said again, his pain a rumbled hitch that broke. "I'm so sorry."

He brushed her hair away from her face, his touch gentle as he drew his fingers through the strands. The action calmed her almost instantly. It took her straight to the quiet moments when she laid in his arms, skin to skin, hearts in rhythm.

Her rocking slowed, stopped. A tear slid out, but she brushed it away with her knee.

"I—" His voice cracked. He dropped his head to hers. Its weight brought another wave of miserable comfort. "I'm sorry. That's all I can say. I'm so damn sorry for hurting you. For driving you to this point. For taking what you hadn't consented to."

Each word filled her with hope when she'd thought it gone. He was sorry. *He* was sorry.

"I don't know how it happened. I would never do that to you on purpose. *Never.*" Anguish spilled from every syllable. It drenched the room in his pain and soothed her own.

He got it. He got *her.*

Wonder glossed over her doubts but not her hesitation. His apology didn't fix her own issues. She swallowed, searching for understanding in the sea of unknown. Exhaustion mellowed resolves she'd once thought absolute. She was tired of being alone, of fighting for something that'd lost its importance.

"I'm the one who responded," she finally whispered. "I didn't have to react. No one else would've. But I did." That was the part she couldn't get over. "It was me, more than you. I did this to myself."

"Oh, God. Ken." He wrapped his arms around her, holding her together when she was ready to shatter. "No." He pressed a kiss to her head, holding it. "No," he whispered. "Don't think like that."

"How can I not?"

He urged her chin up. She didn't resist when she

could've. Instead, she let him cradle her face, raising it until she had to look at him. Pain and sorrow were etched into each line in his brow, highlighting the sadness and regret in his eyes.

"You reacted out of surprise," he told her. She leaned into his touch, her eyes closing as she savored the light stroke of his thumb on her cheek. Did he know he did that? That it silenced the trembling and warmed her when so little did?

That he used it when she gave herself to him?

"No." Her denial came out on a soft note of acceptance. "I reacted because it was you." He was the only one who'd ever earned that level of trust from her.

He dropped his forehead to hers. "You're killing me, Kennedy." His anguish was back, along with the hurt he didn't try to hide. "You trusted me and I fumbled it. I should've been more aware. I should've—"

"Shhh." She laid a hand on his cheek, offering the same comfort he gave her. "It was more me than you." She'd known that all along. Now she had to figure out how to deal with what it'd uncovered. "You're taking blame that isn't yours."

"But—"

"No." She swiveled her head, lifting just enough to lay her lips to his. That was all, but it was enough. The connection filled her with light when she'd been floundering in the dark. Her love sprung forward, a reminder of all that he'd given her. Of the security and quiet. Of the strength without restriction. Of the belonging she'd unknowingly craved. "I won't let you do that."

She eased back so she could be certain he not only heard but accepted what she said. "I am not your exwife." He inhaled sharply, going stiff. "What happened,

happened. We were both surprised and responded poorly. That's on both of us, not just you." She waited for that to sink in. Did he get it? Would he continue to bury himself in guilt that wasn't his to own?

He closed his eyes, winced before he turned his head to kiss her palm, holding it. Her heart did that flutter thing when he opened his eyes. Gone were the doubts and recriminations that'd been drowning him before.

"You are an amazing woman." Awe coated his words and matched the love radiating from him. The love she finally accepted without hesitation or fear. "I hope you know that."

"Maybe." She shrugged slightly but tempered it with a smirk as she wrapped her legs around his hips. "But I can be better—we all can," she added when he started to object. "And—don't let this go to your head—but I think you're helping me with that."

His small laugh eased some of the tension from his shoulders and loosened the ball of worry knotted in her stomach. He dropped a kiss to her lips, lingering to slide his tongue in before he rested his forehead on hers.

"I love you, Kennedy." His declaration pinged at the amazement and fear that vibrated within her, but she wasn't afraid to hear it now. He'd filled the empty spaces without her knowing, and in doing so, had given her more than she'd thought possible. "Your strength drives me to be better, every damn day."

She kept her eyes closed, relishing the glow that built from some place so deep within her she couldn't define it. But it spread on the growing acceptance of what she'd long denied.

She wanted to be loved. She wanted the security he offered. She wanted to rely on him as he did her. She wanted a home instead of a house and the complications that came with it. And a part of her even needed him and all he offered.

Because there were times when she just wanted to be, and he gave her that when no one else ever had.

"I love you, Matt." She bit her lip to stop it from trembling. The leap was scary and exhilarating. Her pulse raced, yet her heart was at peace. "So damn much." She added the last in an attempt to lighten the mood, but she meant it. "You give me things I was afraid to want. It's you who makes me stronger."

His kiss stole her breath and lifted her so high she hoped she never came down. His love poured into her on every swipe of his tongue and mumbled endearment. She took it and gave back all she had.

This right here, this undefinable connection, had started from the moment they'd met. His first touch. That first command. Her first leap into taking what she'd been afraid to expose. His tenderness after. The way he touched and held her.

And she wanted more of all of it.

Heat rose to chase away the last of her chill. The table bit into her tailbone as she leaned back, drawing him with her, his coat providing a barrier from the cold surface.

"Love me, Matt," she whispered between kisses. "Just love me."

"I do." He followed his declaration with another long, bone-melting kiss that backed up his words and left her breathless. "I don't want to stop." He kissed down her chest, taking a nipple into his mouth. He needled the tip, tugging and pulling until she hovered between too much and more.

"Don't stop," she told him, digging her fingers into his hair. "Don't ever stop." She was his, totally his, and she could be that while still being herself. That was the key she'd sought and thought she'd never find.

"I won't." He followed through on that promise with every touch and kiss he rained down on her. The nip on her hip. The hot swipe of his tongue through her pussy. "I won't." The gentle brush of his hand down her leg. The bold thrust of his fingers into her.

"Yes." Her cry was a confirmation of everything he'd given her. She'd never once, in all the times she'd laid on a boardroom table, felt as alive as this. As complete and whole. She wanted to shout it from the rooftops while holding it close at the same time. "I love you." She couldn't stop saying it now that it was free.

He slid into her on a long sigh that confirmed everything she'd already known. Matt was hers. She'd given herself to him and in return, she'd gotten him back.

The exchange was one of dreams, yet the reality was even better than any she could've imagined. Matt had given her the love she'd craved, but more than that, he'd given her the strength to see in herself what she'd been afraid to accept.

"I love you," he whispered, his lips grazing hers. She didn't doubt him, not anymore, not when she'd finally stopped doubting herself. "You're mine, Kennedy."

She was. In every way, she was his. "And you're mine," she told him.

"I am," he agreed. "I'm all yours."

And she wasn't letting him go.

Epilogue

Matt glanced over his small family room, taking in the haphazard piles of open gifts and discarded wrapping paper. The Christmas tree twinkled in the corner, and a football game played on the TV even though his kids were focused on their phones. His mother sat in a chair, contentedly reading amid the chaos.

And within all of that was Kennedy, curled into the corner of the couch, a glass of wine in her hand, watching him.

His heart swelled when he would've sworn it couldn't get any bigger. Her hair was pulled into a messy bun that Dawn had studied when she'd thought no one was watching. Her nod to their PJ day tradition was yoga pants and a sweatshirt. His mother never fully complied either, and he'd upgraded his flannel bottoms to track pants. The kids, however, still embraced the habit that'd started before their mother had left.

He stepped over a toppled pile of new clothes and took a seat beside Kennedy. "Hey," he said, leaning into her, grateful she'd agreed to spend the day with them even if she hadn't spent last night with him. The morning was for his family, she'd told him. He agreed, and he had every intention of her being a part of that family next year.

"Hey," she said back, her cheeks flushed, a quiet contentment flowing from her. He wrapped his arm around her, tucking her into his side. Her head found that spot on his shoulder, her sigh spreading into him. She tilted her face up until her lips were by his ear. "You're sure everyone is okay with this?"

He made a quick check of the three people who'd been his world before Kennedy. Ben and Dawn smiled at each other in the secret communication he'd translated years ago, not that they knew that. They were happy for him. His mother appeared to be lost in her book, but her smirk told him she was very aware of what was going on around her.

He turned to Kennedy and whispered, "Yes. How about you?" Even there, on his couch in his home with his family around them, their bond comforted him.

She glanced around the room before looking back to him. "Yes." Her smile was soft, the love shining beside her happiness.

There were days that he still questioned how she'd come into his life, but he wasn't second-guessing it. Not any of it. "We're not very excit—"

"It's perfect," she cut him off before he could finish. "Truly." She rested her head against his shoulder, cuddling in a little more. "My parents still think I'm in the tropics."

"Have they tried to contact you?" She'd told him about the fallout with her father and her impromptu vacation. His anger still bubbled when he thought of Ray's behavior. He'd signed the contract with Keller Pallet after he'd ensured Ray had a clear understanding of his feelings regarding his daughter and Ray's treatment of her.

Of all the things that'd happened in that meeting that day, that was the regret that still lingered. He should've stood up for her right then. She was so much more than her father saw, and he intended to show her that every chance he had.

"Sort of," she answered him. "My mom sent a text this morning. We're fine." The lack of emotion in her voice said more than her words.

He held a kiss to her temple. "I'm glad you're here."

"Me too."

Contentment mellowed every worry and concern that tried to thread their way into his thoughts. They still had things to navigate, but Kennedy was a part of their lives now. They'd brought her into their fold. He wasn't sure if she understood how special that was, but she didn't need to know for it to be true.

"I have something for you," he said a while later. He set her empty glass on the side table with his, stretching his back as he did.

Her smirk held every dirty thought flowing in her head. "I thought you already gave me your gift." Her words were low and meant just for him, but his kids both snorted their amusement. She ducked her head, her freckles fading behind the blush that crept over them.

"Hush." He shot his kids a glare, but his grin dismissed the reprimand. "I have another." One appropriate for everyone to share in. He'd give her another bite mark tonight, if she let him. He still treaded with caution when it came to their dominant play, wary of going too far. However, he trusted Kennedy to tell him if he did.

He'd never be able to curb the part that drove him to give her what she needed. He didn't need to command her, but he would be there to support her.

He reached under the couch to extract the gift he'd stashed there. "Here."

Her smile lit up the room, her blush fading. "What's this?"

"Open it and find out."

She set the gift down, reaching into her bag beside the couch. She handed him a gift, laughter in her eyes. "Since we're doing this now." She stood, pulling three more gifts from her bag until they each had one. He shouldn't be touched, yet he was. He wasn't surprised that she'd remembered his family, but he hadn't expected it either.

"Oh." Dawn perked up. "You didn't have to."

"I know." Kennedy flashed her a smile. "I wanted to."

Dawn would appreciate Kennedy's spunk, and the fact that she wasn't trying to kiss up as much as be nice.

"Cool." Ben flipped his around in a quick external inspection. "Thanks."

"You guys go first," Kennedy said.

His mother frowned, setting her book aside. "How about we all go at once?"

Kennedy sat beside him, her relaxed movements the best gift he could've received. "Deal." She shot him a wink before she tore into her gift.

Her action sparked a flurry of ripping paper and laughter as the others scrambled to uncover the secrets beneath the wrapping. Dawn's exclamation overshadowed Ben's steady grin, complete with a head bob.

"Wow." Dawn held up the noise-cancelling head-phones. "Thank you!"

"These rock," Ben said, as he ripped the headphone box open. "You are way cooler than Dad."

"Hey!" Matt objected, returning his son's grin.

"These look good, Kennedy." His mother was busy reading the backs of the books she received. "Thank you."

"Matt." The vulnerable tenderness in Kennedy's voice pulled his attention to her. She was staring at the sign he'd had made. She ran her fingers over the words engraved into the stained wood, her lip tucked between her teeth. *Be Bold. Be Brave. Be Strong.*

She looked up, blinking rapidly. "It's perfect."

"It's everything you already are," he said, meaning it. She was all those and so much more. "This is just a reminder."

She squeezed his hand, swallowing hard. "Thank you."

He leaned in to kiss her, unable to hold back. "I love you," he whispered over her lips. If his family didn't know that by now, then they were all blind.

"I love you too." She kissed him again, before pull-ing back. She swiped under her eyes, chuckling. "You haven't opened yours."

His heart was so damn full when he slid his finger beneath the tape on his package, teasing her with his diligent removal of the wrapping paper. She didn't say a word, though, only watched him with anxious eyes.

He flipped the picture frame around, his heart skip-ping a beat when he saw the front. The scripted black frame was small, but the single word set in white on a black piece of clay was huge: *be*. That was it. Just the word *be*.

Emotions swelled in his chest and crowded his throat in their quest for freedom. He ran his fingers over the two letters, letting their meaning sink in.

"I can do that," he told her, remembering their late-night conversation not long ago. *Just be with me.*

She leaned into him, her head coming to rest on his shoulder. "Me too," she whispered, linking her fingers with his.

He let the moment settle around him, at peace in ways he'd never allowed himself to contemplate. Kennedy had brought so much to his life when he'd already thought it was full. He planned on being with her for a very long time, but right then, he was more than happy to just be.

* * * * *

No limits. No refusals. No out.
She'd be his—for one night.

Read on for an excerpt from Signed Over,
a Boardroom memo from Lynda Aicher

Chapter One

"Are you sure about this?"

Jacob Anders studied Bailey with an intense scrutiny she was used to—and so damn tired of. She bit back the sigh that threatened to heave out and returned his appraisal with a steady one of her own.

"Yes," she stated, her voice firm. "I'm sure." About as sure as she could be given the details laid out in the contract before her.

His lips pressed into a thin line, doubt narrowing his eyes before he released his own deep sigh. He shook his head and shoved a hand through his hair, his shoulders dropping.

"You." He pointed a finger at her. "Are going to drive me mad."

Victory danced a jig in her chest, but she withheld her joy to an impish smile. "I have no idea why."

Yet she did. Her happiness soured beneath the weight of that reality. She held her front, though. Held it strong and solid against the jitters and admonishments slamming around in her head. Admonishments she'd heard from everyone from her parents to her last boyfriend.

You're never satisfied. When is it enough? Stop manipulating. Why can't you just be happy?

"Yeah, right," Jacob scoffed, but his scowl lacked bite, just like the tone of his voice. He snatched a pen from his suit pocket and held it poised over the contract.

Hope swelled to shove the air from Bailey's lungs. This was it. The next leap in her never-ending cycle of risks was almost a reality. He just had to sign the damn agreement. Her signature was already scrawled and dated on the bottom of the page. She'd skimmed through it the night before to find the key points she'd asked for.

No limits. No refusals. No out.

She'd be his, and he could do any sexual thing he wanted to her.

Anything—for one night.

Her skin stretched tight with that too-familiar mix of need and fear. Of want and self-ridicule.

Why did she do this? Push for what others didn't understand? Shove when most would be happy with what they had? Cajole and manipulate until she got her way—or simply took it?

Her leg bounced beneath the bar, that insatiable crush of energy escaping in the only available way. Would Jacob notice? Did he really understand what was at stake for her?

He turned his head, his gaze penetrating her before she had a chance to deflect. She swallowed, anxiety creeping in to twist her stomach. Strength built on that unrelenting quest for more kept her from looking away.

She straightened in her seat, spine locking into place against the speculation in his eyes. Blue with flashes of gold that lightened and darkened with his moods, Jacob's eyes were as unique as the man. His classic good looks were enhanced by his easy manner and kindness that appeared open-ended.

"Why me?"

His clipped words shot out to nail her with another rush of doubts. He didn't blink, and she didn't dare flinch. But what did he want to hear? What would get him to sign the contract?

She swept her tongue over her lip in a slow pass, the dry texture tugging slightly before she rolled her bottom lip between her teeth. His gaze never lowered, not even a little, through her attempt to distract him. Her heart did a quick flutter as desire flashed hot and fast.

That right there, that was why him.

"Because you'll give me what I want," she finally answered, her words heavy with the need simmering beneath her skin. His brows hitched up. "And we're good together," she tacked on, her smile knowing.

Their sexual chemistry had been tested and confirmed in multiple Boardroom scenes in the year since she'd joined the exclusive group. The open, hedonistic sex, conducted in boardrooms, between some of the Bay Area's most elite men and women, had fed the crazy need that churned within her, but it was back now, pushing for more.

Something new, daring. Something that would test her.

Jacob was known for his willingness to grant member requests. Yes, others did—they all did when it meshed with their own desires. But Jacob liked to fulfill the unique ones, and he had a reputation for doing so with compassion and tact.

Not that she was asking for either of those.

His lips compressed yet again, sending off another wave of desperation within Bailey. *Please. Don't bail on me. Don't...give up on me.*

She laid a hand on his arm, her plea silent but unrestrained. In a leap of faith, she let it all show. Every aching need and fear that bombarded her until she couldn't think, couldn't…be.

"I want— No." She shook her head. "I need this."

"Have you done it before?" He tapped his finger on the contract without looking away from her.

"No."

"Then how do you know *this* is what you need."

"I just do." Could he understand that when few did?

A silent curse formed on his lips, his nostrils flaring with his quick inhalation. "The risks are—"

"I trust you," she implored, cutting him off. "I do." She squeezed his arm for emphasis, or maybe that was the fear sneaking out once again. "I wouldn't have asked you if I didn't. Don't you see that? I wouldn't do this with someone I didn't trust completely." The truth of that resonated on a clear signal from her head to her heart.

Jacob would take care of her.

Her heart contracted around that nugget of security. He was too kind, too conscientious, too good to be horrible to her. Yet he'd push, right? At least she hoped he would. Why would he go through the effort of getting a special contract created and then approved if he wasn't going to sign it?

"I'm not stupid, nor do I have a death wish," she informed him, sitting back. Her hand was oddly cold when she removed it from his arm. The chill crept beneath her skin to smother the heat that'd just been there. "I want this—with you." *Just you.*

Even she couldn't answer why that last point was so important. It just was.

It had to be Jacob or no one.

That buzzing restarted beneath her skin, humming at an increased frequency that throbbed against her chest the longer he remained silent. Her leg bounced, nerves spiraling until she forced herself to still. Her pulse still pounded and sweat trailed down her side, but she was well versed at hiding the urgency that even she didn't understand.

Questions crowded his expression, but none of them spilled out. Did he think she was crazy? He wouldn't be the first or likely the last.

"Please," she finally whispered, the single word lifting on a plea that felt like her last safe hope.

She could go elsewhere. Hunt down a different guy, place, environment that would feed the urge that never seemed to quiet. But she was actually trying to be smart here. Trying to be cautious when her default was the opposite.

Jacob swiveled his head in a slow arc that could've been rejection or resignation. "I'm not taking this lightly," he finally said, serious. "You'll still have a safewo—"

"No!" Her refusal snapped out before she could stop it. His eyes widened and her hopes dropped. Damn it. She bit her tongue, swallowed. His eyes narrowed again, and she had to clear her throat of the regrets and insecurities before she could finally add, "I won't use it."

"And that right there is why this is so damn risky." His voice had hardened. "You are giving up too much."

Am I? Maybe. Yet she couldn't get herself to back down.

A calm settled over her as she accepted the truth of his words. She leaned in, meeting him halfway in the little space between their bar stools. She made sure he could read the conviction that'd taken root with her determination.

"I'm giving *you* everything." His nostrils flared again on his deep inhalation. She waited for him to exhale. "Only you."

"Fuck." He hung his head, grimaced, but heat simmered beside resignation when he scratched his name over the bottom of the contract. She sat back, her muscles going slack with the relief that swooped in. He'd done it.

The contract was signed.

He pinned her with the steady intent that'd first drawn her to him. He came across as affable, charming even. The easygoing guy who was the first to step up or lend a hand. Yet there was something steady and focused beneath his friendly demeanor, something deep when she felt so shallow.

"Don't make me regret this."

His warning stoked the rebellious side of her that never seemed to die. She flicked her brow up, swallowed the last of her drink before sliding from the bar stool. Her chin was lifted, pride holding her shoulders back when she nailed him with the same hard intent he'd handed her.

"Don't make *me* regret this," she said before she strode from the bar without a backward glance. Her nape prickled with awareness as he tracked her departure, but she held strong in her refusal to show more than she already had.

Jacob Anders was the only man she trusted her life with, and that wasn't her being dramatic. He could seriously hurt her in numerous ways, and she'd just signed a contract giving him permission to do so.

Chapter Two

Jacob set the last tool down on the credenza. The leather straps slicked against the wood in a series of soft taps. He eyed the arrangement and mentally reviewed the use and handling of every item. Did he need them all? No.

But the options were there.

Nerves clustered in his stomach along with the hum of excitement. It'd taken him three weeks to make the arrangements. Three long, intense weeks of research, practice and lessons before he'd felt even remotely close to carrying off this scene.

Bailey was asking for everything, and he planned to give as much as he could.

"Are you ready?"

Jacob snapped his head up. Tension laced through his shoulders when he spotted Trevor James, the Boardroom founder and overseer. "Yes." He kept his voice strong, which was the only way to handle him.

Trevor entered the room, scanning every inch before he stopped in front of the credenza. "I reserve the right to stop this at any point."

"Of course." Jacob hadn't balked at that line in the contract. No, he'd welcomed it. There was no telling where the scene would go or how deeply they'd all sink into it.

Trevor flicked a brow up, but his apparent question remained unasked. He returned to the doorway, his controlled calm weaving into the room to layer over Jacob. He had this, or he wouldn't be doing it. It was really that simple.

And Trevor wouldn't have let him if he didn't trust everyone involved.

"I'll send the men up when they arrive," Trevor said. "Bailey's already here."

Jacob nodded, not at all surprised that she'd arrived early. Bailey Brown was a fireball of energy and sexuality that wasn't tempered one bit. She could be intense, coy and demanding, but she was also funny, lively and exciting. It all depended on what one focused on.

And she'd come to him with this request.

That in itself wasn't unusual. He liked helping people and that included people in the Boardroom. He didn't mind fulfilling scene desires or being the guy people sought out when they needed something unique. But this had been different from the moment Bailey had approached him.

He rolled his shoulders and swung around to study the evening skyline. Trevor had insisted they use his corporate boardroom, and the view was stunning, day or night. Buildings crowded around them to offer the possibility of intrusion without being obvious. Beyond them, the Bay Bridge was a line of lights in the distance over the black expanse of the water.

A deep breath pulled him into the headspace he needed. The darker, harder place that nudged aside protocols and conventional thinking. Right and wrong wasn't always a clear line, especially when viewed from another perspective.

He dug into desires he rarely released, the ones he'd been raised to shun. The ones society claimed to be repugnant. They wove through him on a note of hunger. He rarely engaged in this level of play, yet he understood it, wanted it.

Bailey's request had blown open the door he'd only peeked through before.

"Hey."

Jacob turned to give the newcomer a nod. "Glad you could make it." Another long-term Boardroom member, Drake Hanson had a rougher edge to him that hinted at the dark things he could do.

"I wouldn't miss it." His smirk highlighted the calm eagerness rolling off him.

"Me either," Kellan said as he entered the room. He flashed a smile at Drake, stepping up to shake his hand. "It's been a while."

"I didn't know you were back in town," Drake said.

Kellan gave a dismissive shrug. "It's only been a few weeks." He motioned to Jacob. "It was pure luck that I ran into him."

Had it been luck or fate that he'd literally run past Kellan on his morning workout the day after Bailey had approached him? Younger than Jacob by a few years, Kellan had never come across as such. Hard would be the best term to describe him. He was pleasant enough to most, and deeply loyal to those he called friend.

"Timing's everything," Jacob said, only half joking. He wasn't sure if he would've accepted Bailey's proposal if she'd come to him even six months ago. "Are you both clear on the rules?" He shifted the discussion to the scene, nerves snipping at the edge of his calm.

"Crystal," Drake shot back with his customary snark. He adjusted his tie. "Shirts on or off?"

"On for now." Bailey wanted the power dynamic. "Did Trevor take your phones?"

"No." Drake lifted his from his pocket. "But mine's off, like usual."

"Mine too."

They both flashed dark screens, which didn't mean shit, but he trusted them. "Follow my lead, but feel free to do what comes natural. She's signed her rights over to me for the night, so—"

"She did what?" Kellan broke in, scowling.

Jacob stilled, returning his direct gaze. "Bailey belongs to me." The words alone brought a rush he couldn't explain. Power whispered in his chest and teased at things he'd barely acknowledged until she'd spoken the words to him. *I want you to own me.*

Drake's low whistle broke the tension that'd crept into the room. "You're a lucky bastard." Envy shone unchecked and carried in his voice.

I am. He couldn't disagree one bit.

"I hope you don't plan on using all of those." Kellan flicked his chin at the credenza, his frown still in place.

Jacob's quick snort shot out ahead of his low laugh. "God, no." He wasn't a sadist. He rubbed a hand over the back of his neck, those damn nerves invading further. "Some of those are for you."

The corner of Kellan's mouth curled up in a slow smirk that was both cunning and devious. "I was damn lucky to run into you that day." Of the three of them,

Kellan was probably the most experienced with the tools.

Drake came around the table to study the items Jacob had laid out. "Fucking is in, right?"

"Yes." Jacob inhaled. "If I okay it."

He jerked his head around. "I sure as hell hope you do."

"I bet."

"Oral?" Kellan asked.

"Yes." A visual popped into his head, singeing the images that'd been blasting his mind for weeks. "Both ways."

That smirk of Kellan's grew into a full grin that wasn't at all humorous. Yeah, he'd picked right for this scene. Bailey had joined the Boardroom after Kellan had moved away, so he'd be entirely new to her. Unexpected, an element she wouldn't have been able to anticipate.

A sound came from the hallway, drawing Jacob's attention. His breath hung in his lungs at his first sight of Bailey. To say she was beautiful would be too simple. From her fiery hair to her pixie features that matched her petite form, she was distinct when compared to the standard definition of beauty.

"Gentlemen," Trevor greeted before he receded to the corner at the far end of the room.

"Bailey," Jacob said after he'd found his voice. His pulse set a hard beat in his ears, his longing crashing against the desire he'd held in check since their very first scene together.

The Boardroom was a place for safe, uninhibited sex in a public space. It wasn't a pickup zone or an extreme version of an elite dating service. Exclusivity was rarely applied between members, even married ones.

He had no hold or right to Bailey—except for tonight. This one night.

"Jacob."

The breathy note in her voice twisted around him on the temptation it was. Her hair tumbled over her shoulders in waves of red offset by yellow and orange strategically placed to create the perfect image of flames. Her eyes were outlined in dark makeup to accentuate the sultry smolder in them. The hard tips of her nipples showed beneath her dark green slip dress in a tease that continued to the crotch-length hem. Her bare feet finished the sexy forest nymph impression and had his dick stirring already.

His heartbeat increased in incremental notches as the reality of the moment sunk in. He was finally going to live out his darkest fantasy with the woman he'd love to claim for real.

And then he'd have to let her go.

Don't miss Signed Over *by Lynda Aicher, available wherever Carina Press books are sold.*

www.CarinaPress.com

About the Author

Lynda Aicher is an RWA RITA® Award finalist, RT Reviewers' Choice Award winner and two-time Golden Flogger Award winner who loves to write emotionally charged romances. Prior to becoming an author, she spent years traveling weekly as a consultant implementing software into global companies until she opted to end her nomadic lifestyle to raise her two children. Now, her imagination is the only limitation on where she can go, and her writing lets her escape from the daily duties of being a mom, wife, chauffeur, scheduler, cook, teacher, cleaner and mediator. You can find her online.

LyndaAicher.com
Facebook.com/lyndaaicherauthor
Twitter.com/lyndaaicher
Instagram.com/lynda.aicher
BookBub.com/authors/lynda-aicher